MW00475649

The Day My Mother Cried

AND OTHER STORIES

Library of Modern Jewish Literature

Selected titles from Library of Modern Jewish Literature

Anna in the Afterlife
Merrill Joan Gerber

Autumn in Yalta: A Novel and Three Stories
David Shrayer-Petrov; Maxim D. Shrayer, ed.

Bedbugs
Clive Sinclair

The Day My Mother Changed Her Name and Other Stories
William D. Kaufman

Diary of an Adulterous Woman: A Novel
Curt Leviant

Life in the Damn Tropics: A Novel
David Unger

My Suburban Shtetl: A Novel about Life in a Twentieth-Century Jewish American Village
Robert Rand

The Victory Gardens of Brooklyn: A Novel
Merrill Joan Gerber

The Walled City: A Novel
Esther David

Yom Kippur in Amsterdam: Stories
Maxim D. Shrayer

William D. Kaufman

The Day My Mother Cried

AND OTHER STORIES

With Forewords by

BARUCH FELDSTERN & PETER PITZELE

Syracuse University Press

Syracuse, New York 13244-5290

First Edition 2010
10 11 12 13 14 15 6 5 4 3 2 1

∞ The paper used in this publication meets the minimum requirements of the American National Standard for Information Sciences—Permanence of Paper for Printed Library Materials, ANSI Z39.48-1992.

For a listing of books published and distributed by Syracuse University Press, visit our Web site at SyracuseUniversityPress.syr.edu.

ISBN: 978-0-8156-0955-1

Library of Congress Cataloging-in-Publication Data

Kaufman, William D.
The day my mother cried and other stories / William D. Kaufman ; with forewords by Baruch Feldstern and Peter Pitzele. — 1st ed.
p. cm. — (Library of modern Jewish literature)
ISBN 978-0-8156-0955-1 (alk. paper)
I. Feldstern, Baruch. II. Pitzele, Peter. III. Title.
PS3611.A846D44 2010
813'.6—dc22 2010022322

Manufactured in the United States of America

In memory of my wife, Zelda,
my father and mother, David and Rose Kaufman.

◆ ◆ ◆

And with profound appreciation to my coterie of good friends, readers all, who helped with the production of this book . . . Hilda Breslauer, Carol Montparker, Suzanne McGuire, Frieda Norotsky, Randy Kaplan, and my son Moss and my daughter Carole.

◆ ◆ ◆

Not to be forgotten are the lovely ladies from the Recreation staff who walked that last mile with me several times . . .
Maureen T. Clohessy, Susan Fliss, Susan Glassgold,
and Alice Spiciarich.
Thank you, ladies.

WILLIAM D. KAUFMAN is retired from the Jewish Theological Seminary, where he worked as a professional fundraiser for more than thirty years. His short stories have been published in the *Forward, Moment, World War II Chronicles,* and *Columbia Magazine.* His previous book of stories, *The Day My Mother Changed Her Name,* was published by Syracuse University Press.

Contents

Foreword

Baruch Feldstern

In the 1980s, I was directing a small program in Jerusalem for recent college graduates who wanted to bolster their knowledge of classical Jewish texts. Students lived together in a dormitory in order to free them from time-consuming daily tasks such as shopping and preparing food. Classes were all-consuming and intellectually demanding.

As the 1983–84 academic year approached, I was informed that one of the incoming students would be a recently retired seventy-year-old. I was intrigued but mainly apprehensive. How would such a student adapt to dormitory conditions? Would he be able to interact with students a third his age? Did he realize that classes involving intensive textual analysis filled the day? What would he do when the rest of the students went on occasional study-related hikes? All in all, I was worried.

Then Bill arrived. A compact, easy-going, entertaining adventurer. A polished gentleman in every sense of the word and also what is known in Israel as a *hevreman*—a sociable mixer who integrates easily into any group. Bill became each student's surrogate *zaide,* functioning unofficially *in loco grandparentis.* But more accurately, he was every student's friend. Barriers of age disappeared as Bill took part in every facet of the program. He devoured the classes, contributing his unique perspective to class discussions, occasionally illustrated by anecdotes that I now realize were stories waiting to be developed. He joined classmates on hikes, on evenings out and in endless heart-to-heart discussions about matters sublime and profound. Bill was never tolerated or humored by his young colleagues; he was simply one of them, and a favorite among them at that.

Bill and I hit it off from the start. Of him it can truly be said, "What you see is what you get." He never stood on ceremony, never took advantage of his unusual status. When the year ended, we resolved to stay in touch, a promise that we kept over the next twenty-five years through phone calls, cards, and visits. Nevertheless, I was floored when a package arrived containing Bill's first book of short stories. Not sure what to expect, I started reading and found . . . Bill. Story after story was engaging, imbued with vitality and full of humor. Many of the stories make a point, teach a lesson—but without a trace of preachiness. Bill's characters are real; and invariably they are real characters. The dialogue rings so true that at times you aren't sure if you are reading or hearing it. At the end of certain stories, I can picture Bill telling me about some incident that took place last week or fifty years ago, concluding with an inscrutable hint of a smile on his face, leaving me unsure if I have just been taken into a sacred confidence or just been taken in.

In an inventive interpretation of the convoluted biblical formulation that Sarah's age when the matriarch died was "one hundred years and twenty years and seven years," the rabbis say that at one hundred she was as beautiful as at twenty, and at twenty she was as innocent as at seven. It has been a delight for me to read Bill Kaufman's short stories and to discover that just as his enthusiasm at seventy was on a par with his twenty-something classmates, now past ninety his voice is as fresh as it was at seventy.

Foreword

Peter Pitzele

Let me give you a paragraph from Bill Kaufman's story "Grandfather and the *Poretz*." May I ask you to put aside for a moment your question about what a *poretz* is and your concern that you don't know Bill's grandfather. I just want you to listen to a man playing an instrument he loves and has played a long time. The instrument is called prose.

> Pop loved all fruits equally—with one exception. Plums. He hated plums, despised them. All varieties, shapes, sizes, colors, girths, feels came under his ban. It was an aversion of long standing, a primordial enmity. He even loathed its alter ego, the prune, which is virtually an act of heresy in Jewish households. His animosity to the plum dates back to his boyhood in Russia. To a sunny, gently sloping orchard located only a stone's throw from the tiny shapeless house in which my father was born. What happened? How did it begin?

Now prose, like people, comes in all shapes, and almost anyone, of whatever shape, can be moved to dance if the music is right. But of course not everyone is equally graceful. We have all seen the grace of the gifted ballerina, or the young man with the music in his heart fairly flying. And too we have seen portly men light on their feet, and the elderly surprisingly spry at a wedding. Everyone can dance. A little. And everyone can write prose. So the question is how we, the readers, are moved by prose, to what thoughts and feelings in what manner and intensity.

Let us reread the paragraph above. By its end you will confess you want to read the next paragraph. By its end you will have seen with your inner eye the "sunny, gently sloping orchard" (from a technical point of view, one wants to point out that this sequence of four words all have a stress that rocks them forward, as if rolling down a slope.) You will have smiled at the indispensable prunes in the Jewish household; you will perhaps have admired the choice of nouns that proceeds from shapes, through girths; and you may have remarked at the somber hyperbolic "primordial envy" which takes an alert reader all the way back to the garden of Eden and the first fruit story of them all. But by the end of this paragraph and without being able to tell quite where or how, I wager you will have been completely lulled out of your critical faculties and been put in the mood of a child at bedtime who only wants to read, or hear more.

Prose has done that to you, supple, serviceable, mischievous prose. And there's a whole lot more where that came from in Bill Kaufman's new book.

Who I Am

William D. Kaufman

I was born on November 6, 1914, and according to my father it was one of the luckiest days of his life. Actually, his good luck had nothing to do with my birth. It had everything to do with cabbages.

My father was a huckster of fruits and vegetables who plied his trade from a horse and wagon. The day I was born cabbage was king. It was at its zenith. It was ripe for conversion into its alter ego—sauerkraut. My father's customers were the Russian and Polish coal miners who lived in the villages and townships surrounding our city where anthracite coal was mined.

One of the staple foods on almost every miner's year-round table was sauerkraut. The finely cut up and fermented cabbage is allowed to sour and age in large wooden kegs or barrels. My father had dozens of customers waiting for the delivery of cabbage. Price was no object and my father reaped profits that were unprecedented and, I think, sinful. As long as he lived, my father viewed me as the harbinger of good luck.

I started school at five and stayed with it for the next eighteen years. It was the usual curriculum vitae—kindergarten through four years of college and a year of grad school. Those eighteen years brought mostly good memories. I wrote stories about the pleasant ones and ignored the others.

I had just turned four when the first world war ended. I described the joy and jubilation of the day on our street and synagogue. I also wrote about my friendship with a Civil War veteran who visited our school before Memorial Day when I was in sixth grade. He told us how he lost his arm in the Battle of Bull Run and that he shook the hand of Abraham Lincoln in the field hospital at Gettysburg and that "the president cried."

At thirteen I was bar mitzvah, which was notable only because I delivered two speeches, one in Yiddish in the synagogue and the other in English in the banquet hall. At fourteen I entered high school and chose Latin as my foreign language. Almost at the opening bell I fell in love with the Latin teacher who was as pretty as Clara Bow and probably a helluva lot smarter. We called her "Miss Portia."

In my junior year my parents transferred me to the yeshiva in New York City which was one of the lesser delights of my life. At the yeshiva I was never a very distinguished student, especially in Talmudic studies. My father and my mother, too, expected that I would become a rabbi, which I knew would never happen. I did not have the heart to tell them and when I did, shortly before my graduation, my father was shocked and my mother cried.

I was sports editor of Yeshiva College weekly newspaper and began to write some pretty solid articles. At the yeshiva, there were only two competitive sports—basketball and chess. I began to write a Walter Winchell kind of column, which made me a man to be feared and avoided though that never happened.

After graduation I applied to the Columbia University School of Journalism and because their quota of applicants for the year was filled I was given a provisional acceptance for the following year. That middle year I enrolled for two courses at NYU in reporting and feature writing. I won a medal in reporting and an honorable mention in feature writing. I was ready for Columbia.

My year at Columbia was one of the festive years of my life. Ours was a class of sixty students, most of whom were in the top echelons of their colleges. Among them were graduates of Yale, Harvard, Princeton, Vassar, Columbia, and the University of Chicago. Registered with us was a priest, an ex-managing editor of a popular magazine, a German lady who was a little older than most of us and was rumored to be a baroness, two reporters for the *New York Times* and "schleppers" like me who were ready to try the waters.

The year passed much too fast, at least for me, and when it ended I was ready to take on a job as a news reporter, an editor, a researcher, a writer of editorials, and various positions in advertising. But there were no jobs to be found.

The year was 1938 and the country had been in a deep depression since 1930. There were few jobs available, especially in New York City. Most of us looked hard for any kind of employment. I left New York City for my home town and began the search immediately. There were three local papers. I was given interviews by the three managing editors and two of the three gave me a hurry-up negative.

The third editor suggested I freelance and he would read what I wrote. I was elated of course and in a few days began to write. In our city there were large populations of foreign born. Almost all nationalities had weekly newspapers that were eagerly read. There were two Russian, one Polish, one Hungarian, and a Slovak journal that was published at random intervals.

I wrote about all of them—five to be exact. It took me almost two weeks to do the interviews and research and one day to write the article, which was more than two thousand words. I liked what I wrote. So did the editor. When he completed his reading he took off his spectacles, smiled, and said, "Okay, I'll buy it. Come back on Monday and you'll get a check."

I got to the press room early that Monday morning expecting a warm welcome, a pat on the shoulder, and a sizable check. Maybe not a real hefty one, but in my head it had to be ten or even twenty bucks. When the managing editor stormed out of his little squeak of an office, he lumbered toward me like a bull from Pamplona. He had fire in his eyes. I thought he was going to beat the hell out of me.

He bellowed, "Your story almost got me fired! When the old man read it, he sends for me and says, 'Where do you come to be giving publicity to our competition? Don't you think they sell ads, too, for Christ's sake?'" He stopped to catch his breath. "So I told him it was written by a freelancer from Columbia University.' The old man answers, 'I don't give a shit if it came from F.D.R. himself. Kill it.'"

He told me to go downstairs and pick up my check. I knew I had to say something so I stuttered out, "Does that mean you don't want any stories from me?"

"You can bet your ass on that, you knave." I had never been called a knave before or since. I took the elevator down. At the bookkeeping office I was in for another surprise. I was handed a two-dollar check with my name misspelled. Two dollars! I had toiled two weeks interviewing foreign press editors who barely spoke English, perused their pages (which I could not understand), and then summed it all up in a two-thousand-word article. I had labored at a rate of about five cents an hour, which is what low-caste laborers in India earned hauling logs out of the jungle.

But the Almighty was with me. Not long after my freelance debacle, my sister Dorothy spotted an ad in the newspaper (not the one that jinxed me) that the editor-publisher of a weekly was interested in selling his assets. The name of the paper was *The Abingtonian,* which its owner had started six months earlier in Clark Summit, Pennsylvania.

His assets were a P.O. box in the local post office and a subscription list of a little more than one hundred. It was published by the printer of the Polish weekly I had met earlier. I used him primarily because he extended credit to me and was a very patient creditor.

I wrote the editorials, of course, and hewed closely to the F.D.R. political philosophy, which was not too smart of me because most of the citizenry of the Abingtons were Republicans.

I inherited half a dozen correspondents, all women, who recorded weddings, engagements, deaths, travels, etc. No bar mitzvahs. As expected, much of my time was spent pursuing advertisements. There were too few of these and I was never too successful in solicitation. Things changed for me when I developed a friendship with a minor politician who arranged for my paper to record public notices. These paid a dime a word and kept me solvent.

My newspaper career ended when I was drafted into the Army. It was on November 24, 1941, just two weeks before Pearl Harbor. I served four years and spent most of the time overseas. My Army career was not particularly notable.

I was a warrant officer in the 439th Anti-Aircraft Battalion. Our outfit saw action in North Africa, Italy, France, and Germany. Our mission was to shoot down enemy planes, and we got our share mostly in

Italy. Principally we were assigned to defend airfields, railway yards, bridges, and highways. We also offered protection to artillery. When we were with the big guns, our morale was at its highest because we were close to the infantry, which is the queen of battles. Those were the fighting men, the ones who truly faced the enemy.

Our battalion was converted into an infantry brigade almost overnight. We were assigned to replace an infantry division in Pisa, Italy, which was alerted to make the invasion of southern France. In retrospect, we were proudest of our infantry role. We were in direct confrontation with the enemy and we survived.

One of my favorite stories, "Return to Pisa," is a recapitulation of that action. The battalion was given a commendation by General Mark Clark, commanding general of the Fifth Army, for our infantry role in Italy.

After the war, I stumbled into a job that turned out to be the highlight of my life and my career. I was offered a position as assistant to the director of public relations of the American Zionist Emergency Council. The council was the political and public relations arm of the Zionist movement in the United States and virtually the rest of the world.

I had been a Zionist since my college days and the job was major league for me. The council had meetings that were attended by men and women who became the heroic figures of the Zionist movement and Israel. It was an uphill fight all the way. The battleground was the halls of the United Nations. Most member states were neutral including the United States. There was a bare handful of supporters in the Senate and the House.

Within three years, the tide had turned in our favor. A Jewish state was proposed by the UN and both the United States and the Soviet Union approved the resolution as did a majority of the other nations.

Within a short time the Zionist Council that had employed me was out of business. Finding a job was a little more difficult this time. After three months of search, Lady Luck was with me. I landed a job in the field of fund-raising and my employer was the Jewish Theological Seminary of America. Working for the seminary was perfection for me.

It stands at the head of the Conservative movement, which lies in between the Orthodox and Reform wings of Judaism. It is both a university and a congregation of more than five hundred synagogues. It trains rabbis, cantors, and educators. Its faculty was probably the most distinguished collection of scholars since the academies in Babylonia in the fourth century. I realize this is a rash statement but I hold it to be true. On its faculty were Abraham Joshua Heschel, the philosopher; M. L. Ginsberg, professor of Talmud; Saul Lieberman, the foremost expert of the Jerusalem Talmud; and Louis Finkelstein, the beloved chancellor of the seminary.

My job was on the money end of things and I prospered, as did the seminary. I worked in its development department for thirty-one years and rose to be the head of the fund-raising staff. I left the seminary a few months before my wife of thirty-five years died. She was fifty-seven.

I spent the next eleven months grieving her loss in accordance with Jewish tradition. This involved saying the kaddish for a period of eleven months. This did bring solace to me of a sort. I worked full time and spent most evenings attending classes or meetings.

As the months dragged by, I convinced myself that I should take a year off from work and experience the world. I had always been fascinated by travel, though I had done little, and I now had the money and inclination to experience both.

First came Tibet and China. I chose a tour that was ridiculously expensive. It featured a week in Tibet and a somewhat longer stay in China. Tibet was an eyeful. It was a largely unexplored country with mountains more than three miles high and a population suffused with an inscrutable divinity.

At the head of the country and the religion is the Dalai Llama, who lives in exile in India. Mount Everest, the highest mountain in the world, sits tranquilly astride Tibet's border with Nepal. Everest is 29,028 feet above sea level, which in terms of space is as high as the lateral distance from Commack on Long Island to the village of Northport more than five miles away. Everest sits there like a cathedral of ice.

One incident in Lhasa, capitol of Tibet, that I had anticipated before I left on the tour was the *yahrzeit* of my wife. *Yahrzeit* is the annual memorial service for a loved one. I had supplied myself with a memorial candle and a prayer book. All I needed was a minyan (quorum) of ten Jewish men. There were five in our group including me. There was a couple from Houston with another tour which made seven. I bent the rules and we went ahead. It was something to be remembered.

We sat there, seven men and women in a darkened cubicle of a room, visiting with G-d in one of His highest places. The following morning our guide would not extinguish the candle because it was the candle of life.

China was another story. The year was 1983 and it was a country on the move. Most Chinese dressed and looked alike—white shirts and blouses, black pants, black half sneakers, and smiling inscrutable faces. China looked like a collection of factories. The new hotels were replicas of those in Miami Beach. In Beijing, capitol of China, we stayed at a government retreat, the same where President Nixon and Henry Kissinger had bunked down during their historic visit to China. My roommate and I occupied the Kissinger suite, which was a repository of antique urns, vases, and statuaries.

The face towels in the bathroom were beautifully stitched with crests and Chinese lettering, which overwhelmed me. I had to take one home as a souvenir. I chose not to go the usual route of wrapping it in a sweater or a pajama top. Instead I requested our guide to convey my desire to purchase one. The guide said he would convey my offer.

On the morning of our departure, the guide, the manager of the estate, the chef, and three cleaning girls came to my door. The estate manager who headed the delegation shook my hand and made a two or three minute declaration in Chinese that his establishment and his government chose to give me the towel as a gift. My roommate who came from Alaska and was a school teacher was miffed that I never confided in him.

I responded to the Chinese retinue with a four or five minute reply, in English of course, and I cited the name of Abraham Lincoln two or three times, which pleased them. I believe they were familiar with the name.

My roommate who had more guts than I took unto himself a towel by wrapping it around his middle before we left. A couple of years later I received a note from my roommate telling me he was promoted to principal. After that, he ran for Congress and lost. He was a Republican.

That September I applied to the seminary, my former employer, for entry into its one-year program in Jerusalem. I was accepted. I was sixty-nine years old and the rabbinical students probably averaged out at about twenty-five. I applied for a scholarship and was turned down, which kind of surprised me and wounded my ego. It was a glorious twelve months. A great deal of the time I had difficulty keeping my head above water, but I stayed afloat. I was never a superior student.

My skills in the study of the Hebrew language were weak. My year in the study of Bible would probably put me in the A category. Jewish history was difficult because the lectures were in Hebrew. I think I was a B student in midrash, which was taught by my friend and headmaster Rabbi Baruch Feldstern. I was also a good student in the Talmud and Mishna. Jewish law was my ticket.

There were twelve subjects offered in our program and I enrolled in the whole dozen. The other students were required to take five courses. It may sound like I'm indulging in a little braggadocio, which I suppose I am. Though I never left the seminary in Jerusalem as a savant of Jewish learning, I did, I think, carve my initials on the tree of Torah. Not very deep, of course. At the end of the term, I was honored by the students.

In recent years I have traveled to England, France, Italy, Belgium, Holland, Spain, Alaska, Tibet, Gibraltar, Egypt, India, Burma, China, Nepal, Hong Kong, and Thailand. But never Germany.

I have revisited China twice and Israel seven times. As I write, I am about to turn ninety-four, which is not bad for someone born almost a century ago on the day my father reaped a harvest of cabbages that turned into kings.

Humoresque

One of the great disappointments of my father's life was that I never became another Yehudi Menuhin. Here was this nice Jewish boy from somewhere out there on the West Coast who was stupefying audiences all over the world with his fiddle, and in the process raking in barrelsful of dollars, British pounds, Japanese yen, or what have you. If that nice Jewish boy in the Buster Brown haircut could do it, why couldn't I? After all, we were about the same age. This was Pop's rationale.

My father came from fiddle country. He was born in some unpronounceable village in the Ukraine, not too far from Odessa, which was the birthplace of Jascha Heifetz, Mischa Elman, Leopold Auer, and other violin masters. To hear Pop tell it, every Jewish boy in the Ukraine was teethed on the bow of a fiddle. When I asked him how it happened that he missed out on the violin lessons, he told me that from the age of eight he was obliged to go with his brothers into the marketplace every day of the week except the Sabbath in order to put kopecks on the kitchen table. When I suggested that he might have studied after dark, he gave me his "don't be stupid" look and I retreated fast.

In my time, every Jewish boy on my block and, I often suspected, on every block in the United States was forced to take violin lessons. Whether the boy liked it or not, and most did not, fiddle playing was a "must," like not eating on Yom Kippur. One Friday afternoon, my mother and older sister took me, sullen and complaining, to the Lyceum, as it was called, where I was enrolled for weekly lessons. The first lesson, which I got that very afternoon, was free. It was what they called an orientation and involved giving the new student "a feel of the instrument."

My mother signed me up for twenty-four weekly lessons at one dollar a session. With the signing of the contract I was given a violin and bow and a stained maroon canvas bag with a drawstring to hold the instrument. The bag was big enough, I discovered later, to hold a baseball glove and ball and even a sandwich or two. For the duration of my lessons at the Lyceum, my violin smelled of salami.

In the classroom there were another ten or twelve boys and one girl. If anything, she was even less musical than the rest of us. She invariably stroked up when we stroked down, to the extreme annoyance of the instructor. He was a very young man with a hardly visible red moustache that hovered above a pair of thin lips like a smattering of lint. He imagined himself as something of a wit because he had pasted a large sign on the blackboard that read "Nero Studied Here"—which none of us understood.

The violin issued to me was no bargain, but it was the reason for our overcrowded classroom. At the end of the twenty-four lesson contract, the fiddle became the property of the student. This was a deal that a violin maven like my father could not pass up. It was his estimate that for a $24 expenditure, I could end up with a sound fiddle education plus a sound fiddle worth at least $10. Not a bad investment, Pop said. The violin had a curlicued marking on its bridge that read "Made in Genoa," which thrilled my father who never wavered in his belief that Columbus was a Jew who was born in Genoa.

The Lyceum, which was something of an overstatement, had once been a furniture store. It was partitioned into several classrooms, and novices, such as I, were sent to the one farthest back, which was located next to the boiler room. Our classroom was hot in the summer and even hotter in the winter. The sounds issuing from our room were loud, tuneless, and scratchy. We were sold, at a quarter apiece, squares of rosin that were supposed to keep the horsehairs on the bow snowy white and scratchproof. This never happened with mine, which, almost from the beginning, took on a greenish hue that never went away and emitted scratchier sounds than ever.

One of the early tunes we were taught was the "Humoresque" by Dvorak. The first time we played it, the instructor said, "Boy, isn't that a laugh." He had to explain that his remark was meant to be a joke, but none of us thought it was very funny. Not long afterward he removed from the blackboard the sign about Nero and shaved his moustache. I don't think there was a connection.

The Friday sessions at the Lyceum were not too bad. In fact I began to enjoy them. Not the violin part, of course, but the fun we had when the class was over. I became friendly with the kids, the girl included, whose name was Hannah. She was taking lessons because there was a violin at home that belonged to her father. I soon found out that most of the kids had violins at home, except me, all because my father came from a starving hovel in the Ukraine.

Every night I practiced in the living room but only for short spurts because my playing gave my mother a headache. The one time Pop heard me practicing was when he had the flu and could not go to his store. I don't know whether it was the flu or my scratchy playing of "Humoresque," but he was determined after that to withdraw me from the Lyceum even though I was shy fourteen lessons from permanent possession of the violin.

He told my mother he had a teacher in mind, a Herr Schmidt, one of his customers, who had told Pop he had conducted a symphony orchestra years ago in Leipzig. Herr Schmidt, Pop said, was something of a *schicker* (a drunkard) and was an anti-Semite to boot but for that matter so was Wagner and probably Beethoven as well. My mother observed that a conductor is not a teacher, but Pop assured her that this one was.

My father also said that anti-Semites make the best teachers. When my mother asked why, he told her that anti-Semites never smile. The result is that kids are afraid of them and learn better and faster. I'm not sure my mother accepted the verity of Pop's theories on education, but it was she who was overcome with fear the following Sunday morning when Herr Schmidt showed up at our front door.

To begin with, he came by way of the front door. In those days, nobody, with the possible exception of policemen or doctors on an emergency call, entered through the front door. Everyone came in through the back. So there was Herr Schmidt thumping the front door and my mother bowing him in like he was the kaiser. Speechless, she ushered him into the parlor and hastily put me in his charge.

Herr Schmidt was a large man. He had a bloated beefy face that was dominated by a multicolored walrus-like moustache that curled upward on one side and drooped aimlessly on the other. His eyes were fierce and mildly bloodshot. His clothes smelled of beer and wine, and looked as if they had been slept in the past night or two. He wore a rumpled sweater-vest that covered a somewhat advanced beer belly.

Herr Schmidt demanded to see my Lyceum violin and bow, which my father was determined not to return. He greeted the instrument with the word *dreck* and yelled for my mother, whom he called "Missus," when he laid eyes on the bow. The strands, he showed her, were stiff and "green like snot"—which horrified my mother—and asked her to bring him a basin of warm water, a cake of Fels Naptha soap and a towel. Mama meekly asked if Octagon soap would do instead and he barked a fast "Ja, Ja."

He then proceeded to loosen the horsehair of the bow and washed it slowly and tenderly in the soapy water. He rubbed gently with the soap, rinsed with the water, again with the soap, repeating the process for at least ten minutes. During that time he uttered not a word, but concentrated totally on what he was doing. When he finished, he dried the strands with the towel, tightened the clasp and produced a snow white bowstring. He turned to me triumphantly and said, "Now you can play a fiddle."

Herr Schmidt then shouted "Missus," which brought my mother running in from the kitchen. He told her he would give "the boy" his first lesson next Sunday. He asked for two dollars in advance that she gave him without protest. "Tell your mister, the violin is *dreck* and he should get the boy another one," he said. He told her he had one at home that would be good for "the boy" to start with and would be willing to sell it cheap. When my mother asked how much, he said he would talk to "the mister." He then turned and left through the front door.

I never did get to be another Yehudi Menuhin and probably Herr Schmidt had something to do with it. Sometime later that week Herr Schmidt dropped dead in a saloon in another part of town. There was talk that it happened in a Polish bar just as he ordered his second pitcher of beer. My father was skeptical about the Polish saloon because Herr Schmidt hated Poles as much as he hated Jews. Maybe even more, Pop said.

I returned to the Lyceum and stayed on for those other fourteen lessons. After two or three weeks, my bowstring turned green again and squealed very much like before. Maybe even more. We had a graduation ceremony which my parents attended and, as a solo, I played "Eli, Eli." It was after graduation that my father made the decision to discontinue any further lessons. "Enough is enough is more than enough," Pop told my mother in his most sagacious manner as if he was quoting from the Bible. I still have the violin.

Kaplansky's Troubles

It happened at least a hundred years ago in my father's village in the Ukraine, and people, Jews and even gentiles, were still talking about it when my father left the shtetl in 1910 to seek his fortune and a missing brother-in-law in America. The event, or, more authentically, the collection of events, was referred to as Kaplansky's *tzuris* (troubles).

Simcha Yussel Kaplansky, formerly of Lithuania, was not just another Jew who resided in the miserable collection of hovels that comprised my father's shtetl. He was a name, a big name, probably the most notable and respected name in Romanov, my father's village. He stumbled, literally I mean, into the *yerid* (market) on a market day when the overloaded wagon he drove overturned, spilling Kaplansky and his bags of grain under the hooves of his horse Pyotr. The unlucky nag broke both forelegs and had to be destroyed while Kaplansky lay bruised and half alive in the foyer of the synagogue where they brought him.

Kaplansky survived, of course, and in a week or two started a business in grain and farm machinery. As he told it, he was on his way to Kiev when the calamity in the *yerid* hit him and his horse Pyotr. Of course, there was no call for farm machinery in the village itself. The shtetl people, like my grandfather and his brothers, were tailors, butchers, cobblers, and fixers of all kinds whose houses were located on minuscule patches of land with puny gardens which, if they were lucky, would scratch up each summer some cabbages, turnips, and a few dozens of scrawny potatoes.

The farm machinery was for the many and varied farms in the area that was largely under the domination of a Russian *poretz* (nobleman). The *poretz*, who was a general in the czar's army, was almost always absent from his estate. He employed overseers and retired soldiers to run his farms and properties, but mostly they were botchers, drunks, and thieves and, often enough, a combination of all three.

Kaplansky purchased his wheat, oats, and fruits directly from the *poretz*. In a short time the *poretz* recognized Kaplansky's business talent and made him the agent to handle *his* estate. With his new position, Simcha Yussel the Litvak, as he was now called, was able to expand his business and in time became a rich man.

He also became a dominant figure in the Jewish community and the synagogue. As a young man, he had studied at one of the great yeshivas in Lithuania and was viewed as a scholar even by the rabbi himself. Most evenings he spent in the study hall of the shul where the rabbi conducted a class in Talmud. As Kaplansky accumulated wealth, his contributions to charity increased. He built the community a new *mikvah* (bath house) and took the lead in the purchase of land in the center of the village for the construction of a hospital. With the aid of the *poretz*, the community purchased a small building to house the cheder (schoolhouse), where my grandfather taught.

As Simcha Yussel prospered so did the community. New jobs were created, the *yerid* was expanded, businesses flourished. "He has brought *mazel* [luck] to our village," the rabbi said on more than one occasion.

Within a year of his arrival, a marriage was arranged for him with the beautiful daughter of a distinguished rabbi from Odessa. Three sons were born in the next four years and there seemed to be no limit to the *mazel* being brought to his house.

On his first Sabbath in the shul, while he was still recovering from the calamity he suffered with his horse Pyotr, the rabbi and his congregants were delighted to hear from the Litvak that he was a *kohane* (priest). There were only two other *kohanim* in the town. One was a very old man who had difficulty reciting the blessings when he was called to the Torah. The other *kohane* was a youngish man with tuberculosis who, often enough, was not able to attend Sabbath services.

As a *kohane,* Simcha Yussel the Litvak accepted, with a deferential modesty, the responsibilities and rewards that came with his being a member of the priestly class. In the dispensation of Torah honors, for example, the *kohane* is always called to the Torah first. This was not only on the Sabbath but on the holidays and even on Monday and Thursday when the Torah is removed from the ark.

On the major holidays it is the *kohane* who blesses the congregation. He chants the benediction with the other *kohanim* and the congregants are duly blessed. Simcha Yussel Kaplansky, it must be said, enjoyed considerably the duties and amenities that were part of the priestly role. When he was called to the Torah, he strode to the reader's table like a Roman gladiator presenting himself to Caesar. On holidays he blessed the congregants in a loud melodic voice. He was wrapped like a patriarch in his pure white linen prayer shawl shading his face from public view. The congregants left the shul feeling fully blessed, and so did Kaplansky.

The Almighty blessed Kaplansky with long years, great wealth, and a spotless reputation. After living a half-century in Romanov, his health began to fail and he succumbed two days after Passover. The village people, Jewish and gentile, mourned Kaplansky for a week and would have grieved indefinitely if a letter written by Kaplansky had not been discovered by his youngest son Yechiel.

Yechiel was a Talmud student like his father. It was when he opened the silken sack that held his father's tefillin that his father's letter was discovered. Yechiel read it and fainted dead away. As soon as he was revived, he rushed to his two brothers and after hours of talk, they went to the rabbi's home for his advice. The rabbi studied the letter and asked Kaplansky's sons to allow him time to study it and then render a judgment. On the following day, which was Friday, the rabbi suggested to the sons that a meeting of the entire Jewish community be called for Sunday morning in the synagogue. The rabbi said he would make public the letter and would be prepared to lead the discussion that would ensue.

On Sunday most of the residents came to the synagogue. It was abuzz with excitement. No one knew what was about to happen. When the rabbi rose from his seat, all conversation ceased. He withdrew the letter from his sleeve, unfolded it, and began to speak.

"This is a letter from Simcha Yussel Kaplansky," the rabbi announced in a low grieving voice. "He has written it to his three sons, but it is intended, I believe, for all of us to hear." He removed his spectacles from his vest and read.

> My beloved and compassionate sons. I greet you from the other world where God, I hope, will be merciful and forgiving. I have sinned. I have sinned for more than fifty years. My sin has not been of the flesh, nor of the market place, nor against man or beast. Mine is the sin of deception.
>
> I make my confession now. I have maintained an impersonation ever since I first set foot in our village of Romanov. It began years before you, my beloved sons, first witnessed the light of day, before my marriage to my late beloved wife, your mother Channeh Hindel.
>
> Let me begin with my name. Here in Romanov I am called Simcha Yussel Kaplansky. When I am given an *aliyah,* a call to the Torah, I am called Simcha Yussel ben Yakov Hakohen. And that is an untruth. That is my deception and that is my sin.
>
> My father is *not* Yakov Hakohen. My natural father is Reuven. Reuven was not a *kohane*. Why all this confusion about my name?
>
> At an early age my natural parents gave me for adoption to the Kaplansky family who had no children. In those days—and even now—a family where there are sons will often make arrangements to give one of the sons for adoption to a childless family. The purpose is easy to understand.
>
> The czar will not draft into his imperial army a young man who is an only son. That was the law then and it is the law now. So I become a Kaplansky in every way except by birth.
>
> I make this confession now. My sin is that I should never have allowed myself to pass as a *kohane*. I have performed the duties that belong to a *kohane* and I hope that God will not deal harshly with me. I pray also that my fellow Jews in Romanov will forgive me for being what I am not.
>
> In the other world God will deal with me justly as is His custom. In the world I have just left I have faith that our beloved rabbi will do what he has to do.

That was the end of the letter. It was signed Simcha Yussel Kaplansky.

When the rabbi completed his reading, there was total silence in the synagogue. It was as if God Himself had removed the breath from the lungs of the congregants. The rabbi asked the audience if there were any questions. Reb Velvel Ganz, an elder in the congregation and one who always demanded to be heard, rose from his seat and joined the rabbi on the platform.

"Rabbi, with all due respect," he began in his squeaky voice, "what can we do to repair the damage? On our holidays, Simcha Yussel blessed the congregation as a priest is required to do. Now that he has confessed he is not a *kohane* does that mean that his blessings were just a lot of empty air? And if we were not blessed by him, does that mean we were cursed?"

The rabbi answered in a tired voice, "We were not cursed. You can be certain of that." He raised his voice. "Let us remember whom we are judging. Simcha Yussel was among the best of us. He was generous. He was learned. He was just. His presence in our village was a blessing."

He repeated softly, "A blessing." He paused. "I think we should go back to our homes now. I think we should make our judgments in the privacy of our individual heads." He left the platform and the congregants followed.

That week the name of Simcha Yussel was on everyone's tongue. Even the peasants who came to the *yerid* were buzzing to each other about "that nice Jew who always gave good measure." When the *poretz* heard about the commotion in the village, he was reported to have lost his temper.

"What kind of respect are these Jews paying to the memory of a fine, honest Hebrew who never lied or cheated in his life? I should know. There was not a dishonest hair on his head or beard. May Jesus Christ welcome him to Paradise and seat him with the angels," the *poretz* said with a look towards heaven.

All that week the rabbi prayed for enlightenment. The community was floundering with uncertainty. Was there a need to impose punishment on the house of Kaplansky? Or was that to be left to the Almighty? Was Kaplansky's confession sufficient for atonement as it would be on Yom Kippur eve?

Within the week the rabbi was prepared to meet with the congregation. He summoned his people to a meeting in the shul on Saturday night after Havdalah, the end of the Sabbath. He wasted no time. He flew into the Kaplansky affair as soon as he opened his mouth.

"We know why we are here. Or do we? Are we here to exact punishment on a man because he deceived us all these years? Or are we here to forgive him? Is he worthy of being forgiven?

"To my mind, forgiveness is in the hands of God. Perhaps, at this very moment the Almighty is imposing His judgment on Simcha Yussel. And that is sufficient. That is final. God is the ultimate judge. And that is where I stand and I believe that is where you, all of you, stand. God is the ultimate judge.

"Now as to Simcha Yussel's sin against his community. He entered a priesthood to which he had no right. A violation of our tradition, to be sure. The question is—should we insist on punishment or should we not? Punishment is in our hands, if we choose.

"I have looked into our rabbinical texts. I have delved into our Jewish history. Is there a precedent? Has this ever happened before? The answer—and this will surprise you—is yes. The priesthood has been breached in the past and is still being violated even today. It is not an overt violation; nevertheless it is a violation.

"I have been brought to this conclusion by Maimonides himself who, as you know, is the greatest Talmudic authority in our history. It was Maimonides who stated that *kohanim* are presumed to be priests. I repeat myself. Presumed to be priests. Why *presumed,* you may ask? Because priests are descended from Aaron, brother of Moses, who was designated by God Himself to be the first priest. That took place 4,000 years ago. In those forty centuries, errors occurred. Some were accidental, others were not. During that long period, our people experienced exiles, expulsions, inquisitions, dispersions, some of which are happening at this very moment. In other words, exact ancestry has always been in question.

"It is known, for example, that King Herod, two thousand years ago, appointed as priests men who were not of the house of Aaron. He did this as a favor to Rome. It seems likely that a whole line of priests were descended from spurious priests and are performing their priestly duties this very day.

"You may ask," the rabbi continued, "what does this have to do with Kaplansky. Some will answer—nothing at all. Others will say because our Jewish history has been such a strange one, there is the possibility that all of us could be descended from the house of Aaron. As you all know I have always been a practitioner of leniency and I think, though this is a guess, that Maimonides would agree with my judgment."

He paused and then raised his voice. "I would rule, therefore, that the grievous error of Simcha Yussel be adjudged, not by us, but by the Almighty. We are all in God's hands."

The congregation appeared to be satisfied with the rabbi's judgment though there were some, not many, who disagreed. Reb Velvel Ganz, as was expected, was one of them.

"With all due respect for our rabbi," he began, "I cannot agree with his conclusion. It may be true, as Maimonides reasons, that all *kohanim* are only presumed to be priests, but in Kaplansky's case, he is not only presumed to be a non-kohen, but he confesses to it in his letter.

"I believe our community," he continued, "has been so deceived by Simcha Yussel that his sons should perform an act of atonement of such magnitude that it would erase forever the stain splashed on us for such a long time."

The rabbi sat silent, emotionless. Some congregants took his silence as a sign of approval of Reb Velvel's suggestion. Others thought the reverse. There were no speakers after Reb Velvel.

In two weeks, on the first day of the new month, Kaplansky's sons announced that they would finance the building of a new synagogue and it would carry the name of their father. There was some grumbling but it was only a squeak compared to what might have been if Reb Velvel Ganz continued to harangue everyone, including the rabbi.

The Kaplansky Shul, as it was called, was the most magnificent structure in Romanov. And even today, long past Kaplansky's troubles, it stands as a reminder of the frailty of men and their redemption. A year after the shul was built, the three Kaplansky sons liquidated their businesses and moved to the city of Chicago in America.

In Chicago they went into the grain business and within a matter of years became one of the largest grain exporters in the world. They were helped by the first world war and the devastation of Europe in its aftermath. It must be said that they emulated the life of their father, Simcha Yussel the Litvak. They never turned their back on a friend or kinsman. They helped financially, of course, and assisted many in starting businesses or finding employment.

My Uncle Yankel who was in Chicago for a Zionist convention sought out Yechiel, youngest of the Kaplansky sons. Uncle Yankel was the youngest of my father's brothers. He was the philosopher of the family, my father always said. He was kind, he was wise, but he was a hard luck businessman. Most of his ventures failed badly.

Yechiel, who had changed his name to Y. L. Kapp, proved to be a munificent host. He insisted that my uncle stay at his home, which Yankel told my father was "so big you could fit all of Romanov in it including the *yerid.*" Back in Russia, Yechiel and Yankel had been in the same *Chumash* (Bible) class that was taught by my grandfather.

My uncle would not ask Yechiel for any financial favors. He was too proud for that. "Of course, I was a fool. He was ready to help, I could smell it," he told my father. "I would be a millionaire today, if I had asked," he said.

As if by some heavenly decree, all three Kaplansky sons died within a single year. They were mourned in Russia, France, and the United States and some say as far away as Australia. When my father heard the news, he said it was the Kaplansky *tzuris* all over again. Uncle Yankel was silent. He cried softly for a long time.

Grandfather and the *Poretz*

My father always thought of himself as something of a fruit connoisseur. He often told me he was born with a God-given gift of fruit prophecy. Nothing less. He could, he claimed, glance at a truckful of green bananas and foretell which bunch would ripen sweet and cream-colored and which would end up dry and mottled and fit for the cat. So he said.

My father's first business shortly after he came to this country from Russia was selling fruit and produce from a horse and wagon. The name of the horse was Prince, which was a serious misnomer because the tired old beast was a female. Every morning Prince hauled my father to the outskirts of town where Pop had established a cluster of loyal customers and a reputation for carrying the top fruits and vegetables in the county.

From time to time, he would hoist me aboard the high wooden seat of the wagon, pass me the reins, and let me giddap Prince to the early morning market near the railroad yard where he took on his provisions. There my father went into his customary routine, critically eyeing the bushels, crates, and deep barrels of the newly arrived produce brought in only a few hours earlier from nearby farms. He would sniff, squeeze, tap, shake, and hold to the sunlight the apples, melons, plums, peaches, pears, and other fruits, foreign and domestic, that were on sale. Once I even saw him palpate a coconut, which he told me was hell on the knuckles.

I think Pop was a top-of-the-line fruit maven principally because he loved fruit. Where other hucksters would stop from time to time to smoke a cigarette or slurp a coffee, my father would crunch into a pippin apple, quarter a navel, or, in season, chomp into a Bartlett pear or a white-cheeked peach.

Pop loved all fruits equally—with one exception. Plums. He hated plums, despised them. All varieties, shapes, sizes, colors, girths, feels came under his ban. It was an aversion of long standing, a primordial enmity. He even loathed its alter ego, the prune, which is virtually an act of heresy in Jewish households. His animosity to the plum dates back to his boyhood in Russia. To a sunny, gently sloping orchard located only a stone's throw from the tiny shapeless house in which my father was born. What happened? How did it begin?

One ripe September morning, shortly before the Jewish New Year, my father, who was ten or eleven at the time, and his friend Chotzkel Berel decided that it was much too nice a day to spend in cheder (Hebrew school). They chose instead to take off to the vast hillside orchard owned by the *poretz*, which at that time of year was bursting out with all varieties of fruit. The *poretz* was the local nobleman and landowner—possibly a duke or count, my father was never exactly certain—who governed the village and neighboring hamlets in the fertile eastern Ukraine where Father's family had lived for generations.

Chotzkel Berel knew that the *poretz's* peasants were picking fruit in the north section of the orchard, so the two boys chose to invade the opposite end of the field where the plum trees were begging to be plucked. Pop, the more spritely of the two, climbed the trees, throwing down the choicest of the fruit to Chotzkel Berel. This activity, frequently halted by some enthusiastic gobbling by both boys, had gone on for some time when suddenly and out of nowhere, a peasant from the *poretz's* estate appeared. Chotzkel Berel took off with the fleetness of a Ukrainian wolfhound. Pop was captured immediately.

With a lusty thwack on his bottom, the peasant marched my father northward where the *poretz* on horseback was overseeing the fruit picking. He was told of my father's misdemeanor. Very sternly the *poretz* turned to the trespasser and said, "Explain yourself, boy. Were you stealing my fruit?"

Pop faced him squarely and replied. "I was not stealing. I was tasting the plums. I love your plums."

"You love my plums?" the *poretz* repeated slowly.

"Yes, excellency. I truly love plums."

"And you were not stealing. You were tasting. Is that right, boy?"

"Yes, your lordship," father replied.

"And how did they taste?"

"Very delicious, sir," my father answered.

"Would you like to take some home with you?" the *poretz* asked.

"Oh, yes, excellency."

"Very well, boy. You can carry home a kilo or two. Perhaps more. But in your belly," the *poretz* said.

He then instructed the peasant to feed my father several handfuls of the ripest plums and then release him only after he had "tasted" them all.

Pop ate one plum after another after another. The supply seemed endless. He ate until he could eat no more. He was gorged, bloated, stretched to nausea and soon began to regurgitate. That was when the force-feeding stopped. When my father ceased vomiting and had regained his breath, the *poretz* dismissed him with a wave of his riding crop. "Next time we'll feed you persimmons," he warned. Stained and pale, Pop returned home and, between tears, told Grandfather everything that had occurred. Grandfather, a kindly but just man, admonished him for avoiding the classroom. "One does not miss the study of Torah even for one day, my son," he said. "That was your sin and God punished you, not with lashes or thunder and lightning, but with His bounty of plums. That is God's justice."

The following morning Grandfather walked the long, dusty road to the *poretz's* estate. He pulled the entry bell of the big house and was dispatched by a bailiff to the large storage barn where the *poretz* was instructing his peasants where to stack the barrels of fruit and produce.

"Yes, Jew, what is it you want?" the *poretz* said when he saw my grandfather. "I know your face, but I do not know who you are."

Grandfather explained why he had come. "Your excellency, I wish to make restitution for the plums my son appropriated."

"Forgive me, Uncle," the *poretz* interrupted. "*Appropriated* is not the word I would use. *Stole* would be more like it. If your thieving son were not such a puny monkey, he would have tasted my whip and not my plums."

"A thousand pardons, excellency. I apologize for my son, but I feel obligated to repay you for your loss," Grandfather said.

"That will not be necessary, old man," the *poretz* answered. "The rascal has been punished sufficiently. You may consider the debt paid."

"But the loss, sir. It will be on my conscience," Grandfather persisted.

"Do you have money?" asked the *poretz*. Grandfather answered that he did not.

"Well, in that case, what service can you do for me?" the nobleman asked. "Are you a tailor or a shoemaker? Are you a carpenter? I have repairs to be done in my barn."

Grandfather replied that he had no trade or craft. "I am a cantor in the small house of prayer near the river. I sing praises to the Lord."

"I can do without your praises to the Lord, uncle," the *poretz* said. "Can you sing something lively, something Russian?"

"I'm afraid not, excellency."

"What about sad songs? Do you know any sad songs?"

"Sad songs we are experts in, excellency. With your permission I will sing a psalm that is as melancholy as a Siberian winter," Grandfather replied.

The nobleman nodded his assent and Grandfather began. He chanted a psalm that was really quite joyous, but he sang it slowly and with such solemnity that it brought tears to the *poretz's* eyes. When he finished, he bowed to the nobleman.

"You sang loud and with passion, Reverend," the *poretz* said. "Now it is I who am in your debt."

He ordered his peasants to fetch a pair of horses and ordered them to deliver my grandfather to his home. What a stir there was in the village when my grandfather was delivered first to his house and later to the small synagogue not far from the river.

On the following morning, a bushel of plums was delivered to Grandfather's house. It was a gift from the *poretz*, but it was a mixed blessing. What was to be done with this abundance of already-ripened fruit? And how does one dispose of them? They could be brought to the market place, but the *poretz* was bound to find out.

His plums were large and well-formed while those of the neighboring farmers were wizened and puny and fetched insignificant prices. Nor would it be prudent, Grandfather reasoned, to distribute them to the poor. Their need was for bread and kopecks, not tasty compotes.

It was Grandmother who came up with the answer. She would cook and seethe them in large vats and convert the mass into jelly, and a tart plum butter that was her particular specialty. These products could then be put in jars and sold openly in the market. A windfall of kopecks could then be distributed to the needy of the village. This was Grandmother's solution.

For several days, the stove in her house steamed and sputtered and sang praise to the Lord for His bounty. The wondrous concoctions emerging from the pots were packaged as planned. Then my father and his brothers and sisters made their way through the crooked streets leading to the marketplace. Sales were good, but their luck was bad. One of their early buyers was a kitchen maid in the household of the *poretz*, and a jar of grandmother's plum butter was served at his table that very night. There was instant recognition by the *poretz's* housekeeper. This delicate flavor could only have emerged from his orchard.

On the following morning the nobleman summoned my grandfather to his mansion. There were no polite preliminaries.

"Reverend, you are a disappointment to me. You accepted my gift and then trifled with it. The plums were intended for your pleasure. They were not meant to be peddled in doorways like herring. What you did was an affront to me. Were it not for your station and your white whiskers I would have you flogged like an insolent peasant. I want you and your brats to take those jellies and preserves off the streets. Do you understand that?"

Grandfather bowed as low as his back would take him. "I beg forgiveness, excellency."

"Cow dung, uncle. You are an uncouth old man without manners," the *poretz* shouted.

"A thousand pardons, excellency. I am an unworldly man. Excuse my ignorance," Grandfather whispered.

"No, I will not. You are a man of some years and some learning. You should know how to repay kindness," the nobleman said.

"A thousand pardons," Grandfather repeated.

"You may leave my presence, Reverend. Without delay," said the *poretz*.

Grandfather bowed again. "Before I depart, may I offer your excellency a melody? A song of atonement, perhaps?" Grandfather asked.

"That would be most appropriate but will not be necessary, Reverend," the *poretz* said. "Leave my presence and may God show you the way home. My horses are required elsewhere."

Grandfather was taken to the door by the bailiff and began his long and twisting journey home.

That winter and spring and halfway through the summer, grandfather's family feasted on the plums. Everyone but my father. It was buttered on breads, poured on pancakes, splotched onto blintzes and *varenikas,* mixed into the oatmeal, spooned into the tea, served in ways hitherto untried. Guests gluttonized at grandmother's table. There was not a *simcha* (celebration) in the village that did not bear witness to the glories of the *poretz's* orchard.

During all that time, Pop could never bring even a morsel of the jellied plum to his lips. The sight of it brought on an unease in his belly and a rising of the gorge. Perhaps, my father rationalized, blintzes were meant to be served only with sour cream, and tea with lemon and not jelly. Maybe that was how God planned it (my father was a great one for bringing God into the picture).

One result of the orchard incident was that my father never again skipped a cheder class. True. He never became a scholar like his father, but he did learn one truth that was incontrovertible. It never pays to get caught.

My father's friendship with Chotzkel Berel cooled considerably after the events of that luckless afternoon. In cheder they ignored each other. They took on other friends. They swam in the river from opposite banks. On the Sabbath they went to different synagogues.

Years later, Chotzkel Berel was seen smoking on the Sabbath, was drafted into the czar's army, deserted after several months, emigrated to Brazil, and was never heard of again.

Retribution, my father would say whenever Chotzkel Berel's name came up. A decree from Heaven. A violation of the Torah. What could be more sinful than abandoning a comrade in time of danger? That's how my father saw it. When others would voice the opinion that Chotzkel Berel's disappearance had nothing to do with what happened in the *poretz's* orchard, Pop would answer with a quaver in his voice, "Who knows? Only God knows and He don't say."

Seymour

My friend Seymour Blumenthal was his grandmother's *kadishel,* which means that when she died, Seymour would say "kaddish" for her. Kaddish is the memorial prayer that Jewish men, and even boys, are obliged to recite daily for a deceased relative. If kaddish was not recited, the dead person would not get into heaven. That's what we were told.

Seymour was only nine or ten when we became friends. I think we got to know each other at Hebrew school where we both went, he reluctantly and I less so. "We gotta go. We're Jews," I would say to him and he always answered, "Bullshit."

He was a year ahead of me in school though we were around the same age. He was a good student and so was I, but he was at the top of the class while I was usually second or third. He was a talker and so was I, but never like Seymour. He was in my sister Dorothy's class, and she told me that nobody liked him except the teacher.

He was always raising his hand whenever a question was asked, she said, and most of the time he came up with the correct answer. But not always. One time during civics, the teacher, Miss Bradley, asked the class who was the president of the United States before Calvin Coolidge. Seymour answered Woodrow Wilson, which was dead wrong. The right answer was Warren G. Harding who died in his second year as president.

Seymour argued that since President Harding served only two years, he was just a part-time president and should not be counted. Miss Bradley said, "Nonsense," and when Seymour tried to justify his answer, she ordered him to sit down and stop wasting the time of the class. But that was Seymour. He was a great arguer especially when he was wrong.

My sister who sat next to Seymour heard him say "bullshit" under his breath. "Bullshit" was his favorite curse word especially when he could say it loud and forceful like a baseball umpire.

I liked Seymour. He was odd and strange but he was lots of fun. At least that's how I felt. The members of my club at the Y felt differently. Maybe because he was too bossy, or maybe because he was too smart, or maybe because he was a lousy athlete and would do us no good in the sports competition. I never encouraged him to join our club because I knew our guys would turn him down. I think Seymour realized it too because he joined another club. In six months he became president.

I stuck with Seymour, I think, because of his grandmother. I had a grandmother too, but she was still in Russia. Seymour's grandmother was beautiful the way a grandmother should be. She smiled all the time. She had a mouthful of false teeth that I think were a little too large for her mouth. Mrs. Slabodkin, that was her name, would remove the tops and bottoms after she ate, but she always turned her back on us so we wouldn't see her naked mouth.

Her hair was curly white and was always covered with a flowered *tichel* (a large kerchief). On Saturday when she went to the synagogue, she wore a white one that Seymour said was solid silk. She was a short lady, very short. She not only smiled most of the time, but she was also a hummer. The tunes she hummed were the kind you heard the cantor sing in the synagogue. Seymour said she could have been a cantor if she wasn't a woman.

Seymour was a lousy eater. His favorite food was a *feinkochen* (omelet). This was a fried egg with fried onions. He ate the feinkochen with an onion roll that his grandmother served hot. When it was meal time and I was with Seymour, Mrs. Slabodkin made me a feinkochen too but without the onions. I hated onions but I liked the onion roll. My mother never objected that I ate with Seymour because she was sure his grandmother kept strictly kosher.

As I said, his grandmother's name was Slabodkin, Rochel Slabodkin. My father told me that the Slabodkin name was a very distinguished one. It indicated that an ancestor had studied at the famous Slabodka yeshiva in Russia. It was like graduating from Yale or Harvard, he said. Anyone who had the name had *yichus* (prestige). I told this to Seymour and he said, "Bullshit." His grandfather was a shoemaker and he barely made a living.

It was sometime that summer that Seymour taught us to play poker. We didn't play for money because we never had much. I always had two or three cents in my pocket for an "emergency." Seymour had a nickel. I don't know what kind of emergency could be met with that kind of money, but they taught us in the Boy Scouts to always carry some money in your pocket for an "emergency."

We played poker with cigarette coupons. There were stores in our town that were called "United Cigar Stores." I think it was a chain. They sold mostly tobacco products like cigarettes, cigars, smoking tobacco, chewing tobacco, matches, pipes, snuff, things like that. Also candy. Anything that was bought, they would give the customer coupons. When you had enough coupons they could be redeemed for prizes. But you needed hundreds of them to get anything.

We kids would hang around these stores and when the customers came out, we would ask for their coupons. Most of the time they would give them to us. It was those coupons we used for poker. If you ran out of coupons, you could buy some from one of the guys in the game, five coupons for a penny. Seymour was almost always the winner. Almost any day he would come out with three or four cents' profit. Some of the guys thought he cheated at cards. I didn't believe them. Seymour was an oddball but he would never cheat.

That summer we talked a lot about girls. Seymour was fascinated by girls, as was I, but we were different. He hungered for them while I was just beginning to develop an appetite. Actually there was a girl in our seventh grade who was always trying to kiss me. Her name was Hannah and she was probably a little older than Seymour and me.

Sometimes she would catch me in the cloakroom and put her arms around me and kiss me. It started with kisses on the cheek and then the lips, which really bothered me. Hannah was not Jewish and I thought it was a sin to kiss a Christian girl, especially a Catholic. Our scoutmaster Mr. Goodman once had what he called a "heart to heart" talk with us Cubs and he warned us never to kiss a girl on the mouth. "That's where disease comes from," he told us and he should know because his father was a doctor.

There was a time when Seymour was sweet on my sister Dorothy, which I was not happy about, mostly because Seymour talked "dirty" about girls. He was not a Boy Scout like me. We were taught to be respectful of the female sex. Seymour told me he knew what girls liked and what they didn't. I asked him how the hell he knew so much about girls when he never had one. I had Hannah, I told him, but that didn't make me a professor.

He said he learned all about these things from his older brother Ralph who lived with Seymour's father in Paterson, New Jersey, where his pop was a salesman for a manufacturer. When Seymour's mother died, Ralph was taken by his father and Seymour stayed with Mrs. Slabodkin who couldn't take both boys. So she took the youngest.

That summer I met Ralph and I didn't like him. I think I really hated him because he was a bully and liked punching people. He would hit me on the arm and shoulders and did the same to Seymour. He was four years older than Seymour and wanted to be a boxer like Jack Dempsey. He was on the Paterson High School boxing team and tried to spar with us like we were Gene Tunney. Once he hit Seymour on the face and gave him a bloody nose. Seymour cried like a girl.

Ralph was there less than a week. Seymour's grandmother told me she was relieved when his father took him back to Paterson because he was a *vildah chayeh* (wild animal), and I answered in Yiddish, *"Emes gezukt"* (that's the truth).

When Seymour joined a club at the Y, our friendship suffered. Not greatly, but some. We still went to Hebrew school together. We were beginning to prepare for our bar mitzvahs. Mine would take place two months after his. Even though Seymour was probably smarter than I, I had him beat in the bar mitzvah department. He had a voice like a foghorn in a storm, while mine was as musical as a harp, the cantor told my father.

When we were bar mitzvah, we had parties, of course. Mine had twice as many guests as his, but he thought we came out even. I gave him a fountain pen and he gave me a Boy Scout knife, the official one and not the kind that was made in Japan.

Just about six months after his bar mitzvah, it was late August, Seymour moved to Paterson to live with his father and brother Ralph. It broke his grandmother's heart. I would spot her on Saturdays in the synagogue and whenever she saw me she cried. She was beginning to change. From time to time she came to shul wearing the flowered *tichel* instead of the white silk one that she reserved for the Sabbath.

Seymour visited her a few times, not nearly often enough, I thought. He would come in by bus and stay for a weekend or even a day, like Lincoln's birthday or Armistice Day. He always telephoned and we would meet mostly in his grandmother's house. She would hug and kiss me and cry. Seymour told me he was on the debating team at Paterson High and expected to be captain next year. He also told me, and I didn't believe a word he said, that he was terrific with girls, especially one whose name was Hortense. She was a blond and had big ones, he said.

He also confided that he tasted bacon, which was like ham. He would eat it in a sandwich with tomato and mayonnaise, and I almost puked. Eating bacon, which was really ham, was like turning your back on God. Like becoming a follower of Jesus Christ. That's what I thought.

It was during his first year at Rutgers University that Mrs. Slabodkin died. Seymour and his father came in for the funeral, of course, and left almost immediately afterwards. We spoke for just a matter of minutes.

"Where will you be saying kaddish?" I asked.

"Kaddish," he snorted. "I don't believe in that bullshit."

"It wasn't bullshit to your grandmother," I said angrily.

"My grandmother was a kind but ignorant woman. She believed in God, but I don't." He stopped as if to catch his breath. "Listen, Willie. You expect me to say prayers to someone who's not there? Bullshit!"

We shook hands. I never saw him again.

The Flower of the South

I once shook hands with a man who had shaken the hand, the left one, of Abraham Lincoln. I was a boy of eleven or twelve at the time and the Lincoln handshaker was a Civil War veteran who came to our school the day before Decoration Day, dressed in the blue uniform of the Union Army with an empty sleeve on his right side pinned to his tunic. We shook left hands, of course, which was the way he did it with President Lincoln. It didn't faze me one bit because I'm a lefty, and as I grasped his palm, he said, "Give it a good grab, boy. Squeeze them fingers like you're milkin' a cow's tit." I had never milked a cow before but I squeezed his hand hard enough to make him loosen his grip almost immediately.

In those days, our school had an assembly right before Decoration Day, as Memorial Day was called then, and a dozen or so Civil War veterans would be seated on the stage wearing their uniforms, mostly blue, some gray, and one or two in street suits. I remember one year a real old lady dressed in the stiffly starched white uniform of a nurse was among them. She was pushed onto the stage in one of those ancient wicker wheelchairs by another elderly lady wearing a large hat with peacock feathers that swooped past her head like they were ready to fly off. She was later introduced as the daughter of the one in the wheelchair.

At these assemblies our school principal, Miss Winchester, would introduce the veterans one by one, and maybe half of them would get up from their chairs, which in some cases was an effort, and say some words that hardly any of us could hear. The one exception was a large burly man with a voice the size of his belly who spoke rapid-fire almost without drawing a breath about the first battle of Bull Run. (I never suspected there were two.) It was at Bull Run he told us that he was wounded twice. He got a lot of applause and a few cheers and whistles, which Miss Winchester stifled with one of her steely glares.

The old lady in the wheelchair didn't speak, but her daughter did. She told us her mother heeded President Lincoln's urgent appeal for nurses in 1863 and left her family of three children and a consumptive husband who owned a farm just outside of Stroudsburg. Her first field hospital was in the village of Gettysburg where she spent four months working eighteen hours a day, mostly amputating limbs. She told us there wasn't a night in Gettysburg that "Mama didn't fall asleep on a pillow that wasn't soaked through and through with tears."

Our class had learned about the Battle of Gettysburg some months earlier from our teacher Mrs. Elizabeth Buffington. She was one of the few married teachers in our school and most of the kids didn't like her very much, though I thought she was great. She had this bad habit of giving us tests every day. One day it would be arithmetic, the next geography, the day after maybe hygiene. Once she tested us in grammar, spelling, and decimals all in one day because she said she had an inflammation in her voice box, wherever the hell that is. But I must say her teaching was like glue. It stuck with you as surely as a mustard plaster sticks to skin.

As she lectured, she had this custom of walking around the room and even into the aisles, looking squarely into your eyes while she talked on and on and on. Important things like names and dates she would repeat, sometimes three and four times. When she wasn't circling the room, she would go to the blackboard and sketch maps or charts or little cartoon figures to, as she said it, "put things down in black and white." For some odd reason, she used green chalk.

Mrs. Buffington got real emotional and weepy the morning she told us about the Battle of Gettysburg, which she said took place just about 100 miles south of where we were sitting "at this very moment." She spoke in a hoarse voice like the time she had that infection in her voice box. Not once did she go to the blackboard or walk around the room. She told us that the casualties of that three-day battle ending on the Fourth of July added up to more than 50,000 dead and wounded. "What an irony," she said. "On Independence Day of 1863, 50,000 mostly young men went to their graves or were maimed beyond description. In that terrible battle," she said so low you could hardly hear her, "the flower of the South was lost." And then she repeated it. "The flower of the South . . . gone forever."

Mrs. Buffington withdrew a crumpled pink handkerchief from her sleeve and silently blew her nose and blotted at her eyes. Most of us were overcome too but that didn't stop that idiot Chester Chernowski from asking what she meant by the flower of the South. Mrs. Buffington blew her nose again and said gently, "The youth, Chester. The young men, only seven or eight years older than the boys in this class."

After the Decoration Day assembly, they sent us home early and when we were dismissed I could see that some of the old soldiers were lined up outside the boys lavoratory waiting their turn. One of them had just come out and seemed to have trouble buttoning his fly with his left hand. He was the one who a little later on told me he had shaken the hand of Abraham Lincoln. In between two or three "goddammits," he finished the job and caught me in the middle of a stare. He called me over and asked which way to the street. I said I would take him there and we walked out of the building together. As we walked, he put his one hand on my right shoulder, which he used to slow my pace and to give him balance.

He told me he always came to these things. "Been showin' up the last four, five years and expect I'll be here next year if I'm still standin' upright," he said.

"My grandson Tommy, he's forty, brought me here this mornin' in his Ford pickup, he works for the county, and I guess I'll take the trolley back home."

I asked him where he lived and he told me Green Ridge, which is three or four miles from our school. He said the streetcar would be fine because it would drop him off one long block from his daughter Margaret's house, which was only a hop and a skip away. I told him if he wanted to I would take him to the main post office building, which is where his trolley stopped, and he said he would be much obliged.

As we walked, he told me his name was Evander Billings but that most people called him Eben.

"I'm eighty-two but I'm not braggin' about it. It's no great distinction to get up in years though some of those old-timers on your stage today were disportin' themselves like females in a cathouse. Especially that ellerphant Vince Jones, he's the bag o' wind that told about being wounded at Bull Run."

"Twice," I said.

"Twice what?"

"Said he was wounded twice at Bull Run," I answered.

"Don't believe that bullshit for one minute, sonny. That tub of blubber got himself a ball in the butt so that'll tell you which way he was headin'. The other would come out of his 'magination and not his big ass," Mr. Billings said with real anger.

I was about to change the subject.

"Just a big bag of wind," he muttered.

"I guess you know him from before," I commented.

"Certainly did." He paused. "Used to work for him. Clerkin' in his thievin' shoestore. With one arm, you gotta take what you get. Right?"

"Yes, sir."

"So . . . what do they call you, sonny?"

"William," I answered.

"William! Hell, you're old enough to be called Bill."

"No. Just William. My brothers and sisters call me Will."

"We had a farm boy in our company by that name. Caught a ball square in the face in Chambersberg. Died without a face. What a way to meet the Almighty. Can't recall his surname. Johnson or maybe Jones. One of those everyday names. I'm Evander Billings but folks call me Eben. But I guess I told you that," he said, eyeing me questioningly.

"Yes sir, Mr. Billings," I answered.

"Did I tell you I got my hand shook by Abraham Lincoln hisself? In a field hospital outside Philadelphia. That's where they chopped off my right arm.

"Mr. Lincoln was making the rounds going from one cot to the next. Would say some words of greeting and then maybe shake hands, pat a shoulder or even pat the cheek of some young soldier who was maybe sixteen or seventeen. That was my age, you know. Seventeen. When he comes to my bed, he sticks out his right hand towards mine and then sees there's nothing there. So he looks to my other side and sees that my left arm is tied down to the side of my cot. I says to the orderly with him, there was two of them, 'Would you please loosen me so's I can shake the hand of the President?'

"They done that real fast and he puts my hand into his and we shake. Wasn't really a shake. Just held my hand in his. Then he pats me on the head. His touch was gentle as a prayer and not one word comes out of his mouth all that time. I had the proper manners to say to him, 'God bless you Mr. Lincoln,' and he nods his head and moves on to the next cot. They told me later on that tears was rollin' down his face like the spigot was wide open. When he left our corridor, they tied me down again like he was never there."

"Why would they do that, Mr. Billings?" I asked.

"Do what?"

"Tie your good arm down."

"The pain, boy. When they sawed off my limb, I was clawin' myself real fierce. Thrashin' around like a dyin' cat. Couldn't help myself. So they trussed me up so's I couldn't move. Didn't like it, but they done the right thing."

He stopped talking, I think mostly to catch his breath. We were plodding along slow but sure, his hand still on my right shoulder, pressuring it just a bit to slow up so he could breathe normally without gasping for breath. We were not very far from the post office and I thought he seemed reluctant to reach the trolley stop. When we were almost there, he halted and asked if there were any high bushes nearby where he could take himself a leak. I told him we were right next to the Elks Club, which had lots of bushes, but that he didn't have to do it on their grounds because he could just as easily use their facilities.

"Take it from an old pisser like me, sonny, it's always better to do it in God's great outdoors. Them inside privies you pull a chain that don't always work and then where are you."

Saying that, he hied himself over to the Elks' privet fence and let fly. It took a little time for him to button up. He always seemed to have a problem with the last button. After a brief adjustment, we were on our way.

"So did you like my speechifying today, William? I done it before, you know."

"It was fine," I told him.

He gave me a wide smile showing a mouthful of empty gums. "What did you like about it?"

"I liked it all," I said—and lied. I hadn't really heard a word he said. From where I sat in the overheated auditorium—Miss Winchester refused to open windows because bird sounds were distracting, she said—I could catch sounds coming out of his mouth but couldn't put them together as words. So I gambled.

"'Specially the part about how you got your wound," I added fearlessly.

Apparently this was not what he had expected. He exploded. "You're bullshittin' me, boy. I never talk about that. Never would." He calmed down just a little.

"Told them I volunteered in '61 and they made me a drummer boy. Was seventeen. When I got this in '64," he nodded his head at the empty right sleeve, "I told them I could blow the bugle, but they mustered me out. Too old to be a bugler, they said. I was twenty."

As we approached the post office, he eased up on me and pinched my shoulder lightly (which I think was his way of saying all was forgiven). He told me he had been on the government pension for sixty years, maybe more, which was not overly generous, but no trifle either. His wife Betsy died in 1901 from the dropsy. "Swoll up her legs and arms like they was hams. It was a blessing when the Almighty took her." He wiped his eyes with his sleeve.

We didn't converse any more until the street car rattled up right where we stood.

"Much obliged, William, for takin' me here," he said. "Would've wet my britches if you wasn't there."

He smiled that wide toothless smile and stuck out his hand and we shook. I helped him up the three steps into the trolley and the conductor got him a seat up front. Wouldn't you think he'd skip the fare of a Civil War veteran all decked out in his blue uniform, dinky blue cap and all? Well, he didn't.

The following Decoration Day, it was my graduation year, three or four old soldiers didn't show at the assembly. Neither the old nurse nor my friend with the one arm made it. The Bull Run bullshit veteran with the bullet up his ass was there in full mouth. He told us how he was wounded at Bull Run twice. Yah! Yah!

The Passing of Bubbeleh

Bubbeleh was the family pet. She happened to be a guinea pig, which is not the most fashionable beast in the kingdom of pets, but to my wife she had it all. Bubbeleh was about twelve inches long and weighed in at maybe thirty ounces; her furry body was a tawny brown with white flecks on the head and face and she was always smiling. At least that was what my wife said. The rest of us never saw that smile, but my wife insisted it was in Bubbeleh's eyes. "They smile with the eyes like Mona Lisa," she said with a finality that was thunderous.

The guinea pig came to us by chance. She was brought home by my son from his fourth grade classroom lying timidly in a Florsheim shoe box. My son, who is the humanitarian of the family, especially when it comes to animals, told us that none of the kids in his class wanted "the pig" as they called her.

It was the last day of school before the summer vacation and the guinea pig whose name was Brenda had to find a home. My son raised his hand and was given the animal and the shoe box. My wife was not elated with my son's magnanimity but changed her mind when she set eyes on Bubbeleh.

It was love at first sight. The first thing she did was change her name. In her opinion, Brenda was a name for an overweight cat who lives on Park Avenue. "We'll give her a name with a Jewish ring to it," she said emphatically. "She's such a cute bubbeleh."

And so the guinea pig with the smiling eyes became Jewish and her new name was "Bubbeleh." According to my son and his teacher Miss Ernestine Hobbs, the animal was purchased in a pet shop that sold mostly dogs. Miss Hobbs paid ten dollars for her, a bargain she said, because guinea pigs usually went for twenty. My son said Bubbeleh came from South America, probably a place called Bolivia but he wasn't sure.

"And she will eat anything that is green," he said.

"Green," my wife asked.

"Right. And she defecates a lot."

"Defecates?" my wife said with a furrowed brow. "Where did you get that word?"

"From Miss Hobbs. She says it all the time when she talks about Brenda."

"Bubbeleh, you mean," my wife corrected.

"Right. Bubbeleh. She is quite a defecator, Miss Hobbs says."

"I think we've covered the subject," my wife answered.

"Okay." But he didn't let go. "She eats cabbage leaves or lettuce or celery, but no onions. They make her belch." He paused for a few seconds and then added, "And she defecates endlessly."

"Endlessly?" my wife asked.

"That's what Miss Hobbs says."

"I get the picture," my wife said and terminated the conversation.

Bubbeleh resided in what had been and still is, I suppose, a large fish tank where my son's goldfish cavorted for a while and usually after a week's interval bellied up and died. My son blamed it on the food or the room or the cooking odors or the sunlight or the lack of sunlight or the genus of the guppies he bought almost weekly. Whatever it was, fatality was the end game.

My wife referred to the fish tank as the Castle and kept it spick-and-span except for Bubbeleh's defecatory emissions. It was my job to clean out the Castle every few days and add new nesting materials. I used a mix of cedar chips and sawdust, but Bubbeleh began eating the sawdust so I leaned more heavily on the cedar chips.

Guinea pigs are very timid animals, but smart. To begin with, they never try to escape. My wife would extract Bubbeleh from the Castle and place her on the lawn where she would nibble on the grass. She did her grazing within a small circle and squealed and squeaked all the time she was working on her turf. Mornings around six she would signal my wife that it was wake-up time and chirped and squawked and squished until my wife picked her up and gave her some water. She used a teaspoon and dribbled the liquid down Bubbeleh's mouth, which often caused her to cough. Bubbeleh never bit the hand that fed or watered her. Guinea pigs are not biters, which makes them so popular with kids.

Early in her stay with us, my wife would cradle her in her arms and kiss her on the head, which Bubbeleh seemed to like. Then my wife began teaching her tricks. She would place Bubbeleh in the palm of her right hand and encourage her to scamper up to the bend in her elbow.

This continued for a while, and my wife encouraged Bubbeleh to venture further up her arm and to the back of her neck. And then further until Bubbeleh made it a round trip going from the right palm all the way around to the left palm. Neither I nor my son could get her to go any further than the bend in our elbow. She would remain in the crook of my arm and gaze at me defiantly as if saying, "Look, dummy, she's the one who feeds me."

My wife was continuously experimenting with Bubbeleh's diet. Kosher food, of course. She tried feeding her a few morsels of potato kugel, which Bubbeleh rejected almost angrily. My son thought it was the onions in the kugel. The same with a cheese blintz, which she ignored. I think my wife almost succeeded with a piece of raisin bread, which Bubbeleh nipped at, but she paid the price by vomiting all over the Castle.

I must say that Bubbeleh appeared to relish her stay with us. She showed no signs of boredom though if she did, we would undoubtedly not recognize the signs of guinea pig ennui. On the other hand, she cackled and squealed most of the day, which my wife said was a sure sign of happiness.

Guinea pigs are rodents like squirrels, beavers, rabbits, and of course mice. My wife never accepted the rodent classification for Bubbeleh. She was no rat, she insisted. She didn't look like a rat, she didn't sound like a rat, she didn't smell like a rat. In truth I don't believe my wife ever got face to face with a rat or even a mouse, but Bubbeleh would never be one of those, she swore.

What she was, my wife insisted, was a small pig. A piglet really and a clean one at that. A domestic animal, one that doesn't bite and could be trained not to defecate all over the house. One of our neighbors who was a close friend of my wife, but no longer is, insisted that Bubbeleh was a rodent, according to the *Encyclopedia Britannica.*

"What the hell do they know?" my wife answered. "Look at Bubbeleh. Does she look like a rat?" my wife grumbled. "She's not shifty-eyed. She doesn't have a long tail. Actually she doesn't have a tail at all. She's like a small dog. She has a large head like a St. Bernard and a furry coat like a Pekinese. She's more like a dog than most dogs, for heaven's sake." It was like my wife was defending Bubbeleh's virtue.

The passage of time only invigorated my wife's passion for the animal. She was endlessly petting her, scratching her head, kissing her, cradling her, feeding her domestic fodder like corn flakes or shredded wheat. She was always perched on my wife's neck or the inside of her left elbow. It was a partnership made in heaven.

Time passed and was not especially kind to Bubbeleh. My wife could read it in her eyes, she said. The sparkle was gone. They no longer smiled like the Mona Lisa. They appeared listless, tired, my wife said.

"Bubbeleh is not getting enough sleep. Nor does she eat like she used to," she complained. My son said, "She's not defecating either and it's a different color." My wife gave him a glum look.

We never truly knew how old Bubbeleh was. My wife read somewhere that guinea pigs can live as long as eight years, but she estimated that Bubbeleh was probably half that age.

It was on Yom Kippur that Bubbeleh cashed it in. They say that a death on Yom Kippur brings on a blessing. I don't think that applies to guinea pigs or other pets like dogs and cats. It certainly did not in our household.

I had arrived at shul around eight that morning. At ten the synagogue was still half empty but was beginning to fill up fast. Almost out of nowhere my son came to my seat. He was breathing hard like he had been running.

"Mom wants you to come home right away," he gasped.

"Right away?" I said incredulously. "This is Yom Kippur. What's the problem?" I asked.

"Bubbeleh died."

"Bubbeleh died?"

"That's right. The pig died."

"Bubbeleh died," I repeated. "What happened?"

"Mom said she probably had a heart attack."

"A heart attack? Guinea pigs don't have heart attacks, for Christ's sake," I protested.

"Mom said she did and wants you home right away."

"I can't leave in the middle of Yom Kippur."

"She said tell him to get his ass home right away."

"I don't believe it," I said.

"Her exact words, Dad. She wants you to bury Bubbeleh on the mound."

"The mound. Right away? We don't do things like that on Yom Kippur."

"Mom said you would say that. She told me to tell you if you don't come home now, you can break your fast at your sister's house."

"My sister lives in Pennsylvania, goddam it," I protested.

"That's right," my son said.

I could see this was a crisis not only involving Bubbeleh's remains but me as well. I removed my tallis, went to the parking lot with my son, and drove home. As I entered the house, my wife was seated in the kitchen weeping silently. Her face was splotched with tears. She embraced me tightly like I was heading off to the wars. She was dressed for shul.

Her never-worn Mr. John hat which she had bought months ago was lying limply on the crown of her head. She always looked great in almost any kind of millinery. Her friends told her she could have been a hat model, and she believed them. I did too. I said to her, "I'm sorry, honey."

She answered. "Bubbeleh is in the refrigerator. I wrapped her in a towel."

"A towel?" I asked softly.

"It's a new one. We'll bury her in that," she said.

"You don't want her in the shoe box?" I stammered.

"The towel is better," she answered. She turned to our son and said "Sonny, you know what to do."

Without a word he opened the refrigerator door, pulled out the towel and handed it to me with both hands. It was as if the ritual had been rehearsed. I was a little flustered what to do next. My wife opened the back door and led the way to the mound in the far corner of the lawn.

The mound is a small hillock that I had constructed, largely a shovel job, in a corner of our lawn shortly after we bought our property. It is planted as a miniature jungle of rare plants that had spread over the knoll into a hodgepodge of vegetation that was attractive in a wild sort of way. The mound overlooked a circulating pool that gurgled like a brook and was fashioned like one. It was a pretty scene.

The mound was also a burial ground for the departed pets of my son. It was the final resting place of two baby chicks named Sununu One and Sununu Two, a snake of medium size, and a collection of goldfish who probably ate themselves into the grave.

I shoveled deep into the center of the mound and scooped out enough earth to accommodate the corpus of our beloved Bubbeleh. My wife was silent and was no longer crying.

When the burial was over, she asked me to wait while she put on her Mr. John hat and a pair of white gloves. As we waited, my son asked me if I would say kaddish for Bubbeleh. I told him we say kaddish for human beings and not animals.

"Aren't they creatures of God like us?" he asked.

"Of course," I answered. "But they're not human creatures."

"That's bullshit, Dad, and you know it."

"No. It's not bullshit, Sonny."

"It is and you know it."

"Well," I said somewhat later, "I'll think about it."

"That usually means no, Dad."

"Not necessarily," which was all I could say. I was feeling stupid and guilty and in a hurry to go back to shul. At the synagogue, my son went downstairs to the junior congregation. As he left, he gave me one of those looks that would curdle milk.

My wife took her aisle seat next to me and though her eyes were reddened from the morning's cascade of tears, she looked at peace and regal in her gay, beribboned chapeaux that Mr. John, if there is such a person, created especially for her.

When we reached Yizkor, I included Bubbeleh's name in the kaddish cycle. From time to time during the other holidays, I would do the same. I never disclosed this to my son, but I did tell my wife who kissed me and cried. The following day my son kissed me too, but no tears. He had cleaned the Castle and was back in the fish business with a pair of guppies named Mutt and Jeff.

The Missing Ear

A couple of years ago I wrote a story about my friend Roger; I won't mention his family name because he's been dead and buried these past twenty years and more. In my opinion he would prefer the anonymity of the grave, and one does not trifle with Rog even though he's been resting six feet under for a long time.

We were warrant officers together with Patton's Fifth Army in Africa and later the Seventh in Italy. We shared the same tent for almost three years, which included some sticky service in France and Germany. Roger's expertise, his warrant actually, was in supply; mine was in reconnaissance and later in administration.

Roger looked like a soldier. He was big, six three or four in his bare feet. Strong. He weighed in at about 250 pounds. Powerful. Played tackle on the football team for three of his four years at Holy Cross. He could be as mean as a boil or gentle as a priest, which his mother Mary hoped he would be. He was something of an anti-Semite, though that's another story.

I was probably Roger's best friend in our battalion, though I would put him in my top five or six. Undoubtedly his dislike of Jews played heavy in my estimation though I may have been a little unfair in my judgment. Roger was not only anti-Jewish; he was equally hostile to the British whom he called limeys or worse, the French who were frogs, Protestants of all stripes, Italians, Arabs, the Welsh, and the Middle Europeans who, in his lexicon, were hunkies. I don't know his attitude towards Pakistanis, Indians, and those who came out of Afghanistan but he lumped them all under the rubric of "mutton heads."

When we were in Cassino, Italy, our antiaircraft battalion was paired up with an infantry brigade from Indonesia whose soldiers were Oriental and on the smallish side. It was only natural that Rog would refer to their liaison officer as Mr. Moto.

Roger was a boozer. He liked what he called the "sauce." Any kind would do. He once told me, pridefully I thought, that he was twelve when he experienced his first bout of intoxication. It came out of a carafe of Irish whiskey that was the libation of choice at his cousin Eddie's wake. The cousin, who was really a distant kinsman rather than a relation, was killed in a mine cave-in in northeastern Pennsylvania. The mine was owned by Roger's uncle John.

It was Uncle John, the eldest brother of Roger's mother Mary, who owned the town. He owned the coal mines and those who worked them. Storekeepers, men with trades, politicians, all took orders from the old man and his second-in-command Roger. It was Rog who carried out the edicts of Uncle John.

It seemed odd that it was he who was the muscle of the family rather than Uncle John's sons, but they were softies, more like their mother's side of the family. So it was said.

The miners who worked the pits were mostly of Slavic derivation. They came largely from Poland, Russia, and its satellites. There was a smattering of Swedes and Welshmen whom Roger referred to as the "infidels." He never explained why. Probably because they were Protestants.

The Italian mine workers came mostly from Sicily and of course Roger referred to them as "the guineas." Most of them were proud of Benito Mussolini, which bothered old Uncle John who called him "that fat Eyetalian phony."

As a man and a boss, Roger was well-liked and respected by the miners. When any of their kinfolk came over from the Old Country, it was Roger who was dispatched to get the greenhorn a job either in the mines or from the town's political leaders, who were "owned" by Uncle John. The town was a Democratic stronghold. Uncle John delivered the votes despite his dislike of FDR.

"That smiling aristocrat is owned by the goddam Brits," he would say but never within earshot of the faithful.

It was Roger's job to be present at all celebrations, private and other, of the men employed in the old man's colliery or aboveground. He hardly ever missed a betrothal or a wedding, a birth or baptism, a wake or funeral. He was especially partial to wakes, which could drag on for days and were attended by virtually all of the Irish community.

The wakes were not only Olympiads of drink but also featured the retelling of yarns going back to the old sod. Most were well-known but they were repeated and listened to as if they had just emerged from an Irish throat. Roger was one of the most prolific of these yarn spinners. He drew his material from his uncle's clan and, like Old John himself, started his narration with a deep sigh and the expected opening line of "I mind the time" et cetera and et cetera in the manner of James Joyce.

Though he often ridiculed the Polish-Russian miners, he had a kind of proprietary attitude towards them. He loved to reminisce about the years he spent in his uncle's employ.

"I hardly ever went down the shaft," he told me. "I was the upstairs man. 'Keep them happy,' I was told. 'Be useful. Be their friend.' Most of those hunkies couldn't read or write. These were pork chop people. My job was to keep the pork chops rolling," Roger said.

And he did. What Rog did best was drink with them. There was a saloon named Grogan's Spa where mostly the Irish coalminers and their friends had their swallow. The big tipple took place on Friday night after payday. Grogan set up a table bulging with sandwiches that were on the house.

But mostly Grogan's customers went home first, took their baths, ate their hot corned beef and cabbage and boiled potatoes, gave the wife her food money and then hied it over to the Spa.

The Slav miners mostly had their Friday night bash of beer and whiskey at another saloon run by a Russian named Vladimir Dimitrovsky. It was called Dimmy's. It was very much like Grogan's Spa except that it was a bit larger. The difference was in the music. At Dimmy's there was always an accordion player who kept pulling on the buttons of his keyboard in an unstoppable night of polka dance music. At Grogan's there was a fiddler who was not very good and who became successively worse as the night lengthened. Both bars were jammed with drinkers. They were strung out along the lengthy counters. The floors were sprinkled heavily with sawdust and the walls behind the service bars were mirrored right up to the ceiling.

Both temples of drink were open to midnight. Both proprietors removed their aprons at 11:45 which was the signal that the bacchanalia was just about over. Somewhere around 10:30 a fight would break out in Grogan's like it was written into the lease. The confrontation, which involved fists only, was usually broken up by Roger with the help of the bouncer who was known as the "Elf." Usually there was blood spilled mostly from the nose and maybe a scratch or two on the face.

There were times of course when tempers went into high gear and the fighters wrestled themselves onto the floor where all types of mayhem took place. It was fists and elbows and biting and beard yanking and gouging that clip-clopped across the floor like pigeons at a clambake. It was on such a night—according to Roger they still talk about it even today—that the mayhem known as the Night of the Cousins took place.

Frankie and Padraic Finnegan, cousins by way of Dublin, were locked in combat on the bloodstained sawdust floor of the Spa. No one knew what led to the brawl. Roger and the Elf began to tear them apart when suddenly a scream as from a banshee in labor came out of the mouth of one of the fighters.

Blood started to course out of a still-undefined head. In an instant the source of the bleeding became evident. It came from the right ear of Frankie Finnegan, a handler of dynamite in one of Old John's collieries. His antagonist was a kinsman, Padraic, who was out of work and out of money.

Blood was gushing out of Frankie's ear as from a faucet. Roger was cool and collected as always and asked whose car was parked in front of the Spa. It belonged to a guy known as the Bald Eagle. Roger ordered him to take Frankie to the hospital. A man known as Fangs went with him. The festivities at the Spa were somewhat diminished but not totally.

Just as life was beginning to return to Grogan's saloon, the telephone rang, which was not usual for a Friday night. Grogan took the call and in a few seconds shouted, "It's for you, Roger. It's the hospital."

Roger listened to the caller who turned out to be Dr. Leonard Shapiro. "You say the bleeding's stopped but you're not finished. So what's stopping you, Doc?" Roger asked.

Dr. Shapiro talked for a while, but Roger interrupted. "Sure, it's the right ear, Doc," he said curtly. The voice on the other end sounded louder and angrier.

Roger again interrupted. "Okay, Doc. We'll do that right away." He hung up.

The noise had ceased. The drinkers were silent waiting for Roger to speak up. He cleared his throat.

"Doc Shapiro needs the ear or what's left of it," Roger said slowly. "Padraic bit off a chunk of Frankie's ear and it's lying somewhere on the floor. We got to find it. When we do, we send it to the hospital. So let's move ass and find the goddam ear," Roger said.

One of the regulars piped up, "What's it look like, Rog?"

"Like an ear, for Christ's sake," he answered. "You gotta feel around the sawdust. Don't step on it."

Shane Murphy, a constable, asked Roger, "Why does the doc want the ear?"

"To sew it back on, dumbbell," Roger answered.

"Sew it back on, Roger? You gotta be joshing."

"I'm not joshing. Just find the goddam ear."

Murphy wouldn't let go. "I can't believe he's gonna stitch it back on. It's unbelievable, Roger."

Roger was running out of patience. "How many years have you gone to medical school, Murph? Answer me that."

"None, Roger," Murphy replied.

"Then shut your goddam face and keep looking."

In a matter of minutes, Skeets Moran, a fireman, yelled out, "I think I found it, Rog. It needs washing."

Roger jumped in, "Don't wash the goddam thing. Doc Shapiro told me to rinse it in whiskey. To sanitize it."

Roger was handed the ear very gingerly, and he soaked it in a tumbler of Old Flag, a cheap rye whiskey. The ear came out clean and smelling like a rose. It looked to Roger like a chunk of fried oyster that wasn't quite done.

Roger turned to Sean Murphy and asked if he had come to the Spa on his Harley. When he answered yes, Roger gave him the ear wrapped in toilet tissue and instructed him to rush it to Doc Shapiro in the emergency room. To speed Murphy on his way, Roger poured him a half-tumbler of Old Flag to wet his whistle, which he did in one or two swallows.

Sean told Roger afterwards that Doc Shapiro put the ear to his nose, whiffed it two or three times, nodded to Sean and said, "It smells kosher to me."

"What's with this kosher thing?" he asked Roger.

"Kosher," Roger repeated. "It's like purifying yourself like we do at Confession with Father Kelly."

"Sounds good to me, Rog."

"I knew it would, Murph," Roger said with a smile. Dr. Shapiro who was no surgeon did the sewing. It was a patchwork job of course but it did the trick. In time normal hearing returned to Frankie who said the ear was as good as new. His single complaint was that there were times, especially when it rained, that he heard the ringing of bells.

"What kind of bells?" Roger once asked.

"Like church bells," Frankie replied.

"You mean like in *The Bells of St. Mary's*?"

"That's it, Rog. With Bing Crosby."

From that time on, Roger and the guys at Grogan's referred to Frankie as Bing Crosby. And the name stuck.

Sabbath with the Golem of Prague

The October sun was dropping slowly over the Western Wall in the Old City of Jerusalem. Spectators and worshippers, separated from each other by a solid fence of stone that ran the length of the Kotel, as the ancient Western Wall is called, were eagerly awaiting the coming of the Sabbath.

As the sun descended, the flow of humanity quickened. By now, close to the hour of the Sabbath, the Kotel plaza was filling up with worshippers of all description. Young soldiers still carrying their weapons, Chasidic Jews cloaked in white and black and wearing fur-trimmed headwear, little boys, ringlets of silky hair dripping along their cheeks, Europeans and Americans of diverse sizes, ages, and piety awaited the moment of prayer. They had come to welcome the Sabbath queen.

It was on a Sabbath eve such as this, turbulent, expectant, impatient, that I was to make the acquaintance, in a manner of speaking, of the golem of Prague . . .

I had come to the Wall that Friday evening, as I had on a number of other such occasions, to be picked up by a rabbi, a rather unique rabbi. Baruch, which was the name of this young, rather dapper, ascetic-faced rabbi, had a mission. Baruch's job, his mission, was to save Jews. He concentrated largely on young Jews, though he did not discriminate. "There are no age barriers in Heaven," he told me when he first sized me up.

Where Baruch was unique was in the frenzied zeal with which he tracked his quarry. Anyone who looked hapless or homeless, or simply alone, was fair game for Baruch and his assistants. Did someone need a bed for the night, a Sabbath meal, a pause on the day of rest, a place of study, a counselor, a friend? Baruch would handle it, one way or another.

On this particular late Friday afternoon, I had come there for a Sabbath evening meal. I had done this before and inevitably had come away with an uncommon experience. Baruch knew I preferred being placed at the table of a Meah She'arim family, preferably one where Yiddish was spoken. The Meah She'arim section of Jerusalem was where the extremely devout Jews resided. Their precincts, certainly their homes, were not easily penetrated by outsiders, and being a guest there for a Sabbath meal was one way of crossing the threshold.

On one occasion, I was dispatched to the Old City apartment of an Oxford University graduate, a Londoner married to a lady born in Algiers. Both of them were immersed in Kabbalah, the occult Jewish mysticism, and somewhere between dessert and the grace after meals, my host told me I must never marry again because it would be a luckless marriage. When I asked him how he knew, he shook his head and smiled sadly.

At another time, I was brought into Meah She'arim to a cold flat located on top of a onetime barn. At the top of the staircase, I was welcomed by a skinny, brownish-black and long-bearded Jew, wearing a black hat, black caftan, and an immaculate but worn white shirt buttoned to the throat. He greeted me with a "Good *Shabbos*" twanged out in a singsong Yankee accent. He and his wife, who appeared to be twenty years his junior, were converts to Judaism and hailed originally from Boston. The meal consisted of the leftover meat, potatoes, and canned peaches that had been served at the circumcision that week of their fifth child whom, the wife told me proudly, she had delivered herself.

On the night of this narrative, Baruch selected me for a Meah She'arim host who "speaks Yiddish, but English even better," and put me in the hands of one of his volunteer guides who was to deliver me, along with several other Meah She'arim assignees, to the appropriate families. I was the last one to be dropped off, and when I got there I sensed I was late, quite late.

"What happened, Moishe?" my host, whose name was Zaidel, inquired of the guide. "I expected the guest an hour ago."

"I'm sorry, Zaidel, but you were the last stop. Thank God, we had lots of guests tonight," Moishe answered, departing hurriedly. My host hustled me inside his modest but cheerful-looking apartment. There were two other men in the dining room, *orchim* (guests), as it turned out, from Haifa and Tel Aviv. When I asked Reb Zaidel (which was how his guests referred to him) how it was that he spoke English so fluently, he replied he was born in Montreal and had been a biology teacher there for almost twenty years.

My host was a large man, about sixty years old, burly, a thick reddish beard inundating his white shirt front, a *shtreimel* (fur hat) perched jauntily on his head, and a smile spread across his face, ear-lock to earlock. He told me that he and his guests were Lubavitcher Chasidim who came together on the Sabbath before *Rosh Chodesh* (the new month). He introduced us. He removed his *shtreimel,* exposing a skullcap crushed upon a flushed bald head, filled his silver beaker with wine, and almost abruptly began the recitation of the kiddush (blessing over wine).

After Reb Zaidel had drunk from the wine cup, he invited his guests to say the kiddush, if they wished. All of us declined politely. We followed our host to the sink in the foyer for the hand-washing ritual prior to the *motzi,* the blessing over bread. Zaidel poured a laver full of water into the three-handled copper washing vessel and offered it to me first, a high compliment, I thought. He made me remove my wedding band and the silver ring from the little finger of the other hand, and began to explain the washing procedure. I told him I knew what to do, which, I think, caught him by surprise. I washed, pouring water on one hand, then on the other, and then repeating the ritual twice more, simultaneously reciting the proper blessing. This impressed him even more.

He took the laver from my hand, washed with élan and lively splashing, then passed it to his guests, one of whom laved primly, almost timidly, the other sloppily and, I thought, ineptly. (Is this a clue to our personality, I wondered?)

A word about the two visiting Lubavitch guests. They both could have been outfitted by the same clothier—black hats, long black coats, white shirts buttoned to the limit, hard black shoes, the kind that used to be worn by the New York police. Each man had a full-grown black beard, but of different consistencies. The older of the two had a face that was all beard. It was thick, medium-long, covering both cheeks almost up to the eyes, which were also coal black. The other, who appeared to be in his thirties but was actually ten years younger, had the kind of silken, struggling beard that one associates with an ascetic-faced Chinese mandarin.

The meal had begun with the blessing of the bread. There were the two obligatory challahs, the braided egg breads, which Reb Zaidel placed together, bottom to bottom, and then recited the *motzi*. At its conclusion, he broke off a large chunk of challah, sprinkled it liberally with salt, then proceeded to tear off four smaller chunks that he salted less vigorously and then distributed to his guests. We made the *motzi* too. The fourth piece was left on the chrome challah platter for his wife who unobtrusively came to our table and took it with her to the kitchen. I heard her, just barely, reciting the blessing over the challah.

His wife was a tall, plain-looking woman with beautiful brown eyes. They suggested intelligence, but this is only a guess on my part because she never spoke. Nor did she eat with us. She served the meal, course by course, as if on cue. There was lots of conversation during the meal and she knew exactly when to remove dishes and bring in others.

She was a terrible cook. The challahs were store-bought; they had the kind of rumpled look that comes from an overlong stay in a bakery bin. The gefilte fish, which was homemade, was lacking in salt, pepper, sugar, and taste. The chicken soup appeared to be eked out of an unhappy chicken. Then, of course, there was the joyless chicken in person and an unspeakable potato kugel. The final course was Jaffa oranges, which were good.

The table conversation was unforgettable. It dipped and spun and whirled into strange places and touched upon strange events, always returning to its point of origin, the rebbe, the Lubavitcher rebbe. And his disciples as well. They too, I was told, possessed some of the rebbe's saintliness and charisma. They also were sought for consultation, for the granting of boons, for advice.

Reb Zaidel told of a wondrous event that was reported to have happened recently through the intervention of a disciple of the rebbe's, a doctor who resides in Natanya. He possessed a touch of the rebbe's gifts. The doctor was a consultant physician, not one who sees patients on a regular basis. He had come to Natanya from the United States to study Torah. From time to time, local physicians, Lubavitch and others, would phone or visit him for consultation and advice.

One such doctor, from Petach Tikvah, called to tell him that one of his patients, a pregnant woman due to give birth almost momentarily, had come to his office for examination. She tested quite normal, but when he listened for a heartbeat from the fetus, there was none. The infant was still, no movement whatsoever. What should he do? Should he induce labor and remove the child?

The Natanya doctor replied very calmly. "Send her home," he said. "Wait one hour and then reexamine her. Send her home now."

The Petach Tikvah physician complied. In an hour he went to his patient's home, examined her, listened for a heartbeat and, wonder of wonders, it was restored. In a few days, the infant, a boy, was born and another Jew came into the world.

When I asked for the name of the Natanya doctor, our host said he did not know. "Is that important?" he asked me. "What is important is that these miracles happen. Every day. All the time."

I persisted. "Isn't it difficult for you, Reb Zaidel, a biologist, to accept these stories as truths? The bringing back to life of a dead fetus is not an everyday occurrence. It defies the laws of nature, a system of life that God Himself devised."

"Not at all," Reb Zaidel replied. "There is nature and there is the rebbe. The rebbe has special insights regarding nature. He has insights that even he doesn't understand. How can we? Why should I even try? Our tradition is hinged on miracles—the miracle of our exodus from Egypt, the miracle of Sinai. God took us to His bosom on Mt. Sinai and gave us the Torah. Isn't that a miracle?

"Some of us believe," he continued, "that the rebbe was actually present at Sinai. In another form, of course. Who knows what he learned there? Who knows? Why must you be so skeptical? Why do you question?" he asked.

I was somewhat flustered by his passion. I must be tactful, I thought. I carefully monitored my reply. "It's not that I'm questioning truths, Reb Zaidel," I answered, "but your story about the Natanya doctor sounds, to me at least, very much like a story. It's a word-of-mouth thing. If the event, the miracle happened the way you say it did, it surely would have been reported in the press, on TV, the public would know about it. It would not only be a miracle, it would be a media event. Reporters would be crawling all over Petach Tikvah and Natanya. It would be a flood."

Up to this point, the other two guests were largely silent. The older one appeared to be a gentle, rather timid soul. He had listened attentively to our exchange. It seemed to me that he wanted to get into the act but refrained.

The other, the youngish Chasid whom they called Leibel, was less inhibited. He jumped in with both feet. I had been curious about him. Actually about both of them. When we first sat down at the Sabbath table, we exchanged introductions. Who were we? What were we doing in Israel? Where had we come from?

Both of them were *ba'alei teshuvah*—returnees to the tradition. This younger one was the classic *ba'al teshuvah.* Cleveland born, middle-class, interrupted college career, drugs, drink, petty crime, Chabad House (Chabad is the acronym for the Lubavitch movement), *teshuvah.* He now lived in Tel Aviv where he studied and worked in a bread bakery. He aspired to be a *chazan* (cantor) but I was convinced he'd never make it. Too nasal.

"Reb Velvel," which was how Leibel addressed me, "our prophets of old were given the gift by God to restore the dead to life. It's in the *Tanach.* There was Elijah, there was Elisha. One of them even did it twice. Many of the prophets had the gift. Maybe all. Who knows? The rebbe certainly can if he wants to. Don't you believe what's written in the *Tanach*?" he asked.

"I do, Leibel. Of course I do," I answered. "But I have questions about these things. The Torah is our history as well as our law. The history part is full of legends—Noah, the Flood, Adam and Eve. Whether they actually existed, or happened, is irrelevant. They are lessons, symbols. They teach us how to behave as Jews."

Leibel abruptly switched lanes. He headed for Middle Europe.

"I heard the other day in the yeshiva that one of our Lubavitcher in Prague, a sainted man who visits the rebbe every year, has been bringing back to life the golem of Prague, the same one that was built by Rabbi Loew, who was called the Maharal, many, many years ago."

"You know about the golem, of course," he asked me. I said I did. He ignored my reply.

"The golem was built out of clay, like a giant Frankenstein, by Rabbi Loew two, three hundred years ago and was brought to life by the Maharal with a few magic words learned from the Kabbalah. The rabbi used the golem to defend Jews from attack by the anti-Semites. Whenever Jews were in danger, the Maharal said the secret words and the golem came alive and marched out like an army to destroy the enemy," he told me.

"Everybody thinks the golem was destroyed by Rabbi Loew. But that's not true. Rabbi Loew hid him in the attic of the Altneu Synagogue and restored him to life whenever he was needed. They say that in every generation, a saintly Jew in Prague learned the hidden words and used them to save Jews. The golem is even being used today when Jews are in danger in Prague," Leibel said.

"Why wasn't he used against the Nazis?" I asked.

"Who said he wasn't?" Leibel replied. "You know, of course, that there were less Jews killed by the Nazis in Czechoslovakia than in any other European country."

I said I hadn't known that. Then I asked, "Leibel, you're really not serious about the golem being out there today?"

He assured me he was. The others made no comment. "The golem story is only a legend, a fairy tale, like Cinderella," I said. "It never happened. True, there was the Maharal and he served in the Altneu shul, which still exists today, but the golem part is fiction." I paused. "Don't you agree with me, Reb Zaidel?" I said, turning to our host.

He shrugged me off. "I neither agree nor disagree," he replied. "If I heard the story from someone I knew and respected, he wouldn't even have to be a Lubavitcher, then, of course, I would believe him. But Leibel heard it from somebody at the yeshiva. Who knows who goes to a yeshiva today? He could be a faker, a liar. He could make up a story like that," Reb Zaidel said.

I thought it was time to switch lanes too, away from the golem and back to the here and now. I turned to the other guest, the older one from Haifa. He had mentioned earlier that he came from Los Angeles and that his name was Peretz. When I inquired what he was doing in Haifa, he informed me tersely that his work was confidential and he couldn't talk about it. He told me, almost in the next breath, that he was a physicist and had worked in Oak Ridge and Los Alamos.

I now asked him why he had become a Chabadnik, and I should not have been surprised, but I was, by his answer. He was an only child, born to parents who were Jews, but barely. They were scientists too and practiced no religion. They didn't have time for it; they were researchers. Their work was their theology.

As Peretz became more entrenched in his career, there began to stir in him a need for spiritual calm. His work was demanding, unsettling. Questions arose. He received answers. But the answers gave rise to other questions. He felt that some form of spiritual involvement might lead him to the calm he was seeking.

He began exploring churches, meditation centers, retreats. He was on the brink of conversion to Catholicism when one of his colleagues, a Jew, suggested that he ought to experience his own religion before abandoning it. He introduced Peretz to Chabad. It was not love at first sight, but it blossomed into an infatuation and in time became a passion.

He traveled as often as he could to the Brooklyn enclave where the rebbe and his followers gathered. He felt he belonged; he felt fulfilled. He came to Israel to serve God and the rebbe. Was this his last stop? He did not know.

Peretz completed his discourse. After a short pause, he began to talk again, as if he owed me one further explanation.

"In my work, which is largely theoretical," he began, "we know that when certain elements are put together, they will produce energy. We know also that different forms of energy, harnessed together in exact proportions, can erase a world, and even, possibly, create a new one.

"The universe emerged from God's mouth. He created it with a word, maybe two, who knows? There is a sanctity to words that only God understands. It may be that from time to time there comes along a human being who has solved the mystery of God's words. Maybe these are the men we call prophets. Can they revive the dead with a word? Can they breathe a few words into a mass of clay and make a golem? Who knows?"

Peretz looked at me with a quizzical smile. After that, Reb Zaidel began the winding-down process. Two *z'mirot* (Sabbath songs) were sung, spiritedly and somewhat off-key by Leibel. The *benching* (grace after meals) was led by the host. Afterwards he asked where we were spending the night, and we told him. We left shortly thereafter. I walked with the others as far as Rechov Meah She'arim, the narrow street that runs the length of the sector, and there we parted.

I headed toward Rechov Strauss, which must have been a half-mile away. The streetlights were dim and there was hardly a sound to be heard. It was late, but not that late. Men of all ages and shapes and garb walked towards and away from me, disappearing down side streets and into doorways. Their footsteps were barely to be heard, but the shadows emanating from those dark, fleeting figures climbed walls and buildings and splashed on pavements with an eerie, soundless clatter. The silence that night was heavy and grotesque. This was shtetl country, I thought, my grandfather's country on a Sabbath eve. Rest and repose were there. But also the goblins of the dark, and, perhaps even a golem. Who knows?

You're One Lucky Guy

Yoshke Stein was scared of God. He knew God sees everything. In daylight, when it's dark, even under the bed covers, God sees everything that happens. Yoshke's mother told him all about God when he was a little kid. Five. Maybe four. She said God is everywhere. All over the world. In every house, every room. The cellar too. Nobody can fool God, she said.

Yoshke was twelve. Born November 29, 1914. His mother told him the date. Saturday night, right after *Shabbos,* she said. She didn't remember things, but Yoshke knew the date was right. He read it on the birth certificate. November 29, 1914. Place of birth: Scranton, Pa. Yoshke had a strong memory. He remembered the day the war ended.

His mother always talked about God. God scared her too. She said God doesn't have two eyes like us. He has something that lets Him see and hear everything that happens in the world. He can even read minds. That's because He's God. He knows when you're telling a lie. He knows when you forgot to make the blessing over bread or an apple or a drink of water. God punishes. But only if He wants to.

The rabbi once told Yoshke that most of the time God forgives. That's because He's kind. "Don't worry so much about God," the rabbi would say. "It's His job to worry about you, Joseph." The rabbi was very kind, the kindest man Yoshke knew. The rabbi calls him Joseph. That's his real name. Joseph Stein. His mother calls him Yossel. That's Joseph in Yiddish. All the kids call him Yoshke. He hates that name. He asked them to call him Joe, Joe Stein. He likes that. The teachers in the Franklin Avenue School call him Joseph, just like the rabbi. But everybody calls him Yoshke. Even at the Y.

He goes to the Y every night after cheder like the other Jewish boys. He's not a member of a club. Nobody picked him. Mr. Levine said he would put him in a club if he wanted. Yoshke said no. "I don't like sports," he said. Yoshke knew he told Mr. Levine a lie. Yoshke loves sports. He loves baseball. Nobody knows batting averages like he does. Babe Ruth: 372. Bob Meusel: 315. Lou Gehrig: 313. Tony Lazzeri: 275. The New York Yankees were the best. Better than the Giants. Babe Ruth, the Sulton of Swat. Lou Gehrig, the Iron Horse. Ty Cobb, the Georgia Peach. He was with Detroit. Batted 339 last year.

Yoshke walks to the Y to do business. He is a businessman. He makes money every day. He has the punchboard and the candy box. Two cents a punch. Winner gets a prize. A comb and nail file set in a genuine leather case. Worth three dollars, the dealer told him. Yoshke knew he was full of shit. He saw it for a buck in the Globe Store. He told that to the dealer. "What the hell do you expect for a two-cent punch board?" the dealer said. "Take the nickel board and you get this comb and military brush set. What do you say, Yoshke?"

Yoshke stayed with the two-cent board. He did good business with the candy chances. A kid paid a penny and picked a chocolate-covered patty. If he got the one with the pink center, he won a Baby Ruth bar. Most kids tried to cheat Yoshke. Even the girls. They were the worst. They stuck their fingernails into the chocolate to see if it was pink. Yoshke told them, "Keep your hands off the goddam candy. You touch it and you owe me a penny." Yoshke meant it. He beat some kids. Not hard. No girls. He wouldn't touch them.

Yoshke made money from the whores in the alley. They had lots of money. He ran errands. They would say. "Yoshke, get me a pack of Helmars. Get me a pack of Lucky Strikes. Keep the change." They gave him good tips. Nickels, dimes.

Fat Sally was the best. She liked candy. Hershey's milk chocolate bars. No almonds. Fat Sally gave him a quarter. Twenty cents profit. She called him Joey. She was the best. She bought candy from the box too. Paid him a nickel apiece. Once Yoshke picked for her. Got the pink. Gave her the Baby Ruth. "You're one lucky guy, Joey." That's what she called him. One lucky guy.

One of the whores sent him for chewing tobacco. She spoke funny. She was a dime tipper. She was okay too. But she talked dirty. She would say, "Get yourself a buck, kid, and I'll haul your ashes for you." She laughed a lot. She called him Yoshke. She was the prettiest of the dollar whores.

Once Yoshke told the rabbi he ran errands for the *nofkes*. That was the Yiddish word for whores. "Is that a sin?" he asked the rabbi.

"It's not a sin," the rabbi said. "But never walk inside the house. Do you understand me?" the rabbi asked. "You must stand at the door. Even when it's winter outside. You must *never* walk in," he said. The rabbi looked very serious. Almost angry.

Yoshke always spoke to the rabbi in Yiddish. Once the rabbi asked why he does that. "I speak English too," the rabbi said.

"But you're the rabbi, I gotta speak in Yiddish to you."

"Why?" the rabbi asked again.

"Because you're the rabbi. You talk to God," Yoshke answered.

"God understands English too. He understands all languages," the rabbi told Yoshke.

"But he likes Yiddish better, Rabbi," Yoshke said. The rabbi asked him why. "Because He wrote the Torah in Yiddish. That's why."

"Not in Yiddish," the rabbi corrected. "In Hebrew."

"Isn't Yiddish a Jewish language?" Yoshke asked. The rabbi said it was. "That's why I speak to you in Yiddish," Yoshke said.

Yoshke liked talking to the rabbi. He was always busy. Always busy! Women brought chickens to see if they're kosher. Beggars came for money. Men came with arguments. People brought their trouble to the rabbi. Yoshke had trouble too. The rabbi knew his trouble. He always helped.

Yoshke would be bar mitzvah next year. The rabbi gave him the date. October 29, 1927. "What if my father is—you know where?" Yoshke always asked. "What if my mother is in the Far View?" Yoshke asked that one too. The rabbi said we'll wait and see. Maybe Mama will be let out for the day. Papa too. "You worry too much, Joseph." He always said that.

Yoshke had lots of money. More than thirty dollars. It was hidden so *he* wouldn't find it. *He* was in jail now. Thirty days. His father was often in jail. Or in the hospital. Drunk. Fighting. Breaking furniture. Yoshke was happy *he* was in jail. Papa used to beat him and his mother. But no more. The cops told him next time he beat them, they would put him in the lockup and throw away the key. Throw away the key. That's a good one. That's what they said. His father hated cops. Yoshke hated his father. "Is that a sin?" he once asked the rabbi. "Yes it is. It certainly is." That's what the rabbi told him. Yoshke still hated him. His father was mean. Like Haman. Even worse. Once when he was drunk, his father cursed God. Used the F word. God would get even. Just wait and see.

Business was good. Two candy boxes last week. One punchboard. Money from the whore alley. "Rabbi, I'll have a hundred dollars saved." That's what Yoshke told him. A hundred dollars for the bar mitzvah. Twenty dollars for a new blue suit and black shoes. Eighty for the party in the shul. Boy, what a party he would make. Herring, onions, challah, honey cake, gefilte fish, hard-boiled eggs, wine, whiskey, beer. Soda for the kids. Plenty of food. Don't forget peanuts and raisins. And *arbis,* those little round beans everybody loves. Singing too. Yoshke loved singing. He would show them. Those lousy kids at the Y.

They made fun of him. Tripped him. Laughed at him. Stole the punchboard. How's your father, the jailbird? Is your mother in Far View? Is she still in the Crazy House, Yoshke? He beat the shit out of them. Even the big ones. She wasn't crazy. She didn't talk much. Sometimes she couldn't remember his name. She wasn't crazy. No siree. Not crazy at all. They were crazy. Those rotten kids.

The rabbi called it hysteria. "She suffers from hysteria, Joseph. It won't last." That's what he said. When she was up there, the rabbi would visit. Brought fruit. Oranges. She loved oranges. He peeled them, so she wouldn't eat the peels. He brought candy too. His mother loved candy best of all. Yoshke gave her candy from his box. She picked the pinks. Always. No cheating. No fingernails. Like magic. Always the pinks. Maybe that showed God liked her.

She would come to the bar mitzvah. She would sit upstairs. With the women. The women's section of the shul. When he was done, Yoshke would go upstairs and kiss her. Like all the bar mitzvah boys did. She would cry. Like all bar mitzvah mothers. What a day. Everybody would be happy. Everybody would smile. Even God. His would be the best smile of all. He might even laugh. Does God laugh?

Yoshke was sure he could make God laugh. He'd cross his eyes like that funny guy in the movies. Then he'd wiggle his ears. Nobody wiggles ears like him. That's what Fat Sally said. "You're the best, Joey," she told him and gave him a quarter. He'd make God laugh all right. He'd laugh and laugh until He cried. Maybe not. He doesn't think God cries. Why would God cry? No. God would never cry.

Miller the Shammes

Miller the Shammes didn't like kids very much even though he had ten or twelve of his own. We were never exactly certain how many, nor do I think Miller the Shammes ever kept count. Every year, usually in the month of February, his wife Surke added another baby to the household, more often than not a girl. I don't think the size of his family, nor the gender of his progeny, had anything to do with his dislike of kids, but it was there in full force on Saturdays and holidays, days on which we attended synagogue services in the company of our fathers. Not that he disliked us any less on the other days of the week.

Though he looked twenty years older, Miller the Shammes could not have been much beyond his fortieth year. He was a small, quick-moving man and he wore, at all times of the day and night, a look of strain and anguish on his tight, pinched face. If he ever smiled, it was not very often and never at all at us kids. His eyes were pitch black as were all of his garments with the exception of his frayed white shirt on which was fastened a wrinkled black tie with a knot that defied ever being unknotted.

His outergarment, which he wore in all seasons, was a black loose-fitting gabardine that was flecked and blotted with stains, some of which still had color in them. But what brought eminence to his face and the rest of him was his long black beard that at times seemed to hang mean and ferocious and at others appeared gentle as a velvet scarf.

Miller the Shammes was a shammes. Obviously. A shammes is variously defined as the sexton or synagogue custodian. In some temples, he is referred to as the ritual director and even as the verger.

The latter is the British term for someone entrusted with the care and appearance of the sanctuary, which, of course, is only a minor responsibility in the life of a shammes. If a rabbi is the spiritual head of the synagogue, then, I suppose, the shammes would be its spiritual feet.

Certainly Miller the Shammes would fit into those shoes. A good shammes worth his pay, which is traditionally low, will hardly ever sit down. He is, or should be, in an upright position most of the time doing the many chores necessary for the neat and orderly appearance of the sanctuary. This would include stacking prayer books and bibles, folding prayer shawls, filling the skullcap receptacle, checking light bulbs, polishing ceremonial silver, dusting pulpit stands and tables, checking the ceremonial wine, inventorying whiskey supplies, flushing toilets.

Beyond that he was at the beck and call of the rabbi and cantor, the synagogue president, the ritual vice president and almost any member who paid dues, including those in arrears. In other words, he was everyone's shammes except the kids', with me, foremost I think, on his hit list. I got there, I should add, because he literally caught me with my hand, actually both hands, in the till. This was a different kind of till that probably requires an explanation.

In our synagogue, it was customary to sell pulpit honors during the holidays. This was done by means of an auction that took place during a pause in the service. Some honors were more significant than others and the bidding on these therefore was more active and exciting. The auction was conducted by a synagogue elder with a talent for these things, and when the auction was on there was a flurry of excitement reaching even into the women's section upstairs.

Sales were recorded in an odd way, the only way actually, under the circumstances. Since it was not permissible to write on the holiday, a record was maintained by spelling out the name of each purchaser and the price paid. This was done by assembling letters and numerals printed on narrow strips of paper. These strips were kept in a kind of cash drawer which was divided into dozens of squares. Each square contained a supply of letters and numerals. Thus if Mr. Levy bought an ark opening honor for ten dollars, the keeper of the box would extract letters L, E, V, Y and the number ten.

Miller the Shammes was the record keeper. As each honor went to the highest bidder, he extracted letters and figures and bound them together with strands of white string. At the conclusion of the auction, he closed the box and placed it under the rabbi's lectern. Sometime during the following week, he conveyed the data to the synagogue treasurer who did the billing.

My difficulties with Miller the Shammes began on the morning after Passover. Late that morning, a little before the noon hour, the customary meal time for Miller the Shammes, I sneaked into the sanctuary and removed the alphabet box. I sat myself in one of the forward pews facing the altar and proceeded systematically to untie each bundle of names, returning the letters to the proper receptacle. I did it leisurely and neatly because that is the way I am.

As I unbound the last bundle of letters, I was suddenly seized from behind by two bony fists, both of them belonging to Miller the Shammes. I was not put in jail, which might have been preferable to what happened next. My captor marched me over to my father's store where Pop and his partner and a storeful of customers heard of my act of sabotage. In the telling to my father, Miller the Shammes likened what I did to Absalom's revolt against King David, a hyperbole that to this day I do not understand.

Retribution came fast and heavy. My father decreed that I would not go to Boy Scout camp that summer. I saw that this did not overly impress Miller the Shammes; so did my father, who added the penalty of cutting me off from my weekly allowance, which was piddling enough to cause me no pain. When I got home, the news of my morning's activity had preceded me. My mother cried all that day and into Monday. My older sister predicted that the best years of my life would be spent in Sing Sing. My two brothers felt betrayed that I had bungled the job.

I think I would have forgotten about my misbegotten interlude with Miller the Shammes if I had not run into my friend Boomy Alpert several days later at the Y. Now Boomy is no Einstein, which, I suppose, none of us is, but he more than most. My sister who is not a great one for handing out compliments once said, "Boomy is a good-natured slob at least a notch or two above a moron." This was meant as a compliment.

Boomy was preparing for his bar mitzvah and Miller the Shammes was his teacher. He had arrived early in the evening, but the synagogue service had not yet begun; there were only nine men.

One of Miller the Shammes' responsibilities was assembling a minyan at the synagogue. A minyan, which is needed twice daily, once in the morning and the other in the evening, is a quorum of at least ten men. No congregational prayers can begin with less. The Kaddish, a memorial prayer for a departed relative, could not be recited unless ten men were present.

It was getting late, so Miller the Shammes sent Boomy into the street to find a tenth man. He went out to Penn Avenue and the street was empty except for a lone Salvation Army bum who was smoking a cigarette in front of the Salvation Army shelter. Boomy approached and asked him to join the service. He agreed to go when Boomy told him that it was customary to have a shot of whiskey at the conclusion of the minyan.

So Boomy brought him to Miller the Shammes who never questioned his credentials. Boomy said the man was deaf so that there would be no point in talking to him. When the minyan was over, the bum had himself three fast shots and everyone left happy, especially the bum.

Boomy's story tickled me pink, but there was a bee the size of an elephant buzzing around inside my head. I caught it right off, Boomy not at all, which didn't surprise me. As I saw it, only Boomy and the bum, and now I, knew what had actually happened; Miller the Shammes knew nothing at all. Absolutely nothing. He was still shlepping around in a bliss of total ignorance. Miller the Shammes had to be brought into the picture.

As things stood now, I rationalized, where was the suffering, his suffering? Why wasn't his conscience pulsating with guilt? Why was he not bowed down with the burden of sin? This was not happening because he was unaware of the flawed minyan and the illegal Kaddish prayer. All this had to be revealed to Miller the Shammes with subtlety and without incriminating Boomy. But how?

"You got any ideas, Boomy?" I asked.

"You're the idea man, Willie," he answered.

"Whatever happens, it's got to look like an accident," I said.

"An accident?"

"Yeah. Like it was the bum's fault."

"How do we do that, Willie?"

"He never told you he wasn't Jewish. Right?" Boomy agreed.

"And he didn't say he was a Christian either. Right?"

"Right," Boomy said.

"So that puts you in the clear," I said.

"How does that put me in the clear, Willie?" he asked.

"That makes you a victim of circumstance."

"Sounds good to me," Boomy said.

"OK. Now we got to get the cooperation of the bum."

"How do we do that, Willie?"

"With booze," I answered.

"Booze?"

"That's right. A bottle of hooch."

"Hooch?" Boomy appeared uncertain.

"Whiskey, for Christ's sake."

"Where we going to get whiskey, Willie?"

"No problem. My father makes it by the bathtub."

"Mine too, but he makes it in pails."

"Pails?" I was surprised. "Why not in the bathtub?"

"We use the bathtub to take baths."

"We do too, but not every day of the week."

"My older sister says the whiskey gave her pimples," Boomy said.

I was interested in neither his sister nor the condition of her skin. I had Miller the Shammes on my mind and tucked in right beside him was the Salvation Army bum. I knew exactly how to proceed and explained the plan to Boomy, who at first was somewhat skeptical. He asked whether I was certain he would not be implicated, and I assured him that the plan was as sound as the bank on the corner. (This was during the Prohibition era when banks were as virtuous as Mary Pickford, America's sweetheart.) This convinced Boomy.

We took ourselves to the Salvation Army and had no trouble locating the bum. He had just lit up a freshly picked cigarette butt and recognized Boomy immediately. I got down to business.

"How would you like to earn two pints of freshly made booze?" I asked.

"Freshly made?" he questioned.

"Straight from the barrel," I told him.

"Who do I have to assassinate?" was his reply. We took this as a yes, and Boomy and I told him what he had to do. We haggled on the terms of payment but not for very long. He wanted the whiskey before the action, which we turned down. He then asked for a pint before and a pint after, which we admitted was fair, but we didn't want him performing his assignment with a pint of Pop's booze tucked away inside his head. So we compromised. Two swallows of booze before and the rest afterwards. We shook on it and scheduled the action for the following night.

According to the bum's story, which he gave us in some detail afterward, everything went off as planned.

"I got there real early like you said," he told us. "There was nobody come in yet except that little old reverend in the black coat. I tell you I had him cock-eyed when he seen me wearing the cross. He near fainted. He says to me, 'Weren't you the man who come here the other night?' I said I sure was, Reverend. He says you weren't wearing a cross then, were you? I said I wear it on special occasions. Today is my birthday.

"He asks me in a shaky voice, 'Are you a Jew?' So I say I never was but I'm willing to listen. He tells me that won't be necessary. So I ask him can he use my services tonight 'cause I sure would like a shot of whiskey. He says to me, 'No services. No whiskey. No nothing.' Then he gets suspicious about the other night. He asks me about you," the bum said, turning to Boomy.

"How come, he asks, the boy that brought you in never asked if you was Jewish or not? I tell him I don't hear so good when I got a couple drinks in me and not at all when I'm far gone. So I tell him you asked me a couple questions which I never heard, but I kept shaking my head to whatever you said. So into your church I go."

"All the time the reverend says nothing," the bum continued. "So I ask for a shot of whiskey. He thinks for a while and then tells me he'll give me the shot if I get outta there in a hurry and never mention to nobody that I ever prayed with you people.

"I say to him I wasn't praying the other night. He says never mind. Say nothing to nobody. I tell him OK, but it'll cost him two shots and he goes and gets the bottle. So here I am, boys, and now I want to get paid."

We gave him the whiskey, as we agreed, shook his hand and started to leave.

"OK if I keep the cross for good luck?" he asked me. I told him sure and that now he owes us one. He said "any time" and headed in a direction away from the Salvation Army hostel. I don't think he ever went back to the hostel. It was getting close to the month of May and the bums of winter start hitting the rails going west.

As far as I know, Miller the Shammes never mentioned the incident to anyone. Certainly not to Boomy whom he was teaching two days a week in preparation for his bar mitzvah. Nor to any of the regulars at the minyan. Oddly enough, only weeks after Boomy's bar mitzvah, Miller the Shammes left our synagogue to accept another position in Detroit. He was succeeded by a man we called Herschel the Grabber who, as things turned out, was even worse.

The French Jew

It was great being back in Meah She'arim after an absence of fifteen years. Meah She'arim is the super-religious enclave in Jerusalem not too far from East Jerusalem, the population center of the Palestinian Arabs.

I think what attracted me to this odd place was because it conjured up for me the memory of my father, who had passed on some years before. My father was, to me, the epitome of the shtetl. He grew up in a small village in the Ukraine which he described in Yiddish as being "as big as a *genetz*" (a yawn). Yet it was the center of his universe, as it was for his father and mother, his four brothers and two sisters, and a full complement of cousins and near cousins.

Pop remembered everything in the shtetl, the large synagogue and the small one, the cheder (school), the *mikvah* (bathhouse), the orchards of the *poretz* (landlord). He recalled with a special clarity the graveyard, which was filled with his ancestors of all varieties who were trundled there probably in the century-old funeral dray which inevitably lost a wheel or broke an axle during a funeral.

When I first experienced Meah She'arim, I saw it as my father's shtetl reborn. It was in central Jerusalem but could have been in some insignificant village in Russia. The main street was bustling with black-garbed men and boys wearing oversized black hats, tieless white shirts buttoned to the top, long black coats of indefinite length. The women and young girls were similarly dressed. They wore clothing that covered all parts of the body except the face.

The main street was occupied on both sides by shops catering to the tourist trade. There were stores or stands that sold prayer shawls, tefillin, skull caps, bibles, sets of the Talmud, religious silver things, candelabras, religious souvenirs, and carved wooden ware. There were also restaurants, bakeries, and stores that sold groceries, refreshments, furniture, clothing, lottery tickets, and women's shoes. I don't recall seeing a television store.

On previous visits to Meah She'arim, I always had a reason for making the trip. I enjoyed eating *cholent* (a kind of stew), in the meat restaurant that made one fresh every day of the week except the Sabbath. Or I shopped for souvenirs. Once I bought a medium-sized woolen prayer shawl in the store where I had my tefillin opened and examined by the proprietor. On a number of occasions, I exchanged currency, which was probably something I should not have done.

On my recent foray into Meah She'arim, I was in Jerusalem as a member of a UJA mission and I had a special job to do for my daughter. She asked me to purchase four *claff* for four mezuzot that were to be placed on the doorposts of her new condominium. A *claff* is a square of parchment on which is inscribed three paragraphs of scripture declaring one's love of the Almighty.

I took a taxi to Meah She'arim, and the cab driver let me off at the meat restaurant. I recognized the proprietor, but he didn't recognize me. He was beginning to fill the trays in his display case. It was 10:30 in the morning. I asked in Yiddish when the *cholent* would be served and he answered in English, "Thursday."

"Thursday," I protested weakly. "You served it every day when I was here last. What happened?"

"Nothing happened," he said in Yiddish. "Come back on Thursday." He paused and smiled. "I remember you," he said. "You're older. We used to call you 'der hungriker Amerikaner.'"

We shook hands and I left. About ten stores past the restaurant was a religious articles shop where I frequently changed dollars. I did not recognize the young man behind the counter. He had a squeaky red beard that he fondled as he spoke. He was waiting on a customer who had an odd accent.

The customer had the look of a dandy. He wore a black fedora which was tipped forward at a slight angle. His long black *kapote* (coat) was silken and expensive looking. He wore expensive dark brown pointy slippers, the kind zoot-suiters used to wear on Saturday night. He was in his fifties and clean shaven. The proprietor left his customer and went to the rear of the shop.

I addressed the customer. "You must be from France."

"Why do you say that?" he answered, smiling.

"Well, you do speak with a French accent," I said.

"Yes, I do," he admitted.

"Are you from Canada? Montreal?" I asked.

"No. I am not."

"France?" I ventured.

"Precisely. I was born in Marseilles. My family has been in Marseilles for two hundred years." He paused. "I presume you are here in Yerushalayim with all the Americans who are roaming the streets," he said.

I was somewhat miffed by his casual tone. "We have a number of sessions and meetings with Israelis, in government and in the military," I said.

"Of course, of course," he said hurriedly. He changed the subject. "And what brings you to Chaim's shop?" he asked.

"I'm shopping for four *claff* for my daughter in Boston," I said.

"There are no *claffim* in America?" the French Jew asked somewhat derisively.

"Of course there are, but my daughter thinks they are too expensive."

"I see," he said.

Chaim finished his business with an earlier customer who, after some mild discussion, purchased a large woolen prayer shawl and then left the store. Chaim spoke in whispered tones to the French Jew. Chaim turned to me.

"This gentlemen," he indicated the French Jew, "arrived before you, but because you are an older man, he asked me to take you first," Chaim said with a smile.

"Oh no, no," I protested. "I have lots of time. Please take this gentleman now."

The French Jew smiled at me and began speaking to Chaim in Yiddish. Not surprisingly, his Yiddish had an unmistakable French accent, too. He took off his coat and jacket. He was wearing a sparkling white silk shirt. Chaim gave him a tefillin for the arm, which he began to wind on the right arm.

I thought this was odd. I remarked, "You must be left handed if you are putting the tefillin on the right arm."

"No. My dominant arm is the right one," he said.

"Then why are you putting the tefillin on the right arm?" I asked.

He stopped the winding and patiently explained to me. "There are two modes for putting on the *shel yad,* the tefillin that is put on the arm. One is according to Rashi (the most important commentator on the Bible and the Talmud) and the other is according to his grandson, the Rabbenu Tam. Both of these great scholars differed radically on the way they put on tefillin." He paused, I think to let his words sink in.

He continued. "The Rashi way is how most men today put on tefillin. They put it on the weak arm. If a man is right handed, he will put the tefillin on the left arm. And vice versa."

He looked me square in the eye to make certain I understood. He asked if that was clear.

I replied, "Of course."

"According to the Rabbenu Tam, you start with the left arm and at the conclusion of the service, you unwind the arm tefillin and then put it on the right arm."

He paused. "Is that clear?" he asked.

I said yes and told him I had heard about the Rabbenu Tam method, but never knew anyone who used it.

"Oh yes," he answered confidently, "My father davened that way. My brothers too. It is a family tradition."

He continued winding the tefillin on the right arm. When he finished, he turned to me.

"We believe that even God puts on tefillin."

"Why would He do that?" I asked.

"Do you know the ways of God?"

I shook my head.

He said very casually, "God is God. He does what is right."

"I suppose so," I said. I changed the subject. "It is my understanding that women are not obligated to put on tefillin. Why would that be?" I asked. "Is it because the rabbis felt they were not worthy?"

"The reason given is that women are too occupied taking care of the husband and their children, and keeping a clean house. Therefore a woman is absolved from performing that mitzvah," the French Jew said, rather brusquely, I thought.

"I believe I read somewhere," I continued, "that Rashi's daughters put on tefillin daily. Is that to be believed?"

"I believe it. Also Bruriah."

"Bruriah?" I asked.

"She was the wife of Rabbi Meir. One of the greats of the Mishnaic period," the French Jew said in a formal lecture manner. "It is mentioned in the Talmud that Bruriah was a great scholar, like her husband, perhaps even greater. It is said that she davened each morning in tefillin." He paused. "A superior woman in every way."

I interrupted. "So, may I tell my daughter that she can put on tefillin if she wants to?"

He backed off somewhat angrily. "Are you Rashi? Are you Rabbi Meir? If you were, I would tell you that your daughter could put on tefillin."

I got his point and allowed Chaim to continue his measurement of the French Jew's right forearm. When he was finished, the French Jew spoke to Chaim in a low voice. They were negotiating a price. I moved to the opposite side of the shop. They finished shortly and the French Jew put on his coat.

He extracted from his wallet a calling card and offered it to me. "As you see," he said, "I'm a dealer in diamonds. Perhaps you would want to bring home from Israel a diamond for your wife," he said with a smile.

"My wife unfortunately passed on years ago," I told him.

"I'm sorry," he said in a low voice. "Perhaps there is a lady of your acquaintance?"

I said, "I'm afraid not."

"Well, keep my card," he said. "One never knows what the future may bring."

We shook hands. He left. Chaim joined me. "A fine gentleman. And a scholar," he said.

I told Chaim what I was looking for. He brought me samples. He extracted one that he called superior. He knew the scribe personally, he said, and he does the finest work in Jerusalem. He offered it to me for thirty dollars, which, of course, I rejected. After a minute or two, he retreated to twenty dollars and I bought four.

When I returned to the States, I told my daughter about my conversation with the French Jew. She told me one of her friends was also a practitioner of the Rabbenu Tam method of putting on tefillin. My daughter knew about Rashi's daughters and Bruriah. She suggested that I read about Bruriah in the encyclopedia.

I did. I read that she was reputed to be a greater scholar than her husband Rabbi Meir. Great as he was, Rabbi Meir was odd, a skeptic. There is a story in post-Talmudic literature that he instructed one of his students to try to seduce his wife Bruriah because she was too confident about her virtue and her ability to resist temptation. When Bruriah realized that she had been used and tested by her husband, she committed suicide.

The French Jew never told me about that. I wonder why?

Conversation at a Wake

The great "Bullet" Benny Nolan was the first corpse I ever saw. I was in the eighth grade at the time and a delivery boy in my father's grocery store. The Bullet, as he was called, first at Notre Dame and later on when he was the explosive running back for the Chicago Bears, was one of the immortal athletes of our county. He was right up there with two other local greats—Hughey Jennings, manager of the Detroit Tigers in the early 1900s, and Christy Mathewson, the fabled pitcher of the New York Giants.

I must confess that at the time of his demise, I knew nothing at all of Mr. Nolan's renown as a football immortal. My connection with the deceased was through his wife Margaret whose father James O'Hara was my father's best customer and by far my most generous tipper. The Nolans lived somewhere in that great unknown firmament called out of town. The Bullet had been brought to the O'Hara home for the wake.

Mr. O'Hara was a banker. Actually he owned the bank. He also owned most of the properties on his block including my father's store. But what brought me to look upon the Bullet's last earthly remains that chilly December evening was a clandestine and substantial bribe from Mr. Devine, my father's butcher, who slipped me half a dollar to serve as his stand-in at the wake, which he was obligated to attend but dared not. It. was Mr. Devine who clued me in on the Bullet's football celebrity.

Mr. Devine could not abide the thought of being in the same room as a corpse, any corpse, so he sent me, bearing a decorated Mass card of condolence, as his emissary. He had been a boyhood chum of the

Bullet's older brother Sean, himself now long deceased. Before I left, Mr. Devine gave me these instructions. "Look long on the casket, Willie, and say a proper prayer in your Jewish language for the Bullet in my behalf. You might add a kind word or two for Sean whose game was baseball, God bless him."

I approached the large Victorian O'Hara residence, where the deceased lay in state, with some feelings of uncertainty. I had never seen a dead body before and wasn't quite sure how I would handle the experience. How was one supposed to behave in its presence other than look sad, I wondered? When I asked my mother for advice, she said, "Just use good manners, son, and you'll get by." My mother always said that when she was stuck for an answer, which, in the case of the inert Mr. Nolan, was not very helpful.

I entered the house by way of the front door. This was a first for me. Deliveries were always made through the rear.

Bridey Callahan, the O'Hara housekeeper, made me wipe my shoes on the mat before I crossed the threshold.

"Put it there, Willie," said Bridey, pointing to my overcoat with one hand and the large mahogany clothes rack in the entry hall with the other. I hung my coat as instructed and walked into the parlor where the Bullet was laid out.

I greeted the widow, Margaret Nolan, who was seated facing the coffin at the opposite end of the room. She held my hand longer than I was comfortable with and then patted it. Not a word did she say. Margaret was flanked on one side by a tall magnificent-looking priest whom I had never seen before. He was introduced to me as Monsignor Kehoe. On her left was Miss Ellen O'Hara, her younger sister.

Miss Ellen was the Latin teacher at Central High and was reputed to be hard as nails. Her looks certainly belied that reputation. She was a small elegant lady, late forties, I suppose, a face molded like a Venetian cameo, blue eyes the color of a flawless, waning June sky, and dark red hair gathered taut in a bun at the nape of her high-held head.

Miss Margaret, as we called her, was more robust and taller than her sister. Her once black hair was now silver gray and bobbed in the new fashion. Her face, not unlike Miss Ellen's, had become somewhat fleshy in recent years, and her steely blue eyes were reddened by sorrow and drink. Miss Margaret had her problems. My father and Mr. Devine commiserated over "Miss Margaret's condition" in hushed whispers, but I caught the drift early in the game. From time to time, I would deliver an order after Sunday Mass to the O'Hara kitchen, and there would sit Miss Margaret in her Sunday clothes, a prayer book open on the table, her eyes vacant and incoherent, not seeing me at all as I unloaded several bags on the table. Bridey would be there too, and it was she who would flip me a quarter when I finished.

Miss Ellen took me by the arm and accompanied me to where the Bullet was laid out. I must admit I was surprised by what happened next. And a little frightened. She introduced us. "Willie, this is Benjamin Nolan," she said. Then turning her eyes downward, she addressed the corpse. "This young man is Willie, our neighbor's son. He has come to pay his respects."

I stood there, as Mr. Devine instructed me, and did what I was sent to do. I mumbled a Hebrew prayer just loud enough for Miss Ellen to hear. The only one I knew by heart was the blessing for bread, which I hurried through. I felt confident that Mr. Devine and the Bullet would never know the difference.

I must say the Bullet surprised me. He was not a large man at all. He lay there in stiff repose, which under the circumstances was not surprising, but his flushed face did not appear to be at rest. He looked tuckered out as if he might have just finished a bruising game against the New York Giants.

The rest of him was a blue elegance. He was dressed in a brand new blue serge suit. A sky blue cotton shirt was background to a tie carrying the blue and gold colors of Notre Dame. His hands clasped a silver crucifix bearing a peaceful Jesus. Across his vest was hung a thick gold chain that strung from the left vest pocket through the top button hole to the right pocket where the rim of a large gold watch could be seen peeking out.

Miss Ellen remained patiently by my side as I stood there. I told her I said a prayer in Hebrew on behalf of my family and Mr. Devine. She said that was very nice and she knew of Mr. Devine's "odd incapability," as she called it. She brought me over to sit between her and Miss Margaret.

"What grade are you now in, Willie?" Miss Ellen asked. I told her the eighth grade.

"Are you a good student?" she inquired.

I told her I guess so.

"You're studying Latin with Miss Kinback, aren't you?" she asked.

"Yes ma'am," I replied.

"Do you like Latin, Willie?" she asked teasingly. I then surprised her. I said yes.

Then she surprised me. She tested me. Looking at me somewhat severely, she asked, "How do you say farm?" I answered *ager.*

"Good, very good," she said. "Now, what is the word for woman?"

"Femina," I told her without hesitation.

"Correct. Now say, the woman loves the farm." Again I answered unhesitatingly. She was delighted that I put farm in the accusative case.

The monsignor then joined the game. He asked me some tough ones like soul, light, tears, god, priest, and war. I knew them all except for priest. Miss Ellen told me the Latin word for priest was *sacerdos* and Monsignor Kehoe nodded.

"Have you been bar mitzvah yet, Willie?" he inquired. "I'm scheduled for November," I said and then asked, "How do you say bar mitzvah in Latin?"

He answered immediately, "Bar mitzvah."

Miss Ellen was smiling. "Are you nervous about your bar mitzvah, Willie?"

"Not now, but I will be then," I told her.

"I don't think you'll be nervous at all," said Miss Ellen.

"Oh yes, I will," I answered. "You can't be bar mitzvah unless you're nervous. That's the law," I said with a smile.

Miss Ellen didn't catch on, but the monsignor did. "He's pulling your leg, Ellen." Then turning to me, he said "Willie, you're a scamp."

"What's a scamp?" I asked.

"A kidder, a joker," he said. Changing the subject, he asked whether I had ever been at a wake before.

I told him this was my first. Then I asked, "Why do they call it a wake?"

Miss Ellen answered in a schoolteacher way. "We call it a wake because it is derived from the old English word, *wacu.* This translates as a watch, or a watching. It really means the watching by friends and relatives of a dead person principally at night. Is that clear, Willie?"

I said it certainly was and the monsignor said, "Bravo." More visitors were being ushered in by Bridey, and I thought that it was time to go. I went over to Miss Margaret and took her hand in mine rather firmly and smiled sadly. She said to me very softly, "It was very kind of you to come, William. I will be staying here with Father for a while and I expect we will see each other rather frequently."

Then almost as an afterthought, she asked, "Do you play football, William?"

"No ma'am," I said. "I'm not very good at sports." I mumbled this somewhat apologetically.

"Good. That's fine. It is my personal belief that football is not a game for gentlemen," Miss Margaret stated very emphatically, I thought. She then released my hand and I returned to her sister and the monsignor. Before I left, I had to satisfy a curiosity I could not dispel.

I turned to the monsignor. "Father, would it be okay to ask you a question?"

"Go ahead, Willie. Ask anything you like."

"That gold watch and chain, Father. When Mr. Nolan is buried, will it go along with him?" I asked.

He answered very straight-faced. "No, Willie, that will be removed. It's a family heirloom and will go to Margaret. The crucifix, however, will travel to eternity with Mr. Nolan. Of that you may be sure."

"Anything else, Willie?" he asked as I began to leave.

"Well, yes sir. I'd like to make a donation to charity in memory of Mr. Nolan."

I pulled out Mr. Devine's half-dollar from my pocket, added one of my own and gave them to Monsignor Kehoe.

He took my gift. "You can be sure, young man, that Heaven will take note of your generosity," he said solemnly.

"That's okay, Father," I said as I walked into the hallway to the clothes rack. Bridey Callahan was there and took down my coat from the hook and then helped me into it. I thanked her and said with a grin on my face, "Sorry, Bridey, I'm all out of change."

Bridey didn't appreciate the joke. "Don't get smart with me, Willie," she said sternly. Then dropping her voice to a whisper, she said, "I saw you talking with Miss Margaret. What did she tell you?"

"She thought I shouldn't play football. It's not for gentlemen, she told me. Why would she say that, Bridey?" I asked.

She took me to the door and said rather softly, "Well, you know how it is. She's angry. She's one very angry lady."

"Who's she angry at?" I asked.

"She's angry at Mr. Nolan, of course. That's who," Bridey answered.

"Mr. Nolan? Why would she be sore at him? He died," I said.

Bridey opened the front door and patted me out. "You got it right, Willie," she said as she closed the door.

The *Yerid*

My father was a great storyteller—mostly about himself. His stories were derived largely from his growing-up years in an insignificant village in the Ukraine called Romanov that seemed to have been populated by a mixed bag of thieves, semi-thieves, buffoons, and charlatans. Also beautiful girls.

According to my father, Romanov was known far and wide as the bridal capital of the Ukraine. There was coined the expression "pretty as a bride from Romanov," which was used not only to describe brides but to render judgment on cows, cats, merchandise, cloth, or anything that was on sale or under appraisal. It was like a seal of approval.

The *yerid* (market) was a weekly tradition in Romanov as it was in most Jewish villages in Russia and Poland. Young unmarried men would ride into Romanov on a *yerid* day and take note of the girls, Jewish and gentile, who were behind stalls peddling oats, beets, herring, compotes, or jellies to buyers and lookers. The young men might taste the fruit, squeeze it knowingly, wink at the girls, pat a shoulder or back (never a buttock, God forbid), and pass on to the next booth.

At age eight, my father was a regular at the *yerid*. Not as a customer or spectator, as you might think, but as a merchant, a seller. He was a *yerid* floater, one of those hustlers who rented no stall but peddled his merchandise from the middle of the crowds. His stock consisted of hand-rolled cigarettes, rolled by him, of course, and glasses of seltzer. The seltzer came out of squeeze bottles on top of which there sat an inverted tin cup to contain the liquid. The cigarettes sold for a kopeck apiece, the seltzer for two kopecks a glass.

The day before the *yerid*, my father would stock up on tobacco and cigarette papers and roll out his merchandise. He made them in two sizes—regular and enlarged. The enlarged he peddled two for three kopecks. (Years later, my father claimed, not unjustifiably I think, that he was the inventor of the king-sized cigarette.) The seltzer he bought from a seltzer maker who forced my father to buy four bottles at a time in order to get a special wholesale price. Carting the seltzer was more than my father could handle by himself so he employed his younger brother Yankel to carry the bottles. Yankel was paid a kopeck and all the seltzer he could drink.

The cigarettes he rolled were placed in a small tin box that my father would squirrel away somewhere in the kitchen so that his father might not find them. Grandfather was addicted to tobacco of any kind including snuff, years before nicotine dependency was invented. My father's father was a *melamed* (teacher) of young boys who could outthink, outsmart, and outrun their timid teacher any day of the week. And, incidentally, feed his need for a smoke. Father, of course, was Grandfather's supplier and could not rightly charge him, which made a difference in the state of his business.

My father's success in the *yerid* led to competition from a number of sources, mostly kids like himself. The worst of the lot was Simcha Pavolye, called Shmendrik by those who knew him. Shmendrik sold cigarettes, seltzer, and paperback books of romance written in Russian. He was taller, older, stronger, and more physical than my father and soon occupied the better locations in the *yerid*. These were near the stalls where the prettiest girls were stationed.

It was on a hot June *yerid* day that my father's luck took a turn for the better. On that day the local *poretz*, a member of the Russian nobility who owned most of the village and farms in the county, was on an inspection tour of the Romanov *yerid* and the other *yerids* under his control. It was while he was eyeing the young beauties in the stalls that he extracted from his tunic his bejewelled cigarette case and discovered he was out of cigarettes. He caught the eye of my father and said gruffly, "Boy, let me have one of your *papirosen*." My father offered the *poretz* his tin box and said, "Your highness may take as many cigarettes as you require."

The *poretz* said, "Thank you, boy," and proceeded to select one of the longer cigarettes from the box. He crinkled it between thumb and forefinger, held it to his nose like it was one of those expensive Cuban cigars and reached for a match. But my father got there first. He extracted a match from his pocket, struck it, and brought it to the *poretz's* lips. The nobleman took his first puff and nodded appreciatively to my father. He fished for loose coins in his pocket and offered a handful to my father, who declined to accept them.

"It is an honor for me to offer your excellency a cigarette. I hope you enjoy it. I rolled it myself," he said.

The *poretz* replied, "Well said, my boy. And if I may say so, your cigarette is as tasteful as the *papirosen* I receive from Constantinople."

"Thank you, sire. The tobacco I use comes from Turkey."

"Yes. I thought so," the *poretz* said.

He turned to leave, but before he did, he touched my father's head, smiled and said, "Thank you . . . very much."

My father never met up with the *poretz* again. In time, he became a seller in the *yerid* of herring. These he sold from a wooden bucket he bought new from a hardware store in Romanov. It cost him two rubles and he never forgave the herring for the expenditure. He estimated he would have to sell one hundred herring just to pay for the bucket. This was done before Passover and just in time to peddle Passover borscht (beet soup) that his mother made and was certified kosher by his father.

Many years later, my father loved to relate to us, his children, about his numerous vocations in the *yerid*. His motivation, he told us, was "if I didn't earn five or six kopecks a day, there would be no herring to put on the table with the daily portion of bread and potatoes."

My uncle Benchik, who was five years older than my father and who was drafted into the czar's army when he was sixteen, saw it differently.

"First of all," he said in a professorial tone, "we were not poor. Your father likes to brag about how poor we were. We were poor like everyone else in Romanov. Everybody was on the edge of poverty. We did not need the few kopecks he put on the table for a daily portion of herring. Some days we ate meat. After my bar mitzvah I worked for a butcher and he frequently gave me odd pieces of meat for the table."

Benchik continued, "That part of the story about the *poretz* was true. I was in the *yerid* that very day, and the *poretz* gave your papa a handful of coins and your papa took them. He would have been a *shmegegge* to give them back. Papa was no fool. He took the money because he likes money. Just like everybody else."

Benchik was warmed up by now. In a louder voice, he continued, "The best part of the story your papa left out. That was the part about Shmendrik who used to beat up your father regularly when I wasn't around. It happened a few months after Papa's meeting with the *poretz*. On that day, the overseer of the *poretz*'s farm, a huge, ugly former Cossack, was selling potatoes and he also ran out of cigarettes. He bought one from Shmendrik, and when he lit up the cigarette, it burned like a barn on fire. The Cossack coughed with his first puff and choked like a dog with a bone in his craw. There was bedlam. It turned out that Shmendrik, the moron, was peddling *papirosen* that were half tobacco and half straw."

"Where was Papa at the time?" I asked.

"He was selling herring in another part of the *yerid,*" Benchik replied.

"And what happened to Shmendrik?" I persisted.

"The Cossack flogged him of course and he was never allowed to sell cigarettes in the *yerid,*" Benchik answered.

"Whatever happened to him?" I asked.

"They say he left Romanov a few weeks after the *yerid* business and went to one of the large yeshivas in Poland. He was a gonif, a thief, but he knew how to learn. Years later he became a rabbi and took a position in Brazil," Benchik said.

"That is strange," I said. "Very strange."

"Not if you know Shmendrik," Benchik answered.

The Misbegotten Wedding

I didn't like the rabbi when we first met. He was on the bride's side and was flitting around the buffet tables glad-handing the wedding guests like he owned the place, which I found out later he really did.

Actually it was his father's shul, which, we were told, started out as a storefront that barely accommodated a minyan of ten men and a snarling cat named Murphy. Within the year, the bride's father informed us, the shul was moved into the parlor and dining room of the rabbi's Cape Cod house and subsequently into the entire residence including the property next door.

It became known in that part of the Bronx as Rapaport's shul or Chatzkel's minyan and carried the name, front and back, of the founding rabbi who now spent most of his time in Miami Beach, Florida.

His son, the parambulating rabbi whose name was Harold, was all teeth and exuberance and introduced himself everywhere as "Dr. Hal Rapaport but you can call me Heshie," which no one did. It was the wedding of my nephew Philip, or Pinky as he was known in the family. He was my sister's oldest son who was twenty-one but looked twelve. He was marrying a sweet young thing, a kindergarten teacher a little on the zaftig side who was twenty-three and looked it.

Our contingent of relatives and friends came mostly from Pennsylvania and California and was headed by my father, aged eighty-four and still sharp as a matzo, a cliché he loved to hear and encouraged. He enjoyed being the oldest person in the synagogue or any assemblage, which gave him an opportunity to declaim a favorite aphorism, which in those days was *"Der Oilem is a goylem,"* which translates roughly as "the world is an idiot." This was shortly after the reelection of President Richard Nixon.

In addition to my father, there was my brother, who was the uncle of the bridegroom, as was I; my two sisters, one of whom was the mother of the bridegroom; several cousins, aunts and uncles, and friends, all from Pennsylvania. But Pop was the presumed head of the clan though the real powerhouse was my older sister Dorothy who ruled the family roost even when we were kids.

Our group mingled with the other guests and, as expected, Pop shone. He was the epitome of joy, pride, and sagacity. It was natural, of course, for the young rabbi to seek out my father who, in a way, was expecting him.

"Mazel Tov, *Zayde,* you should have lots of *naches* from the *shiduch.* I know the bride's family well and they are the very best. None better," the rabbi said with a grin the size of Milwaukee.

"Thank you, Rabbi. Yes, she is a lovely girl and has promised to keep a kosher home."

"And your grandson Paul. I have heard good things about him," the rabbi said.

"Philip, Rabbi," Pop corrected.

"Philip?"

"That's his name, Rabbi. Not Paul."

"Oh sure. I apologize, *Zayde.*"

"That's okay, Rabbi, everybody makes mistakes."

"Like I was saying, *Zayde.* Your grandson, I hear, is an accountant, an executive, a good provider, I'm sure."

"He makes a good living, if that's what you hear, Rabbi," my father answered, somewhat annoyed.

"Exactly," the rabbi said. He changed the subject. "Did you notice the chuppah, Grandpa? The best, the most expensive. The flowers are real silk and velvets from France. Not *chazzerai* from China. Cost us a fortune, but it's worth every penny. Real class," he gushed.

My father was not impressed. "So you and your father are the rabbis here?" he asked.

"Partners, *Zayde.* We divide the *avoyde.*"

"Avoyde?" Pop asked. "The duties?"

"You know. Weddings, funerals, bar mitzvahs. Also *milah,"* he answered.

"You do circumcisions, Rabbi?"

"Not me. My father neither," he replied huffily. "We have a mohel, who is a doctor. A real MD."

"A real MD, you say."

"Yes sir. A real medical doctor from NYU, Grandpa."

There was something that was annoying my father and he switched the conversation to a new direction.

"You'll pardon me, Rabbi, but please don't call me *Zayde* or Grandpa or Zydele. I am all of those titles, of course, but my grandchildren gave up using these words when they were three years old."

"Oh sure, no problem, sir," the rabbi said apologetically. "And you don't have to call me Rabbi all the time. I am Dr. Howard Rapaport. I have a doctorate from the yeshiva, and you can call me Heshie."

"Thank you, Rabbi," my father replied. "I could never call you Heshie to your face. If you were selling herring in a delicatessen or worked in a candy store, I would call you Heshie. But you're a rabbi and to me that's something special," Pop said and left.

Almost immediately, the young rabbi sprang to attention. He signaled the bandleader who was also the trumpet player to sound some musical flourishes, which he did loud and off key. The guests moved to their seats. The wedding ceremony began and the nuptials were on track.

The rabbi smiled his way through the service. He was generous in his praises but not too lavish since he was barely acquainted with the groom. His voice was not Caruso nor Perry Como nor even Ringo Starr, but he sounded the traditional words with flair and drama. Heshie was in top form and knew it.

It was when he recited the Seven Blessings that he stumbled. It was not a misstep of giant proportions but it caught my father's ear and mine too. The Seven Blessings, or the *Sheva Brachot* as it is referred to in Hebrew, is one of the two or three climaxes in a Jewish wedding ceremony. The other two are the breaking of the glass by the bridegroom at the end of the ceremony and his repetition of the ancient ritual of the wedding vow—"With this ring you are consecrated to me according to the law of Moses and Israel." This is known as the *haray aht* statement.

In actuality the repetition by the bridegroom of this phrase alone does the trick. With the completion of this wedding vow, the deed is done. The couple is married.

Unfortunately, three Hashems got in the way. Hashem is a vernacular usage of the word for God, which is often questionable. The rabbi, who was no nuclear physicist in the brains department, may have been thinking about other things like girls or feeding the cat as he began his recitation of the Sheva Brachot. In his first three Brachot, he used the word Hashem for the word God instead of *Adonai,* which was the normal word. A serious violation? To my father, yes. When he brought the misquotation to the rabbi's attention, Heshie virtually ignored it. "These things happen, uncle. Yes. Hashem should not have been said, but there was no law broken. They are as married as Abraham and Sarah."

He continued. "I'm a little disappointed in your attitude. You should be giving me a *yasher koach* and all I hear is a complaint. I think you should be ashamed of yourself, Papa," he concluded and began walking away.

My father seized his lapels.

"Ashamed of myself you say, Rabbi? You're the one who botched up the ceremony. You can't wipe that away like a *shmatte.*" He paused. "Maybe you should repeat the Sheva Brachot now."

The rabbi exploded. "Now, now. Are you out of your mind? I would look like a dummy."

"You are a dummy, Rabbi. With all due respect, of course," my father said softly.

"I don't like that, Papa. That's an insult."

"Yes it is," my father said and walked away.

As I expected, after we returned home, my father visited our much respected and beloved Rabbi Goodman. This rabbi was my father's friend and spiritual leader for more than fifty years. Pop explained the questionable circumstances of the wedding ceremony and was given an immediate response.

"David," he said softly, "there is no question about the legitimacy of the wedding. When your grandson Philip stated, without reservation, the *haray aht* vow—"Be thou consecrated to me"—the wedding is done. That is finality." He hastily added, "Of course it would have been preferable if the young rabbi had not used the word Hashem, but believe me, David, God was there and he listened and sanctified the wedding."

My father accepted Rabbi Goodman's interpretation, as I knew he would, and that should have brought finality to this sorry chapter. But it did not remove the demons from my father's head and they lodged there until my father died.

Oddly enough it was my sister Esther, mother of Philip, the embattled bridegroom, who kept the issue alive. When a son was born to the young couple, dissension almost immediately arose with regard to the name. Iris, the mother, wanted to name him Leo after Leo Tolstoi whose book *War and Peace* she quoted like the Bible, while her mother Sandra, a Hadassah lady and Hebraist, wanted him named Aryeh, which means lion.

After a tsunami kind of week, the papoose was given the name Leon, which really satisfied no one. Other problems emerged. Little Leon was a terrible eater and an even worse sleeper. He rejected pablum, squashed bananas, his mother's milk, and baby foods of all varieties and always in full voice. He hardly slept, which was also the status of his parents who required an aide almost around the clock.

In a year's time, little Leon settled down to a diet of onion omelets, which he had three times a day, and those large overblown doughnuts that are coated with a lavish dusting of granulated sugar. It was after her grandson flunked second grade in public school that my sister became convinced that these problems were rabbi-connected.

"It's the curse of Heshie's screw-up," she insisted. "Who the hell flunks second grade, for Christ's sake? Pa was right. That imbecile rabbi bollixed up my grandson's genes. We ought to sue the bastard," she shouted.

She never sued, of course, though she took on the complaining rights that hitherto were the property of my father. He is gone now but in many ways, his memory is still around. He was a devout man but not much of a forgiver. He undoubtedly inherited that trait from his father who was and had been a *melamed* (teacher of young boys) all his life. He taught the five books of Moses and always insisted there should have been six or maybe even seven or eight.

Young Leon is still undersized and a lousy eater, but he is also a Ph.D. candidate at Harvard in Mandarin Chinese poetry. He is red-headed with a face full of freckles and weighs in at about 120 pounds after an onion omelet of three eggs. They say he is a tiger when it comes to women, which, of course, is nothing to be ashamed of.

Don't Blame It on Greta Garbo

It was on a cold and dour day in mid-March during that plodding and violent coal miners' strike in the late 1920s that Mr. Moore, our next-door neighbor, hit it lucky. That morning at about 9:30, while he was having his second cup of coffee, he received a telephone call from Mike Crawford himself, owner of all the movie houses in town, that he had a job for him. He asked Mr. Moore to come in that very afternoon to be fitted for a uniform.

The job he offered and that Mr. Moore accepted without even asking what it would pay was collecting tickets and supervising ushers at the Cameo movie theater, which showed the best pictures in town. John Gilbert, Norma Shearer, Greta Garbo, John Barrymore—the royalty of Hollywood—were regulars at the Cameo.

The job was a comedown for Mr. Moore. No question about that. He knew it and so did Edna, his wife. For more than twenty-five years, he had been a bookkeeper with the Shady Glen Coal Company, but the strike ended all that. At age fifty-five, the going businesses in town, and there weren't too many of those anymore, weren't grabbing at someone of his "mature" years, as Edna put it.

Mr. Moore plunged into his new job with the verve of a West Pointer on parade. With his new uniform, which was immaculately fitted by Mr. Crawford's tailor, he looked like a military man. His pants, which had creases sharp enough to cut through cold butter, were a muted blue-gray serge with a black satin stripe running down the leg. His wool jacket was dark maroon with sparkling gold buttons in front and on both sleeves. His wide lapels were festooned by black braid piping that gave extravagant credence to Mr. Moore's proud, puffed-up chest.

He carried himself with dignity and authority. He was a credit to the uniform and to the Cameo theater.

He was also a credit to us, his closest neighbors. Sometime during his first week on the job, he told my father, "You can tell your kids they can come in free of charge any afternoon I'm at the ticket box. I'll wink them in when the coast is clear and they can pass right through faster than shit through a tall Swede." That was one of Mr. Moore's favorite expressions; he had lots of them.

Now Mr. Moore was not the kindliest man in the world. Not even on our block. We kids learned early in the game to avoid his house on Halloween Eve or when collecting pennies for the Red Cross. He'd just as soon kick you in the ass as greet you with a "good morning." Maybe sooner. I don't think he actually hated kids. My mother who saw good in everyone, including biting dogs, said Mr. Moore was that way because he had grown up in an orphan asylum. Edna once told her that.

Edna was an old friend of my mother's. We had moved next to the Moores seven years ago, but my mother had known Edna Moore many years earlier. Mother, who was a skilled dressmaker, had designed, fitted, and sewn the wedding gown for Helen, their youngest daughter whose name was now Murphy. Until things got real bad for the Moores sometime during the strike, Helen's wedding gown hung in isolated splendor in her old bedroom, which was now occupied by a roomer from Buffalo by the name of Grodsky. He was an engineer with the electric company and Mr. Moore called him "the Polack."

All that spring and summer, Mr. Moore winked us in, but none too warmly. There was a kind of noblesse oblige look on his unsmiling face as he let us pass. It was as if the Cameo theater was his private fief and we were his churlish peasants. But it was worth the humiliation, and my sisters and I rarely missed a movie. I went on Friday after school, they on Thursday. My younger brothers went there once. Their favorite movie stars were William S. Hart, Harry Carey, and Tom Mix and his horse Tony, any one of whom had as much chance of being seen in Mr. Crawford's flagship theater as a "Jesuit priest in a whorehouse," to quote Mr. Moore.

When school started in the fall, Friday continued to be my day of choice, but there was a complication. The Cameo revised its schedule. The first show had always begun at five. Mr. Crawford moved it to four o'clock so that he could get in an extra showing. Mr. Crawford's avarice bothered me not at all, but I was pushed to the limit to catch the four o'clock curtain. School was over at 3:30 and my mother insisted that I stop home first to deposit my school books and wash up—as if it would be a loss of face if Ronald Colman espied me from the screen with a smudge on my nose. Most times I caught Mr. Moore's wink right under the wire. My luck broke the week Greta Garbo came to the Cameo in *Flesh in the Devil.* The movie costarred John Gilbert who, in my estimation, never really deserved Miss Garbo. She was Mt. Everest. He was just another hill in the Poconos. At least that's how I saw it.

Flesh in the Devil was a film not only not to be missed but not to arrive late at. But I did, and with awesome consequences for me, my sisters, my father, and the entire block as it turned out.

It was the Friday of a mass rally called by the striking coal miners at the court house square. The rally tied up traffic for several blocks and I was forced to alter my usual route. I had to go roundabout, running the last two blocks and arriving at the Cameo shortly after four o'clock.

As I passed into its entry, I saw Mr. Moore occupied with a sober looking man wearing a black derby and gray spats. Both men appeared to be engaged in a serious conversation that it was my guess would go on for a while. Meanwhile Miss Garbo was spinning away on that screen while I was cooling my heels waiting for two old cockers to stop talking. I could stand it no longer. When I thought their backs had turned, I darted down that center aisle and seated myself somewhere in the middle rows.

Greta Garbo didn't let me down. She was beautiful in her usual sultry way and her eyelids hung heavier than ever over limpid blue eyes. I assumed they were blue. This picture was not in Technicolor, but they certainly were limpid. In my opinion, she wasted them on a klutzy John Gilbert.

I don't recall my walk home, but I will long remember what happened when I got there. It was a little past 6:30 and there was gathered in our parlor a reception committee consisting of my father and mother, Mr. and Mrs. Moore, all my brothers and sisters, and our nosy neighbor Mrs. Watkins. Old Mrs. Watkins had her knitting with her. This had to be serious. My father spoke first.

"What happened, Sonny? You ran into the movies like a meshuggener and you never got an OK from Mr. Moore. Mike Crawford was there and he saw you go in without a ticket."

Mr. Moore interrupted. "Let me take over, Dave. It wasn't your ass that got fried. I got words to say to your boy and I gotta get them said."

Turning to me, he shouted, "What the hell ever possessed you to rush right past me without even looking me in the eye to see if it was safe? Answer me that, dummy. What was the big hurry? You ran down that aisle like shit through a tin horn."

I sputtered something to the effect that I wanted to see the movie right from the beginning.

"What the hell kind of talk is that, shit heel?" he interrupted. "If you missed the beginning, you could have caught it at the next showing. We do have continuous performance, you know."

"It was Greta Garbo," I said. "I like her. I'm her fan. I didn't want to get there too late. You can ask my sister Dorothy. She likes Greta Garbo too."

I looked at Dorothy hopefully, but she sat mute. She wouldn't open her mouth, which was a first for Dorothy. Not a word in my defense from anyone. I saw I didn't have a friend in the room. A pariah. Like Ben Hur's mother when she was a leper in that dungeon.

Mr. Moore was hardly in a mood for explanations. "Don't blame it on Greta Garbo, for Christ's sake. It wasn't her that got me on Mr. Crawford's shit list. It was you, goddamit. You made a shmuck out of me right in front of Mr. Crawford." (He learned that word from my father.)

I tried to change the subject. "I personally think, Mr. Moore, that John Gilbert was a lousy lover in the picture. You couldn't understand what he was saying. It was like he was talking with his eyes," I said rather boldly.

Mr. Moore interrupted and turned to his wife. "How do you like them apples, Edna? Now the kid's a goddam movie critic. A seventh-grade *pisher*"—my father taught him well—"telling the industry how to make pictures—"

"Eighth grade, Mr. Moore," I corrected.

He refused to retreat. "A seventh-grade *pisher* has the nerve to insult one of MGM's biggest stars. Holy shit! Where do these kids come from?" he said turning to my father.

I could see my father was beginning to get restless. He was always on the brink of boredom when his supper was being delayed.

"What did Mr. Crawford say to you when William walked in without a ticket?" Pop asked.

"What the hell do you think he said?" Mr. Moore answered. "He says to me, Tom, that boy has no ticket. So I told him real fast that he's the cleanup kid. Picks up popcorn bags, candy wrappers, shit like that."

"Then what?" Pop asked.

"Then he says, Good. I like a clean theater."

"Then what?" my father persisted.

"Then nothing. End of conversation," Mr. Moore said defiantly.

"Well, there you are, Mr. Moore," I said triumphantly. "No harm done."

"No harm done? What do you mean—no harm done? I could have looked like a shmuck," that word again. "You can bet your ass that this will never happen again," he shouted at me.

Mrs. Watkins jumped in with both needles. "Mr. Moore is too nice to you kids. Greta Garbo! Where do you come off seeing Greta Garbo, Willie? You're still wearing knickers."

"You stay out of this, Mrs. Watkins. What the hell does his pants have to do with Greta Garbo, goddamit? I don't give a shit what he wears. As far as I'm concerned he can walk in bare-ass naked," Mr. Moore said.

"But that won't happen no more, by Jesus! From now on, none of you—and I mean every last one of you—can come in without a ticket.

No sirree! Everybody buys a ticket from now on. I'm finished putting my ass on the line for any of you."

Then turning to Mrs. Watkins, he bellowed, "And that means you too, Madame Watkins. And your goddam rooming house customers. They'll pay just like everyone else. I don't care if you never knit me another stitch. You can unravel that scarf you're making for me right now."

With that under his belt, Mr. Moore stormed out with poor Edna meekly following.

Old Mrs. Watkins kept right on knitting. Weeks later she finished the scarf and gave it to Edna who gave it to Mr. Moore who almost immediately lifted the ban on Mrs. Watkins. And her roomers. But not us.

My father and mother took the loss philosophically. My sisters were unforgiving. Naturally! My brothers never knew the difference. And as for me—Greta Garbo, wherever you are, you were worth it.

A Coin in a Pinchpurse

I have been with Musa Rahim for fourteen months now and I must admit that I have not always enjoyed the experience, in truth, for truth is the realm of God, according to our beloved rebbe. Musa Rahim is known among us as Moishe Rosenzweig and has been with me, not I with him, for longer than I expected and certainly far longer than Musa had hoped.

I am Velvel Pasternak and I am a follower, a worthy one, I hope, of the rebbe in Brooklyn. I am a dealer in diamonds and Musa is now my assistant. He is a famous writer whose name is cursed by some and blessed by others. He is a fugitive and is in hiding, and I am his hiding place.

When we travel, he carries my luggage and my books. For safekeeping, Musa asked me to transport his notes and writings and his sharpened pencils. He told me he can never write with pencils that are not sharpened to a perfect point. These materials lie in the leather portfolio where my prayer shawl and holy books are kept.

I once asked the rebbe, what if Musa's writings are unworthy or profane? Would that debase the sanctity of my instruments of prayer? The rebbe said there are no profane writings, only profane people. When I told this to Musa, he said, "Tell that to my critics."

I know all about Musa and he knows a great deal about me. He calls me a "born-again Jew," which possibly I am, yet I dislike the inference. In truth, I have been a Chasid of the rebbe's for almost ten years. Before that I was many people doing many things, most of them bad. When I came to the rebbe, I was like a worn-out coat of many colors whose hues had long faded away. I asked the rebbe if I was a born-again Jew, and he said that before there is a flame, there is a spark and the spark never leaves the flame. When I told this to Musa, he said nothing.

Musa Rahim was brought to the rebbe's attention by one of his followers in London. This follower, who calls himself a disciple, is a man of wide fame who is as rich as he is famous and his power even surpasses his wealth. He had known Musa and possibly was his publisher though, in truth, I am not certain of this. It disturbed him that Musa was both a fugitive and a prisoner who was living a life of danger and despair. Musa had been in hiding for more than a year. His enemies had offered a bounty of over $5 million to the man, or woman, I suppose, who would lead them to him.

This powerful man visited Musa in hiding and saw how desperate was his state of mind. He promised to help. He flew from London to New York and asked the rebbe's advice. The rebbe told him, "If you wish to hide a coin, you place it in a purse with other coins. There it will jingle like the rest."

I was chosen by the rebbe to deliver Musa out of Egypt and into freedom. I like to think I was chosen not because I am a diamond merchant who knows London but because the rebbe held me as worthy to do God's work. "The freeing of captives is no less an obligation than honoring one's father and mother," the rebbe instructed me. In truth, I do know London as well as New York or Amsterdam, and if that was the rebbe's reasoning, that too is a blessing.

When I arrived in my London hotel, there was a message that I would be picked up the next morning promptly at nine. And I was, by an undistinguished-looking man driving an undistinguished-looking car. He drove me by a very circuitous route to a not very distinctive residence that I knew was located not very far from my hotel. This was where Musa Rahim was secreted away. I was shown into what would be a small parlor, badly in need of dusting, and in a matter of seconds, Musa walked in. He approached rather unsteadily, I thought, and shook my hand. His handshake was limp, very brief and slightly moist.

I don't think Musa was quite prepared for what he saw. The look he gave me was a combination of skepticism and disbelief, and I think, instant displeasure.

He sized me up, head to toe, like he was measuring me for a suit. First he examined my face, at least the part of it that was not overgrown with my thick bushy white beard. Then his eyes took in the rest of me—the black hat, wrinkled white shirt buttoned to the neck, no tie, baggy black jacket and trousers, scarred black shoes with much too long laces, one of which, I saw, was untied and dragging the floor. What he saw evidently didn't please him very much because he groaned out a distinct, if muted, "Holy shit."

"I beg your pardon?" I said.

"Am I supposed to go around looking like you?" he asked.

"Only if you love life," I answered.

"I meant no offense, you understand," he began apologetically, "but your dress seems a little bizarre. For London, I would think."

"I hadn't noticed," I said.

"No, I suppose not," he said.

We regarded each other without speaking. Musa Rahim was of medium height and build. He was a little bulgy in the belly, a consequence of his year of inactivity, I surmised. He had lots of black head hair though it was thinning above the forehead. He was properly bearded in a young yeshiva student kind of way. His face was not unattractive. The eyes were the dominant feature—strong, piercing, black. Also tired-looking and heavy-lidded. I saw right off that we could do something with this man.

I began to talk. For the next hour, I told him something about our way of life. I told him about our rebbe, our people, our habits, our dress, our purpose, our strange ways, our view of life, our view of others. I told him that here in London there were more than 30,000 followers of the rebbe. Musa listened very intently and, I think, recorded every word.

I told him that contrary to what he might think, we do have tailors here in London, and even barbers. I told him that one of them, Chaim by name, would be brought to him this very afternoon to clothe him properly and do something with his too well-trimmed beard. This caught Musa off-balance.

"What's wrong with my beard?" he asked.

"It's too perfect," I told him.

"Is that bad?" he asked.

"Of course," I said. "A beard should run wild, untouched, uncombed, uncivilized, if you catch my meaning."

"I'm not sure I like that," Musa said.

"You'll get used to it," I told him. "In a month or two, we'll have you looking like one of us." I paused. "You do want to look like me," I said with a smile.

He was gracious; he did not answer. "I would like to wear a tie. Do you people never wear ties?"

"Only when we're buried," I answered.

This startled him. I hastened to explain. "Ties are extra baggage. Our beards cover the shirtfront. Speaking of baggage, Chaim will bring you a suitcase, suitably battered, that will contain all the necessaries."

"Necessaries?" Musa asked.

"Special brands of kosher soap, toothpaste, underwear, shirts, stockings, handkerchiefs, an umbrella, religious articles. Things like that," I told him.

His eyes widened. "Religious articles?"

"Only as props," I assured him. "By the way, your new name is Moishe Rosenzweig. Would you mind repeating it?"

He said it perfectly on the first try. Then I gave him his passport. He examined it carefully, noting the date and place of birth. He looked up.

"There's no photograph," he said.

"You will have one this afternoon. The tailor is also a sometime photographer," I added.

"He sounds very impressive," Musa observed. "What did you say his name is?"

"Chaim. And you ought to remember it well," I told him.

"Why?" he asked.

"Because in Hebrew, *chaim* means 'life,'" I said. I left shortly thereafter.

Three days later, Musa was brought to my hotel by the talented Chaim. I must say that I was almost startled by what I saw. Musa was transformed into one of us. He shuffled into the room with the kind of round-shouldered walk that seems to grasp the rebbe's disciples sooner or later. It is like a Chasidic arthritis—slightly stooped yet nimble. His eyes were dull and lively at the same time. His hat was properly dented and his white shirt, no tie, of course, was an iota away from being on the soiled side. His manner of speech had very definitely departed from Oxford and was now halfway to Eastern Parkway in Brooklyn where the rebbe resides. Musa had arrived.

In our few remaining days in London, I taught Musa some basic things about diamonds. I gave him a loupe and showed him what to look for—color, spots, designs, cuts. The superficialities really. But he was a quick learn, as he called it, and when we arrived in Amsterdam, he was no hindrance at all. At least in most ways. I showed him where and how to secrete our small cache of diamonds and how to comport himself in the backrooms of the Dutch diamond merchants and cutters. I taught him that in our business there is an eloquence in remaining silent. He told me this also applied to literature, which, in truth, I am not sure I understood.

There were times when he was difficult and sullen. On one occasion in our hotel he called room service for a Scotch and soda. I cancelled the order immediately. I explained that we do not drink Scotch. Ordering Scotch or any whiskey, I said, would be highly suspicious.

"What can I order?" he demanded.

"Seltzer water would be fine," I said.

"Seltzer is not a drink." He was angry now. "Seltzer is only the handmaiden to a drink. Sherry, wine, beer—which one is permissible and beyond suspicion?" he asked.

"They are all permissible, but of our own make. When we get to Brooklyn, you can drink as much as you like. A Scotch and soda here could be your last."

We traveled on to Madrid from Amsterdam, and Musa was quite useful here. He spoke the language fluently, which turned out to be a mixed blessing. To avoid suspicion, I asked that he converse haltingly and with an American accent. He obliged, of course, and our business was transacted swiftly and profitably. The days were taken up with business and culture. During our off-hours we toured museums, the Opera, the Royal Palace, and even the Taurine, the bullfighting museum. The nights were slow and tedious and potentially dangerous.

On our second night in Madrid, Musa told me he would like to drop into a "discreet bordello" that he had visited "once or twice" before. I told him that there were no "discreet bordellos" just as there were no discreet cemeteries. He grumbled briefly but acceded to my logic.

Shortly after we arrived in Brooklyn, Musa began to write again. He lives not too far from my home and roams New York City without fear. He largely avoids those places where he had once been known, but he feels quite secure elsewhere. I have no idea what his new literary endeavors are about and though I am very curious, I would never ask.

Musa now appears to be at peace with himself and with the world. I no longer see fear in his eyes. His look is sharp and bold. Shortly after we arrived in New York, I arranged that he meet the rebbe. They sat together in his chamber and were alone much longer than I had expected. When they emerged, they smiled at me, almost as if I had been part of their conversation. Musa's smile was so wide I could see his immaculate white teeth gaping at me. His look was as pure as water.

Not too long ago he inquired whether my business activity ever took me to Jerusalem and when I answered "yes," he said he would like to join me. I told him I would discuss this with the rebbe and Musa smiled and said that would be fine.

Mosquitoes

I am often asked where I get all those odd happenings that turn into my stories. Where do my plots come from? I am likely to answer cryptically, "They come to me from everywhere and nowhere," which is no answer at all. Yet it is an honest-to-God response and it is the answer. Ideas bubble out of my head like steam from a teapot, and most of my stories are true or partially true or somewhat true. They come out of my life.

The other day I wrote a story about my Latin teacher in high school who happened to be equipped with big boobs. Now when you think about it, what's so odd about a female with a big chest? I haven't taken a count, but I would guess that half of the feminine population in the world are endowed with big ones. What made my story readable, I think, was that her pride in her bosom ended up killing her. Yet I don't think this particular narrative was a sad story. Death is not necessarily sad, as I wrote in another story.

I had a friend, now deceased, who was a fabulous joke teller. He never forgot a joke or a punch line. And he loved to be tested. He would defy his audience to give him a topic and he would come up with a joke relating to it. He might be given the word "mosquito," for example, and with no hesitation at all would come up with something hilarious about a mosquito.

Those of us who write or tell stories can pretty much do the same. I know I can. I'm not as gifted as my friend, but I think I can handle the challenge. Take the word "mosquito," for example.

In our town there were no mosquitoes. We were rather high up in the mountains and the climate was pretty dry most every day of the year. We had rains and snow, of course, but they hardly left any puddles. There was never any flooding that I can remember and that good old mountain soil, heavy with vegetation of all sorts, would soak up the wet like a sponge. There was hardly any humidity to speak of and I remember that when my mother hung the laundry on the clothes line, it was dry almost as soon as she put on the clothespins.

Ours was a town usually dry as a bone. A single mosquito would perish out of sheer loneliness if it buzzed into town. That's the way it was until Miss Vanessa Vandross moved into our community. She was the new librarian, pretty in an unobtrusive sort of way, and snappish. She had a way of speaking like she was snapping a whip. Every word came out her mouth like it was shot out of a rifle. And she was opinionated as hell. Often enough, when I would check out a book, she would say to me, "This is not a volume for you, William. Put it back on the shelf."

Miss Vandross came from Baltimore with her dog "Pumpkin," who was huge, almost the size of a small horse. He was immaculate, of course, which is what you would expect from a pet belonging to Miss Vandross. He was odorless, ate his dog chow like he was in Buckingham Palace, was as flealess as one of those show dogs in Madison Square Garden. Pumpkin was to the world of canines as Helen Wills was to Wimbledon or Forest Hills. He was class with a capital K.

Miss Vandross was in town maybe a month or two when people began scratching. It started in the vicinity of Washington Avenue, which was where the library was located, and moved straight up the hill where we lived. At first people thought it might have come from a poison ivy infestation. We had that before, possibly ten years ago, when poison ivy or poison oak was all over the town.

But this scratching outbreak was different. Early scratchers were told that those red angry welts on the arms and face or anywhere else on the body came not from an airborne source but from an animal carrier. Tests by the board of health indicated that the guilty party, so to speak, was not gnats or flies or some creeping species, but the everyday, commonplace mosquito.

Mosquitoes? Hell, we never had a mosquito invasion before, people said. Why now? Where in hell did they come from? Mosquitoes usually come out of puddles or wells or outside privies, which were still in use here and there. Or they could have flown in from New Jersey, which grows just about everything. Or from some goddam salesman selling shoes for Thom McCann who could have carted them in by way of his sample case.

Not to drag out this story more than it deserves, the Board of Health concluded that the mosquito carriers were dogs. But not the old native dogs that have been around our town since the time of Noah. They were largely immune to the mosquito. Something in their hide or hair discouraged the mosquito from taking refuge there. It was the newcomer canines who were the danger species.

The Board of Health printed placards with the picture of some sad-looking hound on it and posted them on every telephone pole in town. Stray dogs by the dozens were brought into the pound to be deloused, if that is the word, by squads of volunteers. There were casualties, of course, on both sides. Some volunteers were bitten by the dogs and some volunteers oversprayed the beasts and there was hell to pay.

Our city, which is the epitome of quietude and peace, had become one big blast of barking. This went on for days until the spray job was done. Dogs were safe again. Mosquitoes disappeared or disintegrated and the town was again the safe haven it always was.

But then, out of nowhere, the shit hit the fan. It was learned that every canine—with one exception—had been mosquitoeized and freed of vermin during the dog sweeps. The pooch that was not detoxified was Pumpkin, the aristocratic canine belonging to Miss Vandross. The newcomer librarian would not allow her pet to be sprayed. She claimed she had papers from a half-dozen veterinarians to vindicate her claim that Pumpkin had a full deck of allergies. He was allergic to sprays and soaps, dog brushes and dairy products, emulsifiers and detoxins, certain meat products and cereals, and there was much more.

"If you would spray Pumpkin in the same way as the other creatures, he would surely perish," Miss Vandross wailed. "He is a delicate dog and is on a special diet," she said.

"A delicate dog you say, Miss Vandross. Hell, he looks about as big as Balaam's ass," Dr. Norton Perkins, chairman of the Board of Health and an authority on the Old Testament, replied testily.

"I object to your language, Dr. Perkins," said Miss Vandross, who was not a Bible scholar.

"For your information, Miss Vandross, Balaam's ass is not what you think. It's in the Bible, of which, I am sure you have several copies in the library. You will find Balaam's ass in Numbers 22, verse 30," he said.

Miss Vandross replied tartly, "Thank you for the Bible lesson, Dr. Perkins, but isn't there something in your Bible about 'show mercy to the beasts in the field'?"

"I am not familiar with that one, Miss Vandross."

"Well, I'm sure it's there if you look for it, Dr. Perkins," she said.

Dr. Perkins answered, "We're not here to discuss the Bible, Miss Vandross. We're talking about public safety. Your dog, I forget what the hell name it goes by, is a hazard to the good health of our community. I have in my pocket an affidavit signed by Judge Maxwell ordering the seizure of your animal to be forcibly sprayed once and for all."

Miss Vandross began quoting the Constitution about all creatures are entitled to "life, liberty, and the pursuit of happiness," but she was cut off by Dr. Perkins.

"That refers to people not dogs, for Christ's sake," he shouted impatiently.

"I am referring to the spirit of the Constitution," she replied angrily.

"The spirit be hanged, Miss Vandross," he shouted. "I am instructing my two bailiffs to take your hound to the pound. Tomorrow what's his name will be sprayed and sanitized like every other pooch in the county." Turning to the bailiffs, he shouted, "Grab that goddam hound, boys, and let's go."

As they seized the bewildered, barking Pumpkin, the librarian began to shout at the vet. "You're a Fascist. In America all creatures are created equal."

"The hell they are, lady. In America a dog will always be a dog and not a man," he answered.

As they drove off, Miss Vandross screamed. "You can go to hell, you murdering son of a bitch." Then she began to cry.

The next morning as Mr. Franklin, the poundkeeper, came to work, he noticed that the rear door to the pound was ajar. He could hear frenzied barking inside. There were three dogs yapping away wildly. Pumpkin was not among them. The hounds looked fierce, Mr. Franklin said, but smug as if they had just eaten a T-bone steak. He thought they were smiling, he told his wife that night. "They seemed to be licking their chops," though he didn't know what that meant.

When Dr. Perkins learned about the missing dog, he and his bailiffs drove to the library to confront Miss Vandross, but the young librarian was nowhere to be found. Nor was she in her apartment, which was cleaned out, her landlady said. The furniture came with the apartment and everything was left as it had been rented originally. And no one appeared to be surprised that Miss Vandross left her premises spotless and shipshape. The bailiffs who searched the flat for some clue as to where she might have gone found a canine brush with a few dog hairs that undoubtedly came off the escaped Pumpkin.

Weeks later Miss Angela Drew, the head librarian, received a letter from Miss Vandross requesting that she mail her unpaid salary check to General Delivery in Boise, Idaho. As Dr. Perkins learned later, and it came as no surprise to him nor to anyone else, there was no extradition agreement between Idaho and Pennsylvania, the Keystone State. In her own genteel way, Miss Vandross told them all to go to hell.

The Lady Who Loved God

Whenever she spoke of God or to God, which she did often enough during the day and undoubtedly into the night, my friend Berdie referred to Him always as Hashem. Hashem is a Hebrew word that translates as "the Name."

Berdie did not invent the word. It's been in use a long time, largely by Orthodox Jews and some others who call Him Hashem without, in their view, violating that part of the Third Commandment that says, "Thou shall not take the name of the Lord in vain."

In my view, saying the word God, for casual usage, or the Almighty, or the Lord, or the Creator, or Yahweh, as the Christians translate Him, does not constitute a violation of the Third Commandment. I'm not an expert on God, nor is Berdie, nor are most, but if I could read what's in God's head, I would be inclined to think that He enjoys the experience of being addressed by any word or name at all.

To take my theory further, I think the reason God cautioned us about not using His name too freely was the matter of intimacy. He wants us, His people, to worship Him but not to the point of overdoing it. After all, He did create us in His image, which gives us a special relationship with Him. I believe that God loves humanity even though, in my opinion, He often has an odd way of showing it. I once expressed these thoughts to Berdie, and I don't think she really understood what I was driving at. Which is okay because sometimes I feel I don't understand either.

Berdie, whose real name Bertha was hardly used by anyone, was a friend, a best friend of my wife. When my wife passed, Berdie felt it was her duty to look in on me from time to time to insure that my clock was still ticking.

It was a benevolent relationship right from the beginning. She believed, and I was hardly the one to disabuse her, that she could best serve me by keeping my refrigerator overflowing with cakes, pies, soups, meat dishes, and a choice menu of kosher delicacies that hardly any Jewish housewife stews up anymore.

Much as I protested, and I swear I did, she kept the bounty flowing. In those days, her husband Irving was alive but failing. It was probably the onset of Alzheimer's though Berdie denied it rather passionately. I think that denial had something to do with her relationship to God, her beloved Hashem. As if Hashem had let her down by imposing the dreaded disease on her husband. Irving was in his high eighties and Berdie was not far behind.

Irving was not able to drive and Berdie never learned. So it was I who took them wherever it was necessary. For me it was not a big deal, but Berdie thought it was and she would muffle my protests by claiming it was Hashem who motivated her forays into the kitchen in my behalf.

I remember one Monday morning I received a call from Berdie inquiring whether my choice of blintzes was cheese or blueberries or both. I was about to say blueberries, but I held back.

"I don't think you should make blintzes just for me," I said sternly.

"Who said they're just for you? We love blintzes too."

"So make them for yourselves," I protested.

"I will make them for me and Irving. But with the same spoon I can make them for you too," she answered.

"So use a smaller spoon and make them for yourselves," I insisted.

"You don't like blintzes, Bill?" she asked.

"I love them," I answered, "but that's not the point."

"So what is the point?"

"The point is I feel you're making blintzes because I drove you and Irving to your doctors yesterday. I feel you're paying me back for my services, which really bothers me," I said.

"How can you say that? I never think that way," she said, a little flustered.

"I certainly hope you don't," I said.

"Hashem knows what's in my heart," Berdie replied.

"So, what's really in your heart?" I asked.

"You should know what's in my heart."

"I really don't," I insisted.

"What's in my heart is to do what Hashem wants me to do," she said.

"Maybe God doesn't want you to do His work. Maybe He wants me to do my own work. Maybe He really doesn't care," I said.

"Maybe, maybe . . . that's no answer. Of course Hashem cares. If He didn't care, He wouldn't be Hashem."

"I'm afraid I don't follow you, Berdie."

"Sure you do," she said.

"Well, maybe I do," I paused. "You think that with all that's going on, God has His hand in everything?" I asked.

"Of course. He's Hashem."

"How about all the bad things? Are they being done by the evil fairy?" I asked. I knew I was being flippant.

"That's Hashem's work too," she answered sadly.

"All the bad?"

"That's right. All the bad."

"Why, Berdie?" I asked.

"Because Hashem wants you to ask why," she said simply.

We never had that kind of conversation again, though in many ways, I suppose, we did.

Irving's condition worsened. There were hospitalizations followed by a brief homestay. He passed away in his sleep. Berdie took that as a good sign. Hashem was listening. Irving passed but without pain.

There was pain, of course, for Berdie. She and Irving had been married for more than fifty years. And they were good years. There were two sons and six grandchildren. They were a close and affectionate family. Berdie grieved deeply but in her own way. She wore a calm face, which was mostly smiling, though there were moments when anger took over and she made no effort to subdue or mask it. These occurred mostly in her relationship with Sisterhood members and the mah-jongg ladies with whom she played every Wednesday afternoon.

In those post-Irving days, she began to lean more heavily on me. I became the burial ground for the disillusionments and complaints she had with friends and neighbors. Berdie was the matriarch of her family. She always had been. There was something majestic, even forbidding in her behavior to her family. They gave in to every whim or request she made. She knew that and it bothered her at times, she confided to me.

I think Berdie was whom she was almost from the time she was born. She was the youngest child in a family where her brothers and sisters were considerably older than she. She admitted she was spoiled by her parents and her siblings. Not very much was denied her though she claimed she never asked for very much. The important day of the week for Berdie was Saturday when she would accompany her father to the synagogue holding on to his hand like it was the Torah.

During the time I knew her, she was a true-blue antifeminist. She believed almost religiously in the superiority of men. Especially in the synagogue. In the issue of granting women equality in the synagogue service, Berdie was one of the few ladies in the opposition. Her rationale was always God-connected. "If Hashem approved of giving more leading roles to women He would have said something about it. Hashem did say 'honor thy father and mother.' He did say honor, which doesn't mean give her an *aliyah*. Like the Indians say," she pointed out to me most emphatically, "God doesn't speak with a forked tongue."

When I pointed out to her that it was the Indians who said that about the white settlers, she replied angrily, "So what!" And that was the end of the conversation.

Not too long after the passing of Irving, the God she loved tested her again, this time even more severely. The oldest of her sons was a diabetic and he lapsed into a number of medical crises. After a short period of convalescences, he died. This time Berdie was not as stoic as before. She wept frequently and profusely. She was near hysteria much of the time. She blamed everyone, including herself, for his untimely passing.

"We all should have recognized his symptoms earlier," she cried. "His wife, his children, his friends, his colleagues at work. He inherited the diabetes genes from me. Maybe it was from my father or my mother. We all contributed. We are all guilty of negligence," she said.

I noted that during that period of semi-mourning and semi-blaming, she never brought Hashem into the picture. It was as if He disappeared from her horizon, that He was marking time elsewhere. The ecstatic look in her eyes when she spoke of God was absent. Much of her day was spent staring at no place in particular and swaying forward and back as if she was deep in Talmudic study.

After months of mourning, she drifted back to her former way of life. She shopped, visited doctors, attended synagogue services, lived her life. She began cooking delicacies for me again. I no longer made pro forma protests. I think that would have saddened her. She was less talkative than before though I knew her mind was spinning like a top. From time to time, I would interrupt her silences with the cliché about a penny for her thoughts and she would smile and say they were not worth the penny. Once she said something about having a conversation with Hashem.

"Is He a good conversationalist?" I asked.

"It's not that kind of conversation," she answered.

"What kind is it?" I said.

"Well, to be frank," she said, "I do most of the talking."

"And what does God say?" I asked.

"He listens. Hashem is a good listener," she answered.

Berdie's health began failing. She was unsteady on her feet and had frequent falls. She was prescribed a cane, which she rarely used. "It makes me dizzy," she would say. Her doctor decided that it would be more desirable for her to be dizzy in the hospital than her home.

Her hospital stay was less than one week. The day I visited, she took my hand and asked whether I still had chicken fricassee in the freezer. I told her it was going fast and she said, "Good, I'll make more."

We spoke very briefly. There were long silences and I knew she was holding a conversation with one close to her. The next day she joined Hashem.

Bluma

I first met my Aunt Bluma at her daughter's wedding. I was three years old and was buried under a pile of heavy winter overcoats on a massive bed in Bluma's bedroom. The wedding must have been on a Saturday night and guests like my mother and father and older sister were gathered in her parlor where the ceremony was due to take place.

I was deposited along with a two- or three-year-old girl named Tootsie on Bluma's bed early in the evening. As Bluma's guests arrived, they tossed their coats, neatly at first, but then haphazard, over me and Tootsie. To their credit, I must say that no matter how they flung their garments, they made certain that our noses were always poised over the morass of coats like a pair of periscopes.

Aunt Bluma was not really my aunt. We called her aunt because that's how she wanted it. She was large and strong and smiling and always kissing me and my sister Dorothy. Much as I tried to escape, she always snagged me and planted kisses on my face like it was a mezuzah. She was a *landsfrau* (kinswoman) of my father, probably a distant cousin, born in the same village in the Ukraine as my father. She was twice my father's age and always claimed she helped deliver him. My father always denied this.

Bluma was undoubtedly one of the early émigrés from Romanov, the village in the Ukraine where she and my father were born. How or why she landed in a small coal-mining city in Pennsylvania is a mystery to this day. My father on the other hand was sent there by his mother. It was his mission to track down and locate his brother-in-law Berel, husband of his sister Bootzie and father of two little girls, who had been incommunicado from his family for more than two years.

It's not as if he disappeared into the mists of northern Pennsylvania. He simply stopped writing and sending American dollars to support his wife and kids. My father found Berel on his first try. He was a boarder at the home of Bluma's next-door neighbor, which happened to be the last address of the last letter he wrote to Bootzie in Romanov.

My father is a peaceful man, a kindly and philosophical soul, but he set aside the philosophy when he laid eyes on his errant brother-in-law. Without a handshake or a *shalom aleichem*, my father hauled off with a left hook (my father is a lefty) to Berel's nose that broke it in three places and made him a believer. Berel carried that pug nose to the grave some forty years later. Within a year, Bootzie and her two girls sailed to this country on the wages Berel earned in a kosher butcher shop.

When my father first arrived, he went to Bluma's house as he had been instructed to do in Romanov. For the next several days, Bluma took charge of his life. He was given space in a bedroom of her house, which he shared with a man named Posnanski. Mr. Posnanski was a devout Polish Jew who arose each morning at four to pray in a squeaky voice to the Almighty. My father arose an hour later, said his prayers hurriedly, was given a huge breakfast by Bluma, and then taken a block away to the wholesale district of the city.

Before she left her house, Bluma stripped her bed of its pillowcase and took it with her. They stopped at the wholesale block that was nearby.

"Good morning, Mr. Levinson," she greeted the owner of a men's and ladies wholesale underwear dealer. They spoke in Yiddish.

Mr. Greenberg was not effusive in his response. "You brought me another greenhorn, Bluma?"

"This is a cousin, Mr. Greenberg."

"I see." He paused. "God blessed you with a fine crop of cousins, Bluma."

"God is generous," Bluma answered.

"The last cousin still owes me twelve dollars. That's money, Bluma. It's not borscht."

"Don't worry, Mr. Greenberg. He'll pay. I guarantee it."

"Guarantee, guarantee. What am I? In the insurance business?" he complained.

Bluma ignored him. "My cousin needs merchandise. He's a peddler. He's going to the coal mines. The wives are good customers," she said. She was out of patience. "Here, take this pillowcase. Fill it with brassieres, bloomers, men's long johns, socks, silk stockings. Whatever miners' wives need. Also things for kids."

She hustled Greenberg. As he and she filled the pillowcase with merchandise, my father asked prices and took into his head what else there was for him to sell. When they completed their work and filled the pillowcase, she took my father to the streetcar and instructed him to get out at the last stop.

"Remember, Doovedel, where the trolley stops. That's where you will get on to come home. These customers speak Russian and Polish. Speak their language. They like it. They always buy. They couldn't buy in the old country so they buy here. Also a lot of them can't count so you must be honest with them. Always give them the right change. Always. Count it out for them and they will know they can trust you."

She paused, probably to catch her breath. "Remember what I said, Doovedel. Be honest. God loves honest people."

My father was honest, not only that day but during his long lifetime. He did extremely well on his plunge into business with only Bluma's pillowcase to his name. He managed to sell everything in that pillowcase and tripled what he had originally invested. Actually he hadn't invested one thin dime because he didn't have a dime. His purchases were "on trust." The following day Bluma gave him a bigger pillowcase.

My father prospered. Most of what he made, he saved. In a month he accumulated a bundle of fives, enough to put a down payment on a horse and wagon. The horse was Prince, a black-spotted white mare who more often than not resisted my father's tug on the reins to whoa. The new transport enabled my father to switch from cloth merchandise to fresh fruits and vegetables, which were a more profitable commodity. He established a regular route that he visited weekly.

Within the year, he earned enough to bring his younger brother Yankel to this country from Romanov. For a time, Yankel lived with him at Bluma's and joined him on the wagon, but he didn't take to it. But that's another story.

Bluma was married to Michel, a meek little man who also hailed from Romanov and who operated a grocery store of sorts in the front rooms of their house. He was overwhelmed by Bluma, as were most people, but he gained a fame all of his own by siring, by way of Bluma, seven daughters. They say that Bluma held him responsible for the flood of females and never forgave him. All of the girls turned out to be beauties, but that too is another story.

Michel had a special problem that required immediate attention. He had three sisters, all unmarried. Bluma accepted most willingly the challenge to provide them with husbands. Most willingly indeed, according to my father. He knew he was a primary target.

As luck would have it, Bluma struck gold on her first try. She arranged a *shiduch* (a match) for the two younger sisters with two brothers, recent arrivals from Lithuania. This left one unmarried sister, Libby, who would be a harder sell. She was twenty-three, somewhat shrewish and no beauty.

For Libby, Bluma cast a roving eye in the direction of my father. She felt confident about this one. On a bright sunny Sabbath, after my father returned from shul and had a good *Shabbos* meal that included his favorite tzimmes, he was on his way to lie down for a nap. Bluma intercepted him.

"Doovedel, I have a little something to discuss with you," she opened.

"A little something?" my father asked.

"Something important."

"Important?" he questioned.

"Yes. Very important."

My father was silent.

Bluma spoke in a low, hardly audible voice, like a rabbi at the beginning of his sermon. "Doovedel, you are here more than a year. Thank God you're making a good living. You're getting older—"

My father interrupted. "I'm only twenty-one."

"I know, I know, Doovedel. Remember, I was there when you were born," she said softly. "It's time to look around for a bride. With your permission. I have someone in mind with all the virtues."

"Are you suggesting Libby?" he interrupted.

"Now that you mention it, yes," Bluma said.

"I don't think so, Bluma, with all due respect," my father said.

"And why not, David?" she asked, no longer low-voiced.

"For a number of reasons, Bluma."

"Such as?" Bluma demanded.

"Well, to begin with, I think she's *prust*." (She's vulgar.)

"Prust," Bluma shouted.

"Prust," my father repeated. "Let me tell you why."

"Prust," Bluma sputtered. "I don't believe it."

"You can believe it, Bluma," my father said almost apologetically. "Maybe you don't see it." He paused. "I don't like the way she eats. I don't like the way she talks. I don't like the way she laughs. And I don't like the way she looks."

Bluma was fuming. "All those things, David. Who do you think you are, Nathan Rothschild? Baron de Hirsch? You're from Romanov. Your father is a *melamed.* Your mother was a servant girl for Nathan the fat man."

My father interrupted, enraged. "My mother was a servant girl—yes. But she was a lady. My father is a *melamed,* but he's also a *talmid chochem* (a scholar). One thing I would never give them is a daughter-in-law who eats like a horse, laughs like a horse, and looks like a horse."

He started walking away, but Bluma would never allow him the last word. She blocked the doorway. "You're not a horse, Doovedel. You're a mule. You're also a *momzer.* I took you out of your mother's womb with these two hands and I'll always regret it." She stopped suddenly. "After *Shabbos,* you can leave the house."

That night my father moved. He became a boarder in the boarding house of a Mrs. Bernstein, Sonia Bernstein. She cooked good meals, but she was a Litvak (Lithuanian). When Bluma learned of his new location, she said, "They deserve each other." In time, no more than a year, Bluma arranged a *shiduch* for Libby, with, of all people, my father's favorite cousin Benny Klein who came to this country on the same ship as my father but who traveled directly to Havana to stay with his brother.

Neither my father nor Bluma enjoyed their breakup, and to Bluma's credit she made the first move that would patch up their severed kinship. She invited him and the lovely young woman to whom he was engaged (my mother) to her eldest daughter's wedding. It took two more weddings before her daughter Ida (the prettiest of the lot) was married. That was the occasion when I met Bluma for the first time. I'm sure she kissed me moistly and then went on to bury me and Tootsie under a swarm of winter overcoats in her massive bedroom on the second floor.

Though she was not my real aunt, she really was.

The Delivery Boy

His name was Sean Mahoney and he was the delivery boy for about ten years in my father's grocery store. Actually it became my brother Ben's store, which he took over when my father retired. My brother not only inherited the store but he inherited Pop's partner of fifty years who, in my estimation, was no great bargain. But Ben is one of those sterling characters who could get along with a snarling bear if he had to, which in my opinion, my father's partner often resembled.

In a way, my brother inherited Sean Mahoney, too. Sean, the delivery boy, which was how he was referred to, was no young kid when he began delivering orders for the store. He was sixty or so, which in those post-World War II days was pretty close to the age when a working man in our depressed area of northern Pennsylvania went into retirement.

There was an inevitability, my brother believes, that Sean would end up working in the store. His mother, Sophronia, was a customer, a credit customer, which means she was "on the book," and while she didn't always pay her bills on time, her credit was guaranteed by her two brothers-in-law Roger and Patrick Mahoney who were probably the most prominent lawyers in the county. When my father's partner would phone them that Sophronia was in arrears—Pop would never make that kind of call—a check would be in the mail the next day.

My father's relationship to them came by way of the Penn Avenue shul, which was being sued by the city for some stupid infringement, according to my father. The brothers, mostly Patrick, handled the case at no charge except costs, whatever that means, and the shul won "handily" as the *Tribune* reporter wrote at the time.

The lawyers were younger brothers of Absalom Mahoney, husband to Sophronia who may have been an attorney too, but he died of "the drink" in his thirties and hardly anyone ever mentioned his name. Whiskey ran in the family genes, Patrick once told my father. "Like some men are addicted to wild women or horses or a pair of dice. Roger and I escaped the family curse, though we enjoy a dram or two of Irish whiskey at a wedding or a wake," Patrick said.

Sean Mahoney's upbringing was not a difficult one, his mother always said. He was a passable student at high school and graduated near the foot of the class. Neither his mother or uncles encouraged college for Sean and it was Uncle Roger who was general counsel for the electric company who got him a job as a clerk in the billing department. Neither the utility nor Sean were too happy with the job, but an accord of sorts was reached. He was never fired, nor was he ever advanced beyond the mail room. The electric company and Sean tolerated each other for more than twenty years, and it was expected that his employment would continue until it was time to retire.

Sophronia and Sean led quiet ordered lives. They shopped every Wednesday evening in my father's store. It was Sean who selected the cookies and jellies and the ice cream, which was usually maple walnut. They attended church services on Christmas, Easter, and Mother's Day. On Saturdays, Sophronia walked downtown, Sean by her side, and they stopped at the two department stores—the Globe and the Stanton Dry Goods Store—and never missed visiting their gift departments but never buying.

From time to time they visited the magnificent offices of Roger and Patrick Mahoney, attorneys-at-law. The uncles would send down for coffee and doughnuts but rarely had time to "visit" as Uncle Roger put it. He was the silent one.

One Saturday afternoon, it was in December, Sean and his mother were in the Globe store and heading towards the gift department when Sophronia sort of leaped up and keeled over, her eyes wide open and staring. It was a stroke, a paralytic seizure. She was not quite fifty and the last word that came out of her mouth sounded something like "Johnny," but the nurse said it could be anything.

At that instant, Sean Mahoney became a man. He became the keeper of the house. He became the keeper of Sophronia. She required varied services for survival. She had to be fed, washed, bathed, changed. Bills had to be paid, shopping had to be done, the apartment had to be cleaned, coal and ice had to be ordered.

Sean left the electric company on the Monday following Sophronia's stroke. The uncles helped in the ways they could, which were considerable and largely financial. They accelerated the process that would put Sean and his mother on the rolls of welfare. Their parish priest Monsignor Cecil Mulvaney was able to secure the services of a former housekeeper in the residence of the bishop. She had been let go because, as the parish priest put it, she was a mite too young and pretty to be doing housework in the quarters of "young, impulsive priests." Roger Mahoney, the less outspoken uncle, opined that she was "fifty-five if she was a day" to which Father Cecil, the priest, replied that "that was young enough."

Bridget Coyne, the housekeeper in question, bathed Sophronia twice each week and took care of the daily personal amenities that no one expected Sean to be involved with. Mrs. Coyne was paid by the uncles. Patrick said she was worth every dime of her salary, which was high but not "outlandish." Sean knew nothing of the arrangement.

He conducted sporadic conversations with the inert Sophronia mostly about the neighbors, or the weather or my father's store where he continued to shop every Wednesday evening. Life droned on. Months turned into years, and Sean became a member of that breed of sons or daughters, usually the youngest in the family, who spend a lifetime taking care of a widowed and sick parent who goes through life like a carousel that never stops. When the music finally ends, the surviving son or daughter is often too old and weary to savor what is left of their portion of life.

When Sophronia died, ten years after her stroke, Sean went through a series of breakdowns. He hardly left the apartment, and when he did it was at night. He became a mumbler; words poured from his mouth like torrents in a squall especially when he watched television, which was constantly. Mrs. Coyne was long gone though she visited from time to time to tidy the apartment.

His uncles urged him to give up his apartment and move to the YMCA. He followed their suggestion and showed no emotion with the change, though he packed his possessions slowly and deliberately like the music had suddenly stopped. That's how Mrs. Coyne told it to the uncles and they cried, she told my father. There were not too many changes in Sean's life at the Y. He was not interested in swimming in the large pool or playing basketball with the younger Y residents or bowling or calisthenics. After he had his half-full glass of Minute Maid OJ and a bowl of Cheerios, he would spend some time in the lobby watching the TV.

After a while, his daily routine revolved around two havens. He began showing up mornings around ten at the law offices of the uncles, who didn't seem to mind too much. They would send him out for coffee or the newspapers or had him deliver documents to the court house, which was a block away. Most of the time, however, he just sat around in the waiting room doing nothing at all, not even glancing at the popular magazines that decorated the shelves.

It was Roger the more or less silent uncle who told Sean that it was not a good idea for him to be sitting around "like a cocker spaniel" in the waiting vestibule on a daily basis. "Take a walk," he said, "go to the department stores, visit the guys at the electric company. Buy some candy at the Globe. Hell, I know you like their Jordan almonds, Sean boy."

Sean was silent as he left, and afterwards, Roger cried silently.

Oddly enough, the other place he was comfortable in was my father's store. My brother Ben came back from the war in one piece and though he knew Sophronia and Sean rather casually, there had always been a common thread between him and Sean. Both were Boston Red Sox lovers, which in our town was not very common. Sean would shop in the store at odd hours of the morning and afternoon. He would come in for a bottle of milk or a loaf of bread rather than the full order he and Sophronia bought every Wednesday night. He prepared his own meals and though he was on welfare, he always had enough money in his wallet to buy himself a steak or a veal chop, which was his favorite.

Sean was always polite and well-mannered. And well-dressed. Whenever he went into the street, summer or winter, he wore the same clothing like it was a uniform. He was tall and angular and resembled a gawky middle-aged Gary Cooper. He wore an old gray Borsalino fedora, a white shirt and somber tie that was always knotted overly tight, a blue cheviot suit with a vest, a pair of white cotton socks, and black shoes with a squared toe, the kind cops wore on the beat.

His suit was well-pressed but shiny. It was at least two decades old, as were the fedora and shoes. At the Y, he was called the shiny professor. Never to his face, of course, since it was known that he lived at the Y at the pleasure of his two big-shot uncles.

He came to my father's store frequently, maybe three times each week. If he was in the store when my father came in from the market, he would go to the truck and help Pop unload. My father resisted at first but saw that Sean really wanted to help. Sean did the same with Pop's partner, who resisted but not too passionately. From time to time, my brother Ben would allow Sean to help him unload cartons of cans or boxes of cereal or sprinkle sawdust near the butcher block. One Sunday, Patrick Mahoney, older of the two brothers, dropped into the store to see my father. "Dave," he said, somewhat nervously Pop thought, "I need something of a favor from you and I hope you will oblige."

"Whatever you say, Mr. Mahoney," Pop started, but Patrick cut him short.

"Not so fast, Dave. Just hear me through." He cleared his throat, which was somewhat restricted. "I want you and your partner to give my nephew Sean a job in your store. He likes it here. He told me so. He just didn't have the gumption to ask you for the job himself."

He continued, "Sean has had a hard life, but you know that. He's in his fifties and it seems to my brother Roger and me that what he really would enjoy in life the most would be to work in your store."

My father wanted to reply, but Patrick cut him short.

"You won't have to pay him a dime in salary, Dave. He would lose his welfare if he got a job. On the other hand, Roger and I would defray any kind of unofficial gratuity you might want to slip him, if you know what I mean."

This time my father interrupted. "Mr. Mahoney, the job is his and for as long as he wants it. How can I ever deny you anything after what you did for our shul?" Pop stopped to interject, "You know what a shul is, right?"

"Oh sure, it's a Jewish church," he answered.

"Right, Mr. Mahoney. We call it a synagogue."

"Of course," Patrick nodded.

"We'll do what is the right thing, and we don't need your money, thank God. Sean will never go home with an empty pocket." Pop then quoted something from Scripture that gave Patrick an opening to make a hasty departure when he finished.

It turned out to be good for the store and its new employee. Sean thrived in his work. Little by little, he learned to do just about everything but butcher meat or wait on trade. He was too timid for that. His principal work was delivering orders in the morning and in the late afternoon in the ten-year-old Ford truck, which wheezed like a ten-year-old garageless vehicle normally does.

Sean had a mechanical bent in him that no one including himself was aware of. He kept the old Lizzie humming like new. When he was not delivering orders or tidying up the shelves, he would go outside to buff and touch up the old girl. It was as if this was his part of the store and he was in charge.

He labored fastidiously and in some ways mysteriously. On his first day delivering orders, he dropped off several bags at the home of a friend of my brother Ben. The lady of the house offered Sean a half-dollar tip, which was generous. Sean refused to accept it because he wasn't certain whether he was allowed to accept tips. He told the customer he would have to check with Ben whether that was okay.

The customer was amused and not quite sure whether Sean was kidding. She phoned Ben who assured her that Sean was serious. He instructed Sean that he was obligated to accept tips because that was how customers said "thank you." Sean nodded and said, "I guess you're right, Ben."

His reply to Ben became a kind of password. He had been taught by Sophronia to be mannerful and polite. And apologetic. It seemed as if an apology was always on the edge of his lips. He would much prefer to agree than disagree. That's how he comported himself in the store. Probably in the Y too but that was another world.

The years rolled on. My father turned over his share of the business to Ben. The partner departed soon after. Sean's uncles retired from the law and then from life. Sean stayed with Ben as long as he was the proprietor. But that ended too. Ben sold the store and Sean would not stay with the new owners though they asked him to. He told them, "I think I'm going to hang up my shoes," and his statement mystified them but not my brother Ben. He remembered this was said by Ted Williams of the Boston Red Sox when he was considering retirement.

Ben would have coffee with Sean at the Y. They didn't talk much but Sean welcomed the visit. Ben would always phone before he came out. There was a time when Ben phoned several times and got a message from the clerk that Sean was still a resident but was on vacation.

Vacation? That didn't sound very much like Sean. He phoned Monsignor Mulvaney who was no longer around, but was connected with his successor. When Ben told him why he was calling, the priest replied almost casually, "Sean Mahoney is dead. He died in the waiting room of the Long Island Railroad Station where he apparently spent his days," the priest revealed.

"He was wearing an odd mix of clothing and they found an ID card in his wallet with a $100 bill neatly folded, which was surprising for a derelict," the priest said.

"He was no derelict," Ben said.

"Well, that's what the police called him."

"Well, they're wrong. He was a good man with a few oddities," my brother said.

"I guess you're right," the priest answered.

"That's what Sean would say," Ben said.

"Would he now?"

"Yes, Father, that's exactly what he would say."

"Well, God bless you."

"You too, Padre," Ben said and hung up.

Sean was buried in the St. Cecelia Cemetery on top of the West Mountain that overlooks our town. He lies there next to Sophronia, which is where he belongs.

The Day My Mother Cried

Almost a lifetime ago when I was nine or ten and my sister Dorothy was two years older, we, jointly and not singly, made our mother cry. My mother never cried, not even when her best and oldest friend Channe Shtein who grew up with her in Verzhbalov, Lithuania, died after a long and crippling disease.

Mama loved Channe Shtein. They were neighbors in the village where they were born, were taught to be seamstresses under the supervision of the same master tailor, came to America on the same ship, settled in the same coal mining town in Pennsylvania, became brides on successive Fridays and almost within the year began to produce children as proper Jewish brides are obliged to do.

In my mother's case, five children came out of her and possibly an equal number who didn't. Channe's output was two sickly twin boys, Eddie and Seymour, who barely made it through their circumcision and were a whining, scrawny pair all their lives. My mother always blamed their disposition on Channe's husband Nachman who was born in Galicia and was a huckster like my father except he peddled junk.

As I said, my mother never cried. Even in the synagogue during Yizkor (the memorial service), my mother sat dry-eyed according to my sister Dorothy who sat next to her in the balcony. "Mama would move her lips and close her eyes like she was talking to God," my sister said, "but no crying, not Mama."

My mother was good and kind and gentle and was almost always smiling like she knew something we didn't. She was a tiny lady, never more than ninety pounds though she went down to eighty-five when my sister Esther was born. After Esther there were no more kids.

Mama had red hair that she wore in a bun and eyes that seemed to be blue at times and brown at others. My father who was no giant, maybe five feet six, seemed to tower over her like Goliath over David. He said more than once that Mama was *azoy groys vie a genetz* (as big as a sigh), which was a compliment though my mother didn't think so.

The day my mother cried those bitter tears was on a Friday. In those days, Friday in most Jewish homes was spent preparing slavishly for *Shabbos* (the Sabbath). Mothers awoke early and allowed their children to stay in bed longer than usual; they got a head start before the hustle that came with getting the kids ready for school. There was the kitchen floor to be hand scrubbed, the coal stove to be blackened and polished, the pantry to be put in order and the food to be properly drawered.

On the outside of the house there were front and rear porches to be swept and hosed down. In those days visitors entered a house through the back porch. The front door was for the postman, the doctor on a house call, the police (God forbid, of course) or strangers. Neighbors or friends or trades—people came in through the rear. This was the custom from way back when housebreaking was almost unknown and violent behavior was there but not too evident.

At any rate, on that particular Friday morning, my sister and I got out of bed later than usual. I always managed to get to the bathroom first. This was like a peace agreement between Dorothy and me. It was necessary that I get to the toilet first because I could not say the morning prayers with a soiled face and unclean hands. Girls are more fortunate than we of the masculine gender. They were exempt from reciting the morning prayers. In fact, they were not required to say the afternoon and evening prayers either, which to my mind was unfair.

On that morning, breakfast was on the table as usual. There was an orange cut in half, a buttered roll, and a glass of Postum, which was like coffee but sweeter. My sister had the same breakfast except her orange was bigger than mine. My mother once explained why. It had something to do with girls maturing earlier than boys, which was okay with me because we have them beat in other ways.

The rolls came to my father's store from Wolfgang's Bakery, which was the largest Jewish bakery in town. We ate mostly the big rolls, which for some reason were called Kaiser rolls. Gentile kids called them "Jew rolls."

My sister Dorothy liked onion rolls and I didn't. She said the onion on top of the roll, which we called a kuchen, kept the roll fresh. My mother called that silly but wouldn't argue about it. She hated arguments. She said quarreling and fighting killed families like they did to the Franchettis down the block. All because the grandmother Josephina went to the cathedral for Sunday Mass with her sister Consuela while the rest of the family prayed at St. Catherine's. The family was never the same after the two old ladies abandoned St. Catherine's.

It was in March just about a month before Passover that the roll situation became the St. Catherine's for Dorothy and me. As I said, it was Friday and it must have rained most of the night though it was sunny and clear when my sister and I sat down to eat breakfast. Our meal was on the table, the oranges cut in quarters, the Wolfgang rolls and the lukewarm glasses of Postum.

Everything was normal except for the clock. We sat down ten minutes later than usual. I charged into that orange like it was my enemy. Juice splashed out of my mouth and gurgled all over my chin. Dorothy ate more sedately.

We made up some time but hardly enough. It was a ten-minute walk to school and we could probably make it on time if we ran, which, of course, my sister would never do because it was not "ladylike." She used that word like she invented it. We had eaten about half a roll apiece.

My sister whined to my mother, "Ma, we're gonna be late. Can we take our roll with us and finish it on the way to school?" My mother didn't answer. It was as if she hadn't heard Dorothy. She was in the middle of buffing the oven part of the stove.

"Can we eat it on the street? We're gonna be late, Mama," my sister pleaded.

"Late as hell, Ma," I added.

My mother turned and gave me a severe look. "You know we don't use that word in our house, William," my mother said in a near whisper.

"I know, but . . ." I began but Dorothy interrupted.

"So what do you say, Mama? Can we go now? We will finish our rolls on the way to school." Dorothy was begging. My mother shook her head. It was no.

"We don't eat in the street like wild Indians," my mother said. "That is not the way we behave."

She paused and was silent. My sister and I thought the conversation was over, but we were mistaken. My mother stopped polishing the stove, turned around and faced us. "You can take your rolls and eat them on the way to school. What kind of face will I have with the neighbors? They will see my children eating on the street like beggars. Like dogs chewing on a bone."

She paused as if to catch her breath. "Go. Go," she repeated. "This will never happen again." We grabbed our rolls and scurried out of the house. I ran like hell and got to school on time. Dorothy arrived late but her teacher Miss Collins liked her and made no fuss. School was school that morning and dragged out like a bad movie. Finally lunch.

My sister and I, actually all the kids in our classes, ate lunch at home. We were due back at 1:30. Dorothy and I loved the lunch we ate on Fridays. That was the day my mother prepared chicken for the Sabbath meals. She would render the fat and skin so that the fat would ooze out and the pieces of skin would crackle. The ooze part was called *schmaltz* and the skin part was known as *gribenes.*

Our lunch consisted of slices of rye bread on which had been spread an avalanche of *schmaltz* and an accompanying plate of *gribenes.* Often interspersed into the saucer of the cracklings was a scatter of *arbis* (chickpeas). The accompanying beverage was seltzer (carbonated water), which came out of a glass bottle with a siphon lever that was fun to squeeze.

Dorothy and I entered the house with the usual Friday expectations.

We came through the back door as always and my mother was sitting at the kitchen table red-eyed and weepy, a grim look on her face. Spread out on the table in front of her was a page of the newspaper on which were sitting two half-eaten rolls. One of them I could see had evidence that it had landed in a spill of horse manure. It was Dorothy's onion roll. My roll was unmarked.

My mother greeted us with an outburst of tears and wailing. "I was walking to the store and saw your rolls lying in the gutter like *shmutz*. How could you children do this? It's a sin, a sin against God. Throwing away bread is an insult to God. You did a terrible, terrible thing."

Dorothy interrupted. "We had to run to school, Ma. It was so late we had to throw away the rolls. We did eat most of them as you can see." Dorothy pointed to the onion roll that was sprinkled with horse manure.

I jumped in. "It wasn't such a big sin, Ma. Wolfgang's bakes hundreds of rolls every day. Maybe thousands. That's what Pa says. And every day they throw out the rolls and breads that aren't sold. Is that a sin, Ma?"

My mother dabbed at her eyes. She had stopped crying. "Of course it is, son. You should understand that," she said patiently. She rose from her chair and declared in a loud voice, "You children do not understand what I'm talking about. Wolfgang's didn't make those rolls. God made them. God gives us our daily bread. He taught us to take the wheat from the fields and turn it into bread. When you throw bread or rolls in the street you are insulting God."

She stared at me. "The first *brocheh* you learned in cheder was the *motzi*, the blessing for bread. The three meals we eat each day are started with a *motzi*. Only after the *motzi* do we eat the meal. Bread is God's way of giving us life. Is that too difficult for you to understand, children?" my mother asked.

She appeared to soften as she spoke. "Maybe it's my fault," she said. "Maybe I should have told you long ago what it's like to be hungry.

"My father died when I was one year old. My mother raised me alone. She had no skills to earn money so we were always hungry. We were a house without bread, a house without luck."

She sighed and began to cry again. "Our neighbors were poor but they gave us scraps from their tables. For the Sabbath we were given a few pieces of challah, some potatoes, maybe a piece of kugel. Once in a while a few clumps of *cholent*.

"Whenever there was a *simcha* in our neighborhood, my mother was there. She took home what she could hide in her garment. We were beggars. Hungry. Alone. I cried, but not my mother." She wiped her eyes and repeated slowly, "My mother never cried."

She folded her handkerchief and placed it in the pocket of her apron. She spoke clearly, deliberately like she was reading from a script.

"This was my life until I was eight years old. At that age I was apprenticed to a master tailor who was a neighbor. He taught me how to sew, how to stitch, knit, baste, how to measure a garment. I was a good worker. I had to be. My mother received a ruble each week I worked for the tailor. The ruble put bread on the table. On Purim and Chanukah, the tailor gave me an extra ruble. On Passover, my mother and I sat at his table for the seder. We were people again. We were no longer beggars. God gave us bread."

My mother picked up the can of stove polish, turned her back on us and began to blacken the oven. Our lunch was on the table. The Friday menu: challah, *schmaltz, gribenes, arbis,* and the siphon bottle of seltzer. We didn't do much talking during lunch. When we finished the meal, my mother kissed Dorothy and then me. She gave each one of us a stick of Juicy Fruit gum, which she had never done before.

Of course, we never ate a roll again in the street and my mother never shed another tear. Except once. It was on the morning I entered the Army in 1941. I remember she cried a torrent of tears. Like a dam burst in her head.

Of course I cried too. But that's another story.

Yom Kippur at Twelve

I insisted on fasting on Yom Kippur when I was twelve even though I was not obliged to refrain from eat and drink until I was thirteen. My father thought it was a good idea and gave me a hasty okay. "So what if he becomes a man at twelve instead of thirteen. Will Moses turn over in his grave?"

My mother, however, fought me hard. "You'll be fasting on Yom Kippur all your life, why start now when you don't have to?" she said with some heat. Hers was the utilitarian argument that made sense, of course, but my pride was on the line and I persisted. She tried compromise by suggesting I eat an apple or banana in the early afternoon. I told her that was not fasting. We argued back and forth for a while, and though she resisted, I could see that it was not Custer's last stand with her. I could see that she was ready to surrender.

I knew I had her beat when she removed her eyeglasses, blew on the lenses, and wiped them with her apron. She always did that when she needed more time to think. Subsequently she gave in but not without a final warning that I would regret not eating around two in the afternoon. How right she was as I will relate later. Mothers! You can't beat them.

There is a sameness to the Yom Kippur service in the Penn Avenue synagogue as I suppose there is in most Orthodox shuls. Beginning around 7:30 or 8:00 there are morning prayers that are led by the *ba'al tefillah* (a sort of minor league cantor) who is marking time for the number 1 cantor to appear, often with a male choir. Young people, like myself and older, arrive later when the real action begins.

Before the Torah scroll is removed from the Ark, an auction of the honors of the day is begun. This has always fascinated me because like all auctions they frequently generate heat and passion and a competitive élan that is not normally associated with a shul. Certain significant Ark openings often inspired frenzied bidding. I remember one such Ark opening that was being sought by two of our heavy money members. The final and winning bid was $500, which was unheard of at that time. The buyer, a shady character who had connections in the bootlegging and bookmaking business, gained instant fame by giving the Ark opening to the rabbi. They say that when the bid reached $400, the purchaser's wife, who was sitting upstairs in the women's section, fainted dead away. After she was revived and learned that her husband won the bid, she passed out again.

My father often tried to buy an Ark opening that had some special meaning for him, possibly relating to the memory of his father. The time he succeeded it cost him $18 and my mother never forgave him. "For two dollars more," she whined, "I could buy Willie a suit with two pairs of pants and a nice cap." My father was too angry to reply.

Yom Kippur was always hard on kids whether they were eaters or fasters. The services in the synagogue went on all day. There was nowhere to go. No point going home; there was no one there. Mothers and fathers were in shul where they belonged. The kids had to fend for themselves. They were restless. Kids went in and out of the synagogue like they were playing tag.

Sometime around noon there was the Yizkor (memorial) service, which was one of the highlights of Yom Kippur. Basically Yizkor is a memorial service for the dead. Usually the rabbi's sermon, which could go on for an hour, preceded Yizkor. There was a lot of free time for the kids, most of it spent outside the shul. Next to the shul was a blacksmith shop that was always going full force.

There were several horses waiting to be shod by two big-bellied blacksmiths who were stoking separate forges. Deep in the red-hot forges were three or four glowing horseshoes that were being readied for the horses. These were huge dray horses with wide chests and rather delicate legs for such giant-sized animals.

When the horseshoes were judged to be ready, the blacksmith would bend a foreleg to himself, fish a glowing red-hot horseshoe out of the fire with a clamper and fit it onto the hoof. A geyser of smoke came from the hoof. When the smith adjusted the shoe to the proper fit, he nailed it with middle-sized nails to the hoof. The horse appeared to be indifferent to what was going on. But we kids were not. This was theater. We were viewing life from another page, another book.

Some of us waited around for the next shoe, even some of the girls. They covered their eyes when the smith applied the iron to the hoof, especially when it steamed up. I was standing closer to the older blacksmith. Turning to me, he asked with a smile, "You like what you see, boy?"

"Yeah," I said. I hesitated and then asked the question that was puzzling me. "When you put on the red-hot horseshoe, do they feel it? Does it burn the hoof?"

He answered. "It ain't supposed to, but once in a while when the shoe isn't set on right, they'll kick."

"Were you ever kicked by a horse?" I asked.

"Twice," he said.

"Twice."

"Yep, twice," he answered. "I been shoein' horses for better than twenty years and only been kicked twice and that ain't bad."

"Where did they kick you?" I asked.

"Both times in the face."

"Wow," I said.

"You can say that again, boy."

He finished shoeing and reached into the forge for another shoe. He examined it carefully and then spit on it. The shoe steamed up and he put it back into the forge.

"Why did you put it back?" I asked.

"Cause it didn't steam right," he replied.

I paused. "So you got kicked in the face twice?" I asked.

"Yes siree. You want to see where?" he asked.

"Sure."

He pointed to his right cheek. There was a long scar shaped like the letter J. Near his ear was a blunt scar that looked unhealed. "Not too bad, eh, boy?" he said with a smile.

"Yeah. Not bad," I said and left.

When Yizkor was over, I reentered the shul where all over the place young kids were gorging themselves on a variety of snacks—grapes, cookies, Italian plums, gross chunks of honey cake, anything that could be stuffed into their faces. I could feel the juices stirring inside me; I was getting hungry. I stayed next to my father, mouthed a few prayers, then left for a bathroom stop. Returned to my father, who I noticed was getting a little drowsy. I left for the outside.

Strung out all over the place were groups of young people laughing, talking, gossiping. There was always one or two in the crowd who bragged that they could fast right into next week. I could see Maxie Leventhal, dressed like a pimp, and his buddies garbed the same way, guffawing at some off-colored joke that he probably told dozens of times before. His father was one of Pop's closest friends.

For years, Maxie and his buddies would while away the two or three hours of Yom Kippur afternoon at the burlesque theater in town located only two blocks away from the shul. They called it taking a "breather." After the performance, they would return to the synagogue and coast through the waning hours of Yom Kippur.

Hunger was fast overtaking me. My belly was growling; my tongue and mouth were like the Sahara. I remember my mother's suggestion that I break up the day with a banana. That banana was looking more seductive by the minute. So I did the unthinkable. I confronted Maxie Leventhal.

"Can I go with you guys?" I asked.

Maxie answered in a hurry. "Hell, no. You're a kid."

"I got the money," I said.

"You're not old enough. You're not big enough," Maxie told me.

"Old enough?" I shouted. "I'm fasting, for Christ's sake."

"You may be fasting, but you're not even bar mitzvah," he said.

I replied. "Your brother Joey is going and he's not bar mitzvah."

"Yeah. But Joey's six feet tall. You're a shrimp. What are you? Five feet?"

"Never mind my height," I shouted. "I'm ahead of Joey in school."

"So what? So you're smarter than him," he said more softly. "Besides, they wouldn't let you in. You got to be sixteen to get admitted to a burley cue."

"Oh, yeah. So how will Joey get in?" I asked.

"I know the guy at the door," Maxie whispered.

"Well, then you can get me in," I protested.

"Forget it, Willie. You're not going." He started to walk away, but I caught him.

"You know, Maxie, you're a bastard. We're almost cousins, for Christ's sake. Your father and mine lived next to each other in the old country. They went to cheder together. We're family."

Maxie softened. "That's exactly the point, Willie. If your father or my father found out that I took you to the burlesque on Yom Kippur to watch some shiksa twirl her ass and her boobs, they'd kill me. Murder in the first degree. That's what would happen, and you know it."

I started to walk away. Maxie overtook me and said softly, "Look, Willie. In four years or so, if we're still around, we'll go to the burlesque. I promise."

I must say Maxie kept his promise. When I was sixteen, he made the offer and I declined. By that time, I was in the yeshiva and couldn't see myself watching some shiksa with oversize boobs twirling them like she's leading a parade. Especially on Yom Kippur.

My Father's Mother

When I was fifteen or sixteen and a junior in high school, I learned a lot about old age from an honest-to-God expert on the subject. His name was Cicero, Marcus Tullius Cicero to be exact, and he wrote an essay, in Latin of course, which he titled "De Senectute"—"Concerning Old Age."

It was written forty-four years before the birth of Christ when Cicero was sixty-two years old and I don't think he made it to sixty-three. The year of his demise, sixty-two or sixty-three or whatever, put him in the category of having reached a ripe old age for that period of time when most folks shuffled off to eternity in their forties or fifties. His essay was a mite on the bragging side, but modesty was never very high on his personality chart.

Incidentally Cicero was a politician most of his life and was assassinated while trying to escape the wrath of his political enemies. That was the way politics was practiced in those days, which, if you ask me, has some merit.

At any rate, Cicero is only tangentially part of the story I am about to write. I bring up his name because I received an A plus in that Latin course, which was the only A plus I ever received in high school, college, or grad school and the reminiscence is fodder for my ego.

This past November I turned ninety-four and have been wearing it ever since like a badge. Or a medal. I like being ninety-four. I like the ring of it. Ninety-four. When you say it slowly, it comes out like poetry. At least it does to me.

I suppose that when I turn ninety-five the music will stop. It will be back to the world of arthritis and stool softeners and perambulating walkers.

Or maybe not.

I am more or less sound of life and limb. And I think I'm still pretty sharp in the upstairs department. I feel, I really do, that we *nonagenarians* (the ninety-year-olds) got a break being born when we did. Growing up in the Twenties was a mixed bag, but it leaned more favorably in the good direction. It was the time of Prohibition and gangsters, but it was also a time when the nations were talking about peace. Permanent peace.

As early as 1921, when I was seven, just three years after the end of the first world war, there were begun talks on disarmament. World War I ended with 10 million men killed and perhaps four times that many wounded. 50 million casualties in all. I remember when I was a kid in grade school, we saw newsreels in the movies that showed battleships and cruisers, ours and those of other nations, being towed to the middle of the Atlantic Ocean and sunk. It was disarmament in the raw, a whiff of peace. It never lasted but it was there. One brief moment but it was there. . . .

On this old age thing, it may be that a strand of longevity is lodged in my genes. At least on my father's side. Pop and his mother Sarah, my grandmother, got as far as eighty-nine, which is a pretty respectable score. Especially for my grandmother who was born, we think, around 1860. We never did know her exact day of birth.

In the Ukrainian village where she was born and raised, there were no birth records extant. There probably were at one time stored in the synagogue but the ravages of fire destroyed them. A fire in a single dwelling could cause the whole village to go up in flames. This included birth and marriage records.

My grandmother came to this country in 1924 when I was ten and my sister Dorothy was twelve. We called her *Bubbeh* as we were instructed by my father, but the *landsleit* (folks who knew her in the old country) called her *Soorkeh,* which we learned later was not pleasing to her. She thought it was a *prust* (vulgar) name and instructed my father to let the world know of her displeasure, which he never did.

She arrived together with her son and his wife, our Uncle Benchik and Aunt Broocheh and their children Marian and Sam. They were met at the ship by Uncle Yankel who was the Yankee of the family. Our Uncle Yankel, who was something of a luftmensch (someone with his head in the clouds), was drafted into the U.S. Army towards the end of the first world war and spent the duration as a baker of bread in Texas.

His view on Texas was somewhat muddled. There were Jews there, he said, who spoke Yiddish that he barely understood and English that he didn't comprehend at all. It was a place, he complained, that was populated by giants who never smiled "even when they laughed."

Uncle Yankel was *Bubbeh's* youngest son and probably her favorite. He was given the job by my father to meet the family in Ellis Island and bring them home. My father had rented a flat for them that was partially furnished. It was located in a dumpy part of town, but was not too far from where we lived and there was a shul located a block or two away.

Aunt Broocheh and Uncle Benchik liked the place until they learned that the house next door was the workplace for a half-dozen whores. There was a steady traffic there during the evening and late night that was distracting to my cousins Marian and Sammy who spent their evenings and most of their lives doing homework. Years later each one graduated high school as a valedictorian, a distinction no one in my family ever attained.

My father was the leader of the clan principally because he had more money than his three brothers and his sister, my aunt Boozie. Benchik and Mottel were junk peddlars and Yankel, the luftmensch, was involved in several business ventures all of which failed. Aunt Boozie, who was the firstborn of my grandmother, was married to Berel whose track record in the earnings department was as miserable as his flaccid personality. He was lazy and sly and shiftless and though he was trained as a butcher was unable to cut meat because his vision was bad. So he claimed.

On the afternoon of their arrival at the Lackawanna railroad station, all of us, my mother included, waited patiently for the train of deliverance. Of course, my grandmother became the center of attention. She was short and stout and was wearing a wrinkled black cotton dress over which was a small girlish tea apron also in black. My mother could not understand why the apron.

Covering her head and part of her face was a flowered *tichel* (kerchief) that looked like it was just recently pressed. The part of Grandmother's face that was uncovered showed bright blue eyes and an unlined face that could have been painted by Rembrandt. It was sopping wet from tears that gushed like a fountain over her cheeks and mouth.

Later when her face was dry, her bubbling mouth, which was working overtime, appeared somewhat sunken and for good reason. She didn't have a tooth in her head. My father said with a break in his voice that she used to have teeth like jewels. "And so strong she could bite through nails."

After Grandmother completed her greetings to the grown-ups, it was the kids' turn. She took me first. She hugged and kissed me with several sodden kisses, the kind that stay with you for hours. She cried anew with my sister and cousins and just as moistly.

As she hugged us, she said three mystifying Yiddish words I did not understand though I was conversant with Yiddish—*"Mir zoll zein,"* which translates literally as "me shall be." My father said it meant you are mine or you belong to me or you should be like me. He was never too sure. Whatever its meaning, it was her trademark and a way of greeting her grandchildren. Often it was the watery kiss first and then the three little words. As she aged, the kisses were there but the moisture factor was diminished.

Almost from the day she arrived, my grandmother lived with her daughter Boozie. For a price, of course. My father and his brothers picked up the tab, which at first was modest. It grew in proportion to the squabbles that took place between my grandmother and Boozie or her daughters or her husband Berel. My father was convinced that the arguments were inspired by Berel, who profited by each impasse.

An early crisis came when my grandmother insisted on going to the synagogue on the Sabbath. Boozie lived miles from the shul and transportation had to be found to deliver her on Friday to the home of Aunt Broocheh, who lived near the synagogue. My father found a retired coalminer with an ancient Ford that did the trick. Pop paid him with groceries from our store.

There were other emergencies—Grandmother was a demander but not very heavy in the follow-up department. She wanted teeth but would not go to a dentist. She said that people back in the Ukraine ordered teeth by mail. She demanded a new dress for the holidays but would not go with Boozie's daughters to the department store. My mother, who was a seamstress, sewed her a new silk dress that Grandmother never wore. She never even tried it on, my mother said.

She insisted to her sons that the grandchildren visit her regularly, which we did none too enthusiastically. We would arrive, receive the *mir zoll zein* benediction with the damp kisses and then she would fall asleep. A slight buzz would come out of her throat. It was not a full-scale snore, more of a steady drone that was a signal for us to escape.

There was one visit that stays with me even today though I am past ninety. I visited her alone; my sister took the afternoon off. Grandmother was in a reflective, talkative mood. She told me that her parents died when she was four and she was raised by her grandmother.

It was a typical snowy Russian afternoon, she said. The snow was piled deep against the door and it was blowing outside with windy screams. Her grandmother told her that it was on a day like this that she heard the news that Napoleon had invaded Russia. My knowledge of history and music told me that Napoleon's troops had crossed into Russia in 1812, almost two hundred years ago. I was thrilled by the reminiscence. It was like this was an event I had personally experienced, as if it had come from my great-great-grandmother's mouth directly to my ears.

My grandmother is no longer around, of course. She had become enfeebled by the time factor and succumbed to it at eighty-nine, which is not a bad tally. I recall my last visit. I had just been discharged from the Army and was still in uniform. She blinked at me unknowingly but out of habit she reached for my cheek and gave it a dry kiss. There was no *mir zoll zein,* which she probably forgot.

She looked at me somewhat confused but there was a moment of recognition. In her quavering voice she asked, *"Bist noch altz in der Yeshiva?"* "Are you still in the Yeshiva?" I said no and she nodded.

As we looked at each other in silence, I took her shriveled hand, kissed it, and said in a low quavering voice, *"Mir zoll zein."* She opened her mouth as if to reply but nothing came out of her lips. After a few moments, she fell asleep and I left.

At the Rebbe's Tish

I think I was the one and only nonbeliever in the maelstrom of frenzied dancing and whirling men, young and old, who were participating in a Friday night *tish* (dinner) with a Chasidic rebbe on an unforgettable Sabbath eve in Petach Tikvah, Israel.

The rebbe, I cannot recall which town or village in Poland his name is associated with, was seated on a throne-like chair at the head of the table holding his head in his hands, moving it right to left and back as he kept time to the *niggun* (melody) that was being sung loud and lively by the dancing Chasidim and onlookers, such as myself, my host Rabbi Mottele Spitalnik, and about a dozen other visitors.

Mottele, as I called him, was associated with the seminary in Jerusalem where I was a student. He was considerably younger than I, half my age actually, and we had struck up a friendship, a strong one, that was rooted into our natural curiosity about one another. He was trying to understand why an old geezer like me had returned to study after a half-century hiatus. As for myself, I was using Mottele as my personal encyclopedia into the myriad pathways of Jewish learning.

I knew I was getting the better of the bargain. Accepting his invitation to spend the Sabbath with him and his family in Petach Tikvah was part of my learning itinerary, though I must confess I mounted the bus to Petach Tikvah that Friday afternoon with mixed emotions.

A few days earlier, Mottele had piqued my imagination and my abdominal juices with the casual mention that after shul on Shabbat, we would return home to a meal of his wife Essie's *cholent*. For me, a *cholent* properly made, and even improperly made, is a *meichel* (delicacy) for which there is no equal. It is a kind of stew that has been simmering in an iron pot containing a mix of barley, lima beans, potatoes, onions, and meat. It is cooked over a slow fire for twenty-four hours or thereabouts and what emerges is a mélange of sheer heaven.

When Mottele disclosed that his wife was something of a *cholent* aficionado, I reacted fast but skeptically.

"So you say that Essie makes a good *cholent*?" I asked.

"One of the best," he answered.

"One of the best, you say?"

"I guarantee it," Mottele replied.

"You guarantee it?"

"You have my word," he said.

"OK," I said, adding, "I hope you're right."

Mottele then switched gears. "Before the *cholent*, Bill, I am going to take you to a sort of banquet on Friday night."

"A banquet?" I asked.

"Well, not exactly a banquet. I will be taking you to the rebbe's *tish*."

"The rebbe's *tish*?"

"That's right," he answered.

"Isn't a *tish* a table?" I asked.

"Exactly. But it's more than a table, much more. It's an experience."

"Can you be more explicit, Mottele?" I asked.

"Oh, sure." He paused. "This rebbe has followers, Chasidim, mostly in Israel, but spread all over the world. America, Argentina, Canada, England, France, and other faraway places. Wherever they are, they are under his influence. They conform to his belief in God, his teachings, his belief in humanity. They seek his advice and take it. Are you following me?" he asked.

"Of course," I answered.

He continued. "On Friday nights he invites his Chasidim to a *tish*, a table, which is really a celebration, a happy celebration, where his followers eat and drink, sing, dance, and then listen to the words of the rebbe. Nothing is really rehearsed. His words, they say, are dipped in Torah."

Mottele was excited. "Most of his Chasidim, probably all, are convinced that what comes out of his mouth was put there by God Himself.

He is God's messenger. He is more than a holy man. He speaks to God and God listens." He paused. "That is what his followers believe."

Mottele stopped talking. I think he was a little embarrassed by his passion. "I am not one of his Chasidim, you understand. Nor do I believe that God sits on his shoulder as his followers do. I believe you will find the *tish* interesting and enjoyable and you will learn something."

I mumbled a few words about looking forward to the experience and, as things turned out, I was not disappointed.

We had a very good Friday night meal at Mottele's apartment with the conventional menu. Wine, gefilte fish, chicken soup, boiled chicken, and a dessert of Jaffa oranges. We sang *z'mirot* (Sabbath songs), rested, and at about 9:30 left for the rebbe's *tish.*

We entered a large auditorium-like room. It was filled with Chasidim of all sizes. Some were wearing their severe black hats, others, mostly the younger ones, wore *kipoth* (skullcaps). Almost everyone was garbed in long black coats with a sash of sorts girdled around the middle. There was activity; dancing, laughing, and singing with some Chasidim doing all three simultaneously. I did not join the dancing circle, though Mottele did.

At the extreme part of the room there were small bleachers, maybe fifteen to twenty feet wide with three tiers of seats, which were sparsely occupied by younger Chasidim. Mottele introduced me to a few. One was a visitor from Argentina, Reb Avrom Musikant, who had arrived that day for his annual visit with the rebbe. He was the wildest dancer in the circle. He was kicking, stamping, singing, and clapping like a drunken gaucho cavorting on the Pampas.

After a short interval, the word came that *"Der Rebbe kimt,"* the rabbi is coming. The announcement was in Yiddish, which was the language of the *tish.* Apparently there were advanced seating arrangements as well as designated standing assignments behind the chairs. Mottele and I stood behind Reb Avrom, the Argentinean, who sat at the opposite end of the table facing the rebbe and his two *gabboyim* (attendants). It was one of the best seats in the house.

We had full view of the rebbe. He was not an old man, possibly sixty, though he appeared to be in his late seventies or early eighties.

Mottele had told me about the rebbe's earlier life. He was a Holocaust survivor who had been kept alive by the Nazis for some reason known only to them, possibly for purposes of ransom. He was fed only enough to keep him alive. He was beaten regularly by his jailers, who spoke Polish, a language he understood. He was told by the Nazis that his wife died of cholera, which he never believed. After the war, he learned from an Auschwitz survivor that she perished in a gas chamber.

From where we stood, we could see the rebbe very clearly. He wore a black hat that sat on his head as if it was a size or two too large. His dark eyes bulged heavily in their sockets like they were on the verge of falling out of his head. His cheeks and chin, which once carried a full beard, was now a patchwork of white tufts of hair that stood like spots of grass on a bare field. The Nazis had yanked his beard so often it left his face a tableau of angry unshapely scars.

Yet from that chaotic face there emerged a voice clear and soft and sweet as if from a whispering stream. The rebbe had begun a *niggun* that was apparently unfamiliar to his Chasidim, but which they caught onto in a few moments. When the singing died out, the rebbe turned to one of his *gabboyim* who went into the kitchen and brought out a large braided challah (Sabbath bread). The rebbe broke off a large segment of challah and tore it into bite-size pieces that were passed down the table and given to sitters and standers alike.

No blessing was said for the challah. Mottele explained that during an earlier Sabbath meal, blessings were said for the wine and challah and the rest of the meal, but there was no *benching* (blessings at the end of the dinner). The *benching* was deferred to the conclusion of the *tish*.

After the challah was disposed of, the rebbe's other lieutenant went into the kitchen and brought out two roasted chickens. With both hands, the rebbe tore the chickens apart and proceeded to send down pieces of chicken, some with bones and skin, to the sitters and standers. I was given a chicken wing, Mottele a leg, and I was not certain that I could chew and swallow my portion, which had been handled by so many Hasidim. But I did. Reb Avrom, the Argentinean, ate his portion with gusto and, turning to me and Mottele, said, "Whatever comes out of the rebbe's mouth will be blessed by God."

The next food brought from the kitchen was a large platter of steaming egg barley. Mixed on top of the egg barley were small pieces of *gribenes* (chicken skin cracklings). The rebbe dutifully spooned out for himself a mouthful that he swallowed. With the same spoon he dipped again into the egg barley and passed it down the table. He did the same with another spoon, and then another. When the spoons were returned, he refilled them again and again so that all attendees received a portion.

As the spoons began to head in my direction, I decided that I was going to get away from the *tish* in a hurry. I had no intention of putting that much-used *leffel* into my mouth. Who knows what was nesting on that ladle waiting to invade an innocent mouth like mine. Undoubtedly a dozen Chasidim had left their deposits of toxins on those infested spoons.

I tugged Mottele's sleeve and whispered "Let's get out of here."

With a wide-eyed and desperate look, he answered, "No, we can't do that. It would be a slap in the face to the rebbe and his Chasidim."

"I can't eat that egg barley," I protested.

"You have to," he said.

"I can't, I just can't," I insisted.

"What are you afraid of?" Mottele asked.

"The spoon," I said.

"The spoon?"

"Yes, the goddam spoon. That spoon is teeming with herds of germs, bacteria, viruses, and God only knows what other strains of disease. I'm not putting it into my mouth."

I could see Mottele was losing patience. "Don't worry about it," he said, an angry look on his face.

"I am worried about it, dammit," I said.

He changed tactics. His voice had an edge to it. "Are you afraid you'll catch a cold?" he said sarcastically.

"Worse than a cold," I answered.

"Worse. Worse," he mimicked.

The spoon was on its way. It had already reached Reb Avrom, the Argentinean. My spoonful was next. I began to retreat. So I'll catch a cold, I reasoned. What's a cold? I've had hundreds of colds. You gargle, drink cups of hot tea, and you're home free.

But what if I got more than a cold? I thought. Influenza? Pneumonia? Tuberculosis? Those are big time. Or worse! Diptheria, food poisoning, meningitis. My God! I could die.

The spoon arrived. I held it. Eyed it. My fingers trembled. I brought it to my mouth. I swallowed last. The egg barley went down smooth as ice cream. The die was cast.

On the way home, Mottele explained the facts of life to me. "The rebbe," he told me, "is regarded by his Chasidim as God. They revere him. They love him. They obey him. They worship him," Mottele repeated in a loud voice. "When he passes out pieces of challah, they know it was torn apart and passed out by his hands. The same with the chicken. It was ripped apart by his fingers.

"The egg barley is the high point. It was fed to them with a spoon that came out of his mouth. His mouth," he shouted. "What could be more meaningful to them than food that literally came out of the rebbe's mouth? What excitement there was for the Chasidim that something of the essence of the rebbe was now part of them. What a blessing!"

I did not reply. What could I say?

In the morning, we went to Mottele's shul and then returned home to a *cholent* that was everything he said it would be. I gorged myself shamelessly almost to the point of being embarrassed by my gluttony. But I wasn't.

Two or three days later I was ballooned up like a basketball from that *cholent*. All kinds of sighs and sounds and growls escaped from my insides. The noises ceased after a while but not the gas.

As to the other hazard to my health, nothing happened. Absolutely nothing. Not a cough or sneeze or hiccup. Not a stuffed nose or tickled throat or swollen gum. Normalcy was the word and I remembered what Reb Avrom Musikant, the visiting Argentinean, said. "Whatever comes out of the rebbe's mouth will be blessed by God."

You can say that again, Reb Avrom.

I Am Not She

My friend Bernice and I traveled to the city just about every Saturday or Sunday. Mostly Saturdays. With us it was like a religious rite, one of those thou shalts which was not only easily doable but cheap.

We would catch the LIRR around ten, get to Penn Station three-quarters of an hour later, take the Fifth Avenue bus uptown to the Metropolitan Museum, and arrive in time to catch the cafeteria line that started moving around noon. Most times we packed our own lunch and just ordered coffee.

From time to time, I would bring with me a miniature bottle of Scotch whiskey, usually J&B, and toast myself gloriously with a Scotch and water prior to unfurling our tuna sandwiches and prune Danish. Bernice was never too happy with my miniaturized happy hour, which she said gave me a two- or three-hour buzz that, in her words, slowed me down to a crawl.

I never thought it did slow me down, but one does not argue with Bernice about anything relating to the Met. She and her late husband, who had been a painter and a pretty good one, I thought, spent their Saturdays and most of their Sundays ambling through the museum like they were the landlords. And in a way I suppose they were. They hardly ever missed an exhibition, even those where there was an extra fee, which never sat well with Bernice. She paid of course but not without a grumble. It's not that Bernice is a grumbler but she was never very happy spending money even if most of it came out of my wallet.

I was always amazed, as I still am today, how much data on the Met has been sequestered into Bernice's head. I am not referring to the special exhibitions and collections that were transported to the museum from all parts of the globe. Most of these were augmented by films either created by the Met or by the countries from which the collections came. There was no admission charge for these films, which pleased me, of course, but left Bernice ecstatic.

Additionally there were audio devices rented to viewers that guided them through the exhibition. There was a modest charge that Bernice never allowed me to spend.

"Don't you think I can give you a tour of the exhibition as good as the manufacturer who makes these goddam things?" she would ask quizzically. I never answered.

It was not only that in her head were stashed away the facts and figures relevant to the exhibitions, permanent or temporary. She knew where everything was or should have been. She knew the locations of all the museum restaurants, elevators, staircases, benches, sales areas, bargain sales areas. She knew shortcuts to the toilets, elevators, escalators (I think there was only one), rest areas, water fountains. She was an encyclopedia.

One of our oddities, I suppose, was that whichever way we went and whatever exhibits we visited, we would end our day's tour inevitably and unchangeably at the Temple of Dendur. The temple was built in Nubia in approximately 15 BCE by the Roman emperor Augustus. It was given to the United States by Egypt in 1965 and in 1967 was turned over to the Metropolitan Museum. In 1978 the temple was installed in the Sadder wing of the museum.

To Bernice and me, it was a kind of watering spot to rest and rehabilitate ourselves after the multihour tour we completed. It was not that we were exhausted by the day's jaunt, but it was always deliciously restful. No crowds, hardly any sounds or noise, no walls, no gapers, no gawking.

And a bounty of space. The temple and its large gateway extend over an expanse of more than an acre, I would guess. There's lots of sunlight. The outside wall of the temple area is all windows. There is a small parapet, perhaps two feet high, that extends over most of the temple space. This serves as seating. And for meditation, at least for

Bernice and me. After the Dendur experience, it was back to the Fifth Avenue bus.

From time to time, largely on weekdays, we would change our itinerary and visit a museum other than the Metropolitan. Not very far from the Met were the Whitney, the Guggenheim, the Museum of Modern Art, and the Frick, which was Bernice's favorite "small" museum.

The Frick was neither small nor was it called a museum. It is known as the Frick Collection. It was established by Henry Clay Frick who in my college days would have been referred to as a "robber baron." He was one of the original robbers, like Jay Gould, J. P. Morgan, Andrew Carnegie, and John D. Rockefeller. Frick bequeathed his Fifth Avenue mansion and added $5 million to convert it to house his magnificent collection of Rembrandt, El Greco, Bellini, Hals, and other great classical artists. He added $15 million as an endowment for the collection.

Bernice loved the Frick, as did I, but for a different reason. Bernice adored the art, the collection, which I did too but what fascinated me most about the Frick was the quietness of the place, the silence, the absence of noise. It was a refuge from turbulence that museums like the Metropolitan lived with especially on weekends and holidays. In time we knew our way around the Frick. Visiting there was like consuming a delicious dessert after a trencherman's meal at the Met.

There was no eating place at the Frick, which should have been a negative but wasn't. After we left the Frick Collection, we would gnaw on our tuna lunches as we walked down Fifth Avenue to Fifty-ninth Street, where we took the subway.

There was one Frick visit that was unforgettable. It was like a dividend, a payback for all the trips we took there. It was on a June day, possibly July, and it was in the late 1980s. We had only just arrived and were going through the galleries systematically as was Bernice's way. After an hour, we rested in a large rectangular room that I think was a combination lecture hall and music room.

There were four small benches in the four corners of the room. One of the benches was occupied by an elderly lady who was wearing large owlish sunglasses. She was dressed plainly and wore a light gray sweater, which was not strange because the area was excessively air-conditioned.

Bernice and I took the bench on the same side as the elderly lady and thumped down on it in relief. We were tired. We sat quietly and enjoyed the rest. After a minute or two, Bernice tapped my arm.

"You see that woman sitting there?" she asked.

"The one in the corner?"

"It's not exactly the corner," Bernice observed.

"You're talking about the old lady with the hat."

"Right. But that's not a hat. It's a beret."

"To me a beret is a hat. So what about her?" I asked.

"Isn't there something familiar about her?"

"Familiar?" I asked. "You mean the shoes?"

"No. Not the goddam shoes. The face. I'm talking about the face."

I reached for my distance glasses and adjusted them so there would be no glare. I looked at the woman, and Bernice was right. I knew that face. I had seen it before. "You're right," I said. "There's only one face like that."

"I can't believe it," she said in a whisper. "Sitting there alone like she's nobody, like she's one of us."

"She is one of us, Bernice. She hasn't just flown in from Mars," I said brusquely.

"I know but I can't believe it. We're making a big mistake. It can't be her."

"I think it is," I said firmly. "She's supposed to live here in New York. Somewhere on Fifth Avenue."

"Yes, that's true," Bernice admitted. "What about her feet?"

"Her feet? What about her feet?" I was getting annoyed. "She's supposed to have big feet, they say. I didn't look at her feet."

Bernice was silent. Something was cooking in her head. "Would you go back and look at her feet? Pretend you're on your way to the john," she said.

"Hell no," I answered. "Why can't you pretend you're going to the john?"

"Because you know I never use the restrooms in museums," she said.

"She doesn't know that, for Christ's sake," I replied.

"You would make it look more natural," Bernice said.

One never argues very long with Bernice. She will always overcome. So I got off the bench and walked in the direction of the mystery lady. I concentrated on her shoes, which seemed ordinary enough to me. They were the comfortable style footwear that old ladies like my mother wore when she was on her way to the synagogue.

I did go to the men's room and used its facility. I was impressed by the ferocity of its flush. It roared like a small Niagara.

Returning past the mystery lady was a bust. Those dark glasses hid the eyes and forehead. The beret covered the hair so that not a wisp was revealed. She owned a shapely chin and her cheeks were lightly wrinkled. The nose, which looked noble, was also despoiled by the sunglasses. I reported all this to Bernice who I believe was happy with my reconnaissance.

"Honey, I think you got it," Bernice said. "Now I'm sure she is Greta Garbo."

"Garbo?" I said passionately. "I thought we were talking about Marlene Dietrich."

"Marlene Dietrich," Bernice scoffed. "Impossible. First of all she's a clothes horse. She wouldn't be caught dead in a sweater like that. Or old lady slippers. Besides, I think she now lives in Paris."

"You know, honey, I feel like I know Marlene Dietrich. When I was a soldier in North Africa, she was part of an entertainment unit. And of all things she played a saw. A goddam saw. Would you believe it? She played 'Yankee Doodle' with a violin bow and a saw."

Bernice was not impressed. "She's no Marlene Dietrich. That's for sure."

"You really think she's Greta Garbo?" I asked.

"More than ever," she said.

"If you're so sure she's Garbo, why don't you go over to her and shake her hand or ask for her autograph or some kind of shit like that?" I suggested.

"I couldn't do that," she answered hurriedly.

"Why not?" I said.

"I don't have the nerve. That's why."

"Sure you do. Look, sweetheart, it's your turn."

"I know. I know it's my turn, but I don't have the guts."

I sensed she was wavering. "You can do it, Bernice. You not only have guts. You have chutzpah," I said.

"No, I don't," she replied hurriedly.

"Sure you do. Aren't you the one who told the rabbi his sermons were too long?"

"He knew I was kidding," she answered.

"And that they were repetitive," I continued.

She hesitated and then answered lamely, "That was just a jocular remark, for heaven's sake. He knew I was joking."

"So why don't you go over to the lady in the corner and ask her in your best jocular manner if she is who we think she is. And while you're at it you can size up her clodhopper feet," I teased.

"Clodhopper?" Bernice asked.

"Large, oversized. Big feet," I answered.

Our conversation, while not heated, was no longer conducted in whispers. I think our mystery lady sensed that our conversation related to her. I detected a fidget. And then a couple more.

She rose from her bench. She carried a small but sloppy purse and started walking toward us. She still wore her dark glasses. Her beret was taut on her head. As she approached Bernice and me, I thought I detected the flicker of a smile on her lips. When she reached us, she stopped for an instant and said in a soft musical voice, "I am not she," and then continued her departure. She couldn't have advanced more than a step or two when Bernice said, "Sure you are."

Our lady stopped, turned around and smiled. I am confident it was a smile. Then, à la Charles Laughton in the film *Witness for the Prosecution,* she lifted her right forefinger and tapped it on her right nostril and winked. And then smiled, showing a mouthful of perfect teeth.

As she walked away, Bernice whispered to me, "Ten."

"What's with the ten?" I asked.

"Size ten shoe, dummy. She has clodhopper feet."

Remembering Uncle Shloime

My uncle Shloime is gone almost forty years now and I don't think of him very often, but every now and then, under the oddest of circumstances, his small bearded face and black-garbed figure will invade my memory and I will stop and think about the disheveled, mumbling little man whom none of us, not even my mother, his youngest sister, ever understood.

Not too long ago, I was at the circus with my grandsons when, in the middle of the trapeze act, Uncle Shloime popped into my head. How he got there, in that jumble of hurling bodies, I cannot imagine. Uncle Shloime was as far distanced from the world of clowns and sawdust as he was from the crumbling yeshiva in Poland that was his habitat and mother for more than fifteen years. I suppose a perceptive analyst would come up with the thought that it was the itinerant side of circuses that plugged me into the recall of my odd and, in many ways, mysterious uncle.

Uncle Shloime was an itinerant bookseller. His stock of books consisted of the thin volumes of talmudic insights and discoveries that he himself researched and recorded. How profound his scholarship was none of us will ever know. In those days, it was not uncommon for impoverished scholars to publish pieces of their scholarly output and travel from town to town, selling their wares, very much like a peddler of notions or pots and pans. Their customers were the well-to-do Jews of the towns and cities they visited.

It was a form of dignified begging, and no one knew this better than these wandering mendicants themselves. But it was a living, pure and simple. Why Uncle Shloime chose this route, no one really knew, not even his wife, Ruth. That's what she told my mother on her one and only visit to our home.

There was never any need for him to squeeze out a livelihood through the sale of his books. In fact there was no need for him to earn a living at all. Uncle Shloime married into a family of wealth located in one of the large cities in upstate New York. A condition of the *shiduch,* the arranged wedding match, was that he would be forever exonerated from the burden of supporting his wife and future family. He would be free to spend his days and nights in study and research.

His wife, Ruth, was blind from birth and was viewed by her stern but very devout father as being unmarriageable. Under the circumstances, he "bought" his daughter a bridegroom, a scholar. A learned man who would spend his life unraveling the mysteries of the Torah, that unravelable document of God. That was how Aunt Ruth's father planned it. Uncle Shloime turned out to be no bargain, however. After several years of study, during which his books were published and his children were born, an unease and restlessness seized him and he began to explore the outside.

In the beginning, Aunt Ruth told my mother, he would depart for a few weeks at a time. Then a few months. After that, he would stay with his family for the holidays only. No one ever really knew his exact routes of travel. He probably never ventured beyond the neighboring states and Canada. His occasional postcards to Ruth were postmarked from the East and usually were requests to ship him more books.

Our town in Pennsylvania was part of Uncle Shloime's circuit. I think it was his favorite stopover because of my mother, though he never said so. Actually he hardly knew his youngest sister. He had been sent away to a yeshiva in Poland when he was ten or eleven and his visits home were infrequent. Mother was at least eight years his junior.

I remember his visits very clearly. Uncle Shloime would arrive unexpectedly and out of nowhere, usually on a Friday when mother was in the midst of her preparations for the Sabbath. He usually entered, without knocking, by way of the back kitchen door, silently set down his scarred satchel and parcel of books, and with great gusto proceeded to clear his throat and blow his nose. This took a little doing. He would never embrace my mother; that would be unseemly. He would limply shake her hand. Then he would ask for a glass of tea.

Mother would busily put on the kettle, steep the tea, pour it into a glass and lovingly serve it to him with several slices of lemon. As he drank the tea, spoonful by spoonful, sucking noisily on the lemon, he would tell us where he had arrived from. It was usually from Wilkes-Barre or Allentown. Uncle Shloime traveled by bus wherever possible. He could sleep on a bus, hardly ever on the train. After the tea, he would take a laxative.

Uncle Shloime had tried them all. Ex-Lax didn't work on him. Feenamint worked, but it was undignified for a Jew to chew gum. Castor oil was strictly for emergencies and not to be taken when one was on the road. His favorites were Boll's Rolls, a pressed fig concoction packaged like Life Savers, and that old reliable citrate of magnesia. He often shared his cache of Boll's Rolls with me. I loved them. They were better than candy. The citrate of magnesia, which fizzed mightily when freshly opened, tasted just like lemon soda. Maybe better.

Then Uncle Shloime would take a bath. Mother made it scorching hot, which was the way he liked it. Uncle Shloime always said the only mistake God made during Creation was he made the oceans cold. Mother would then unpack his satchel, gather his soiled laundry, lay out a clean shirt and underwear, and smooth his wrinkled black tie, which he never wore. She would brush his stiff hat and steam his long black coat, which had absorbed more than its share of Pennsylvania dirt and coal dust.

At the Sabbath meal, she would serve her brother the choice morsels of chicken and noodle pudding she usually put on Father's plate. She ladled into his soup plate the yellow unformed little chicken eggs that boiled hard in the chicken soup, much to the chagrin of my brothers and me. These had always been our exclusive booty. Mother was attempting to fatten up Uncle Shloime overnight. He was so skinny, she complained.

Her brother's health, mostly his stomach, worried her. His diet on the road consisted principally of hard boiled eggs, rye bread, cheese, and tomatoes and cucumbers in season. It was little wonder, she said, that he was addicted to laxatives. After the Sabbath, she would launder and mend his clothes. Mother performed these rituals dutifully and lovingly. Was it not our obligation, she would ask wide-eyed, to honor and serve a scholar?

Uncle Shloime seemed to be totally oblivious to Mother's concern and hospitality. In the house he would walk from room to room, mumbling to himself, occasionally clearing his throat to give voice to a piece of liturgy, which he sang flat. I remember asking him why he was always praying. He told me he was speaking to the One Above. "Every free moment we must speak to God, even when we are asleep." When I asked him how that was done, he nodded his head several times, as if that answered the question.

From time to time, Uncle Shloime would ask me what I was studying in cheder (Hebrew school). I would tell him and he would shake his head up and down several times, which I interpreted as approval. Then he would ask whether I enjoyed studying the Torah, and I would answer somewhat tentatively, "Yes, Uncle Shloime." He would nod again and pat me on the head.

On one visit, I must have been eleven or twelve at the time, he skipped his usual preliminaries and inquired, "Why do you think God put people on earth?"

I answered immediately and very confidently, "To serve Him."

"Is God a boss who created people so that they would be His servants? Why would He need people or animals or birds or fishes to serve him? He is God. God serves Himself," Uncle Shloime declared.

"I meant to serve Him by performing His commandments," I replied.

"That is the answer. But why?" he persisted.

"Why what, Uncle Shloime?" I asked, perplexed.

"Why did God create people?"

"I just told you why, Uncle Shloime," I answered very perplexed.

"Yes," he said. "You gave me the answer. But it is also the question. Do you understand?"

"No," I answered.

"Good. Very good," he said and he began to hum some undecipherable piece from the liturgy.

Some time during the period of Uncle Shloime's wanderings, Aunt Ruth paid us a visit. She arrived by bus accompanied by her daughter Miriam. My sister and I met her at the bus station. There was instant recognition. She put her fingers through our hair and identified each one of us. She told me my hair was red and my sister's brown.

Aunt Ruth was a wondrous guest. She delighted my mother with her wit and liveliness. She brought my brothers and sisters gifts that she had made herself. Mine was a skullcap made of a red fabric. "Some day you will be a cardinal," she said jokingly, but I didn't get it. My sister was given a pink hair ribbon shaped like a flower that she never wore.

I remember in particular a cozy conversation she had with my mother. I was in the kitchen at the time and they were in the dining room, and I heard every word. My mother brought up the subject of Uncle Shloime's traveling. "Why can't you force him to stay at home and give up the book peddling? He's so frail, so small. How long must this go on?" she asked Aunt Ruth.

"I used to say the same thing to him every time he returned home," said Aunt Ruth, "but I no longer do. He always gives me the identical answer. 'This is what God intended me to do,' he would say. After a while I stopped asking."

"I think none of us truly knows him," she continued. "He never talks about the past, your mother and father, the yeshiva, his brothers and sisters. As if he was created only for the present. No yesterday, no tomorrow."

Then in a soft conspiratorial voice, which I could barely hear, she told Mother, "I never said this to anyone before, but I think Shloime is a prophet—"

Mother interrupted, "What did you say, Ruth? I couldn't hear."

"A prophet," my aunt repeated.

"You mean a prophet like Samuel and Elijah? As in the Bible?" Mother asked.

"Yes. As in the Torah," Aunt Ruth said.

"How can you say something like that?" Mother scolded.

"I know exactly what I am saying." Then she whispered something in Yiddish that I couldn't hear.

"But what proof do you have?" asked Mother.

"Evidence, Rose. Evidence is what I am talking about. Did you know that he told me a few days before it happened that my father would die and that I must prepare myself?" Aunt Ruth said with some excitement.

"But your father was a sick old man," Mother countered.

"He was never sick a day in his life. Father passed away in his sleep—just like that," she answered.

She continued, "The children. As I was carrying each child, he told me, never directly, of course, that our first three would be boys and the last a girl," Aunt Ruth answered.

"What did he say exactly, Ruth?"

"He told me I would be a mother like Sarah and Rebecca. Sarah gave birth to Isaac, and Rebecca had Esau and Jacob."

"And how did he tell you about the girl, about Miriam?" Mother persisted.

"He said I would soon have someone who would help me bake cookies," Aunt Ruth answered.

"Well, that doesn't sound very convincing," said Mother.

"Maybe not, Rose. But he also said I could see if I knew how to look. He said God gave me spoiled eyes, but a healthy brain and that one doesn't see with the eyes but with the brain."

Then she added, "I do see things, Rose. In my own way. I know how my children look and I know how you look."

"How do I look, Ruth?" Mother asked.

"Kind. Very kind," she answered.

Aunt Ruth and Miriam took the bus home the following morning. I don't think my mother took that conversation too seriously, at least from what I was able to observe. She never repeated it to my father, nor to anyone else as far as I know. Uncle Shloime continued to make his periodic stopovers, but they were less frequent now. Mother never ceased overfeeding him, darning his socks, mending his shirts, and brushing the grime off his scuffed black shoes. As the years piled up, Uncle Shloime got skinnier, hummed louder, and, I think, sold fewer books. Then, almost abruptly, he traveled no more.

Uncle Shloime's generation is gone now. So are the itinerant book-peddlars. I don't know whether they ever added much to the edification of talmudic insights of their well-heeled customers, but they left their footprints. And maybe a legend or two. And maybe even a smile, or a sigh.

I like to think that from time to time I catch sight of Uncle Shloime somewhere out there in a world now long gone. I can see him sitting in some dingy, unheated bus station, his scarred satchel and tattered packet of books at his feet, waiting for the ride that will take him to the next town. He is cloaked still in that long black frock coat, its sleeves stained and torn waiting for my mother's needle. On his head is perched the battered black hat peppered with particles of coal dust that in the sun flash like jewels on a crown.

And then I hear Uncle Shloime clear his throat long and mightily and start to chant something from the liturgy that comes out with fervor and, as always, out of tune.

Interlude in Bangkok

It was my last weekend in Bangkok so naturally I went to the synagogue. I had been doing the synagogue circuit whenever possible during my three-month travels through Southeast Asia and the search was often more exciting than the visit. In Rangoon, as an example, I was taken to a disheveled century-old synagogue, not listed in my guidebook, that was sitting anonymously on a street teeming with cobbler shops and stalls, some of which were the property of the synagogue. On the day of my visit, the temple door was bolted shut. My guide knew exactly where to find the custodian who produced the key with the aid of a new United States dollar bill.

The interior of the old sanctuary matched the street, dank and dusty, its floor and benches strewn with sacred debris—worn prayer shawls, tattered loose pages from Bibles and prayer books, pamphlets, newspapers, soiled skullcaps. It was a depressing experience.

Bangkok was going to be the end of the line for me and I was dead set on finding the whereabouts of a synagogue with the unlikely name of Even Chen, which translates as Rock of Charm. Getting there was no easy chore. At the YMCA where I was staying, not one of the lovely young women behind the long service counter knew, or even had the faintest idea, where the Jewish temple might be located.

At my urging, the prettiest of the lot phoned a Christian clergyman who conveyed a wisdom that had eluded me. He suggested that I get in touch with the Israeli embassy. This call yielded instant dividends. I was given a name and address. The location was in the Warner Theater office building in downtown Bangkok where I was assured there would be a Sabbath service.

I was not let down. Even Chen was indeed a Jewish house of prayer, though office of prayer would be a more accurate description. The synagogue occupied a small suite of offices on the first floor, which was actually the second floor by American count. I timidly entered and surprisingly there was not a Thai, Indian, or Oriental face among the worshippers. I learned that this was a makeshift minyan something like a convenience store, established and maintained by Jews from the West who had business involvements in Bangkok and Asia. The service was no different from a Sabbath worship in the States.

When the service ended, I felt no compulsion to linger on.

After a few exchanges and introductions, I muttered some innocuous amenities to the red-bearded man, an Israeli, who had led the prayers. He told me in faultless English that a Sabbath luncheon would be available very soon, but I declined his invitation and departed.

I left the office building, which fronted upon a large square plaza extending to the street. On my right was an outdoor café with half a dozen tables shaded by gay-colored beach umbrellas. The plaza was baked by a hot glaring March sun, which induced me to turn immediately in the direction of the café and a tall chilled glass of lemonade. As I approached, I was greeted by a tinkly little voice. "Hello, mister," it said as if it were tumbling out of a music box. It came instead from a very pretty young Thai woman seated at a table, a Coke can in her hand. She was wearing a modish flowered dress, somewhat revealing but not too much, and a gentle smile. Planted within a mound of black silky hair on top of her head was a single white rose that seemed to light up the lovely gleaming face below it. She was twenty or twenty-one, I would guess.

I answered, "Hello."

"You do business inside building?" she inquired with a smile.

"No, do you?" I asked, a smile on my face as well.

She said, still smiling, "I do business outside."

"Are you a hooker?" I asked.

"What is hooker?"

I told her that a hooker is a girl who sleeps with men for money.

"I not sleep with men," she said. "I make love with men. I make love with you, yes?"

"No. I don't think so," I answered.

She frowned. "You not like me?"

I replied quickly, "I like you very much. You're very pretty. But I can't go with you."

"No. You not understand," she said. "I go with you. To hotel. What hotel you stay?"

"I'm not at a hotel. I'm staying at the Y. The YMCA."

She smiled anew. "I know that place very good. I go there all the time."

I was startled. "You go to the Y? With men?" I asked.

"Not with men. Holy Jesus! I go to Bible class. Me Christian like you."

"I thought you were a Buddhist," I said.

"Him too. I smile with Buddha all the time. You see?" she said pointing to her smiling face.

"You have a nice smile," I said. A waiter came over. I ordered lemonade and sat down opposite her.

"You lovely man," she said.

"No. I'm not lovely. I'm old."

"You not old. You got wife?" she asked.

"No. My wife is gone," I said.

"You get new wife. You marry me?"

"I don't think so," I replied.

"You want woman more old? You marry my mother."

I laughed. "Is she pretty like you?"

She answered very seriously, "No, she pretty like you."

"She sounds wonderful, but I'm afraid I could never marry you or your mother. You're not Jewish," I said with a smile.

"What means Jewish?" she asked.

"It's my religion. You know what religion means?" I inquired.

"Yes," she said. "Jesus Christ."

"Jewish means an old religion," I explained. "Before Buddha, before Jesus. Two thousand years before Buddha. You understand?"

"Yes. I understand. Him a very old god. Me Catholic. Hail Mary, full of grace. No?" she asked.

"No. Jews are different."

"I think you same as me," she said.

"I really don't think so."

"I think so. You very nice man. I like. You like me?"

I said I did and changed the subject. "Where do you live?" I asked.

"I live very far. With mother and son. Mother take care of son. Him five. Name Samuel. You like Samuel?"

"Definitely. My grandfather's name was Samuel. What's your name?"

"I not tell my name. Bad luck. You call me Lizabeth, like Lizabeth Taylor."

"Why is it bad luck?" I asked.

"Gods not like name. It makes me bad luck. You not understand," she said.

"What gods do you mean? You have Jesus and Buddha. Do you believe in other gods too?"

"Oh sure. Have lots more. I very religious. You call me Lizabeth. You know Lizabeth Taylor maybe?"

I told her we had never met. I rose from my chair.

"Look, Elizabeth, I'm sorry but I've got to go. I wouldn't want any of the men upstairs to see me talking with you. They might go away with the wrong idea."

She asked, "What is wrong idea?"

"Well, you know. That I'm making a date with you. "

"You not make date with me. Today no good. Tomorrow we make date. I come to Y. I take taxi. We say good-bye now, but not good-bye Charlie. You understand? Not good-bye Charlie," she repeated.

"Not good-bye Charlie," I repeated. "I'm afraid I don't get it."

"We ladies say good-bye Charlie to man we not like. You understand? Good-bye Charlie mean goodbye for always. Never see again," she explained.

I told her I understood. I told her I had to leave; I was scheduled to be on tour most of the day. "Tomorrow morning I'm taking the boat to the floating markets. That takes a long time," I said. "In the afternoon we are going to the Grand Palace and the Royal Chapel to see the Emerald Buddha. I don't know when I'll get back."

It was as if she hadn't heard me. "I see you tomorrow at YMCA. I take taxi. We go to Bible class. We have good time," she said. She beckoned to the waiter nearby and pointed to the empty can in her hand. He brought her another Coke; I waved good-bye and left.

The following day, my last in Bangkok, I did tourist things as if there were no tomorrow. There really wasn't. The floating markets were interesting in a tourist trail kind of way. There were exotic flowers and strange fruits and vegetables, but there also were cheap souvenirs, busy street hawkers, inflated prices, and sizzling unidentifiable chunks of meat and fish. I bought something hot and spicy.

The Grand Palace was a revelation. The Emerald Buddha was not emerald at all; it was a delicate Buddha figurine two or three feet high, carved out of a single piece of jade. To top off the day, I had an expensive dinner at the Oriental Hotel. It was a string quartet night and an unforgettable buffet table. Late that evening, I took a taxi back to the Y. I asked for my room key and there was a small stuffed envelope in the box. I took it to my room and opened it.

Inside was a familiar white rose. There was no note. I put the rose in a glass of water and went to bed. I slept fitfully.

I rose early the next morning. My bags were already packed. The rose was limp and drooping, its petals scattered on the desk. I removed the rose and dropped it into the trash basket. It made a dull, muffled sound as it hit bottom. I scooped up the petals, which were browning at the edges, and let them fall into the basket. They fluttered down like demure snowflakes and made no sound as they landed. I unlocked the door, went down to the desk, paid my bill, and then left for the airport. It was good-bye Charlie.

Being Prepared

I was a Boy Scout for just about two years and tried super hard to live up to our slogan: "Do a Good Turn Daily." I tried hard. I really did. In my case it wasn't that easy. Other Scouts could grab themselves a fast Good Turn just about any time they chose. They could volunteer to their mother or dad to go to the grocery store to buy a loaf of bread or a quart of milk or maybe a dozen eggs or some crap like that because mothers are always running out of food one way or another.

It so happened that my old man owned a grocery store and brought home whatever it was that my mother ran out of.

I did delivery orders for Pop, of course, but that was like a job and not in the category of a Good Turn. I was a money earner, like working in a bank or a gas station. I got tips from his customers except for one or two cheapies who were always out of change.

We had a scoutmaster; his name was Harvey Golden and he was the son of Max Golden, the richest man in town. Mr. Harvey, which was the way he wanted to be addressed, asked us at every Scout meeting what Good Turn we had done today. Today, for Christ's sake. Who the hell did he think we were, Dick Tracy?

I would argue with Mr. Harvey, but it was like he was in another county. "Mr. Harvey," I would say earnestly, "we go to school till 3:30. Then I go to Hebrew school until 6. After that I go home to eat supper, change into my scout uniform, shine my shoes, brush my teeth, and then show up for our Scout meeting at 7. Where would I find time to perform a Good Turn?"

"That's why you're a Boy Scout, dummy. Scouts get things done even under adverse conditions," he lectured me. "Take Charley

Lindbergh, for example. Would he be able to fly the *Spirit of St. Louis* if he couldn't find the time to fill his goddam gas tank?"

Harvey was the kind of guy who loved to call celebrities by their first name or close to it. Even noncelebrities like me. The first time we met, he called me Billy Boy, which would be fine if I was a horse running in the Kentucky Derby. When I told him I wasn't crazy about that moniker, he asked, "What about Mary Jane or Hortense? Or Marlene?"

So I shut up and he called me Willie—which I liked. As long as I knew him, he referred to President Herbert Hoover as Herbie or Horton and to President Calvin Coolidge as Buster or Smiling Cal. We Scouts referred to Harvey as Mary and I don't know why.

Don't get me wrong. Mr. Harvey was not a geek. He went to all our bar mitzvahs and gave each of us a tie with a naked woman on it. They say it cost him two or three bucks. But of course he was a rich man's son and most of the time behaved like one.

I remember the time he led us on a hike in the Poconos. He got one of those oversized trucks from his old man's factory to transport us to a mountain named Big Pocono, which was about twenty miles from our town. We Scouts were members of the Hyena Patrol. There were eight of us plus Mr. Harvey. A patrol is usually named for an animal and has an official yell associated with it. Our yell was a combo of a scream and a hysterical laugh. Like a loony would sound in a horror movie.

Our hiking plan was to get to the top of Big Pocono, which was 2,200 feet high, build a fire Indian style (no matches) and then cook a meal in the embers.

Mr. Harvey led us on that hike until we were about halfway up the mountain. We followed a path onward and upward until the path disappeared. We had reached a dense forest and could no longer see the mountain top. We wandered through brush and bush and pines and oaks but we were traveling blind. We didn't know where we were.

After about a quarter of an hour, Harvey blurted out, "I think we're lost, guys." One of the senior scouts, Monty Cohen, took up the slack. "Why don't we sound off with our patrol yell? We're the Hyena Patrol, right? Any of you guys ever hear a hyena?"

Mr. Harvey said he'd heard an animal he thought was a hyena when he was in Wyoming. "It sounded like halfway between a bark and a laugh. Something like this." He began to bark like a bulldog and then giggled like a bride.

We all joined in, and in about two or three minutes a forest ranger about a mile high came out of nowhere and shouted, "What the hell is going on here?"

Mr. Harvey tried to mollify him with a half-assed explanation and a five dollar bill which the ranger did not accept.

"Sorry, buddy. We don't take tips like a waiter." He gave Harvey directions to the top of Big Pocono and after about twenty minutes of climbing, we were there. Mr. Harvey began to issue orders like he was General Pershing.

"You, Monty, are in charge of making a fire. And you," he said, pointing at me, "find us a place to take a leak."

There was one of those ancient outhouses about fifty feet from where we were and Harvey got there first. Monty Cohen, the fire maker, made a small slanting tepee of wood shavings, dry leaves, tree bark, and paper. When Harvey was out of sight, he ignited the tinder with a wooden match, and in a matter of seconds we had a roaring fire that would have made old Daniel Beard, the founder of American scouting, proud of the Hyena Patrol (except for the wooden match).

With the fire under control and surrounded by a phalanx of bricks that Monty Cohen found on top of Big Pocono, we removed from our knapsacks the provisions we had for a meal. Most of us brought hot dogs which we stowed into the fire to brown and sizzle. Others brought yams and potatoes and ears of corn. One of the guys in our patrol brought a can of baked beans, kosher style, which brought on the usual vulgarities about the potencies of the baked bean. The chow was scouting at its best.

Mr. Harvey did not stinge when it came to food. He told us as he unwrapped a cache of tissue-wrapped packets of edibles that a meal is a meal and not a sandwich. He pulled out of his sack a brand new small frying pan, a small bottle of olive oil, bread sticks, potato salad, and a Sunkist orange the size of a small basketball. The main packet, however, was a steak big enough to sate the palates of the entire Hyena Patrol.

As he poured olive oil into the spotless frying pan, he said, "This is the way British Scouts camp out. It's all in the beef. A good cut of meat is the center of the meal. It's fried by the older Scouts but tended by the Cubs. That's scouting."

I broke into his reverie. "I think I saw the movie. It was a documentary." I hoped he would catch the sarcasm in my voice, but apparently he didn't.

"They even had folding tables and chairs during the meal," Harvey added.

"What about cigars?" Monty Cohen said under his breath, which Harvey heard.

"That's not funny, wise guy," Harvey said. We could see he was miffed. We knew for sure that Harvey had a taste for cigars, the big fat ones that came out of his father's humidor. Several of us spied him at the Y on a Saturday night puffing on one of those fat stogies that they say went for a quarter apiece. He was with a girlfriend, really a beaut, who looked like Clara Bow.

"Sorry, Mr. Harvey," Monty Cohen said in a low voice. "If I offended, I apologize."

Harvey did not reply. He continued to sizzle his steak like he was in the kitchen of the Waldorf-Astoria. We were on that mountain top about an hour mostly eating and it was time to depart. We extinguished the fire with a variety of liquids, policed up the place, as they say, and moved out. Our descent down the mountain was uneventful and pretty fast.

That summer most of our patrol went to Scout camp. I didn't go. I was the exception. There was a question as to the kashrut (kosher observance) of the camp. According to my father's partner, who was not one of my favorite people, the facilities were not kosher. This was the decision of our rabbi. He ruled that the meat was kosher. Indeed, the meat came from the same butcher we all used. What was not were the pots and pans and silver, which were the same ones that were used during the regular season.

My father was as disappointed as I. He really was. But he would never question our rabbi's decision. Pop's partner Milton said he would never send one of his kids to a camp where they extinguished fires by pissing on them.

The Sunday morning the patrol left the Y for camp, Mr. Harvey took me aside, patted me on the shoulder and said, "Billy Boy, the name of the game in scouting as well as in life is just four little words—be smart and be prepared."

He took out of his pocket one of those Swiss Army knives with a dozen blades and put it into my palm. To this day, that knife occupies my back pocket like it was born there.

Harvey's scoutmaster days were limited. He remained an official a little longer than I served as a Scout. In time I became a Star Scout, which is no big deal. It requires five merit badges and I picked the easy ones. In a couple of months I earned badges in Cooking, Dog Care (I used a neighbor's dog), Coin Collection, Weather, and Theater, which was my favorite.

Around the time of my birthday in November, my father sent me to the yeshiva in New York City where I was no genius. The vagaries of Jewish law escaped me. I was more adept with the rules of poker than with the rationales of *Bet Hillel* and *Bet Shammai.*

Mr. Harvey worked in his father's factory after graduating from Penn State. A year or so after Pearl Harbor, he took over the management of the total family properties after his father suffered a severe stroke.

Harvey's phenomenal success as a supplier of parts that went into tanks during the war did not surprise me. Any guy who roused a forest ranger by sounding off like a hyena gets my vote anytime.

I also still have the tie with the naked lady he gave me for my bar mitzvah. I wore it only once. It was at the Purim ball of our temple, a night of fun and gaiety. My tie was the hit of the evening, which I think would have pleased Mr. Harvey.

Going Home

I got home from the war on November 24, 1945, which was a Saturday. I had celebrated Thanksgiving two days earlier in Fort Dix, New Jersey, where I was billeted with several thousand GIs of mixed ranks. I think, though I'm not exactly sure, that most of us disembarked onto good old American terra firma in Camp Edwards, Massachusetts, which is not too far from Boston.

I think, and here too my memory is a bit scratchy, we spent the night in Camp Edwards. Most of us had departed from Le Havre, France, on a Liberty ship ten or twelve days earlier. There was lots of wine and some whiskey aboard ship that kept most of us pretty well oiled and, I think, a little on edge. Most of us had been overseas two or three years and there was an uncertainty on how we would be accepted at home or how we would greet the world we left.

On the following morning, we departed Camp Edwards for Fort Dix though I can't recall how we got there. It could have been by railroad or bus or truck or even by ship. I do remember we got there in time for lunch, which was a cold meal of mostly sandwiches.

I was pleased, really delighted, that Fort Dix would be my ticket out of the Army. In a way it all started there for me. Our antiaircraft battalion, almost three years earlier, took off from Fort Dix for a destination unknown that ten or twelve days later turned out to be Oran, the second largest city in Algeria. The first, of course, was Algiers, which I always connected with Charles Boyer and the Casbah.

We were informed by one of the information officers who greeted us that the climate and temperature of Oran was very much like that of Los Angeles, which was highly questionable according to my friend Jerry Leff who was our supply officer and who had resided in the City of Angels for several years. Jerry was probably my best friend in the battalion, and though we got along like the Bobbsey twins, there were differences.

Where we were alike was that we were both Jews and proud ones, I think. Beyond that the differences were gigantic. Jerry had lots of money, was a handsome dog with a smile to match, and was a super salesman with a super salary. He was one of those who was paid a salary by his employers as long as he was in the service.

I was the editor of a weekly newspaper that was always losing money. My appearance was not very impressive. I stood five feet four inches in my combat boots. Almost everyone including Jerry called me Shorty except the colonel, who addressed me as "Hey you."

During our first stay in Fort Dix, the name of the game was "toughening up." This was done largely through daily hikes. We started off with a five-miler lugging a rifle and knapsack. This was followed on the next day with a ten-miler and then a fifteen-mile hike with a full pack. The twenty-miler was like a graduation exercise. The following day was calisthenics and first-aid classes. This was like a day off. Then we would start training anew with the five-mile exercise.

The training was tough but the nights were *delizioso* as they say in Naples. There was an officers' club but Jerry and I avoided it. We were on the lookout for the more sublime treasures. Women. There were lots of them around the base. Young, old, pretty, plain, married, unmarried—all varieties. Serving the base mostly as clerks or medical personnel was a cadre of girls, women, and even grandmothers who were pretty good practitioners of the social arts.

It was not surprising that Jerry landed the sweetheart of Sigma Chi, the clerk in our barracks who was a beaut. Her name was Beulah but she preferred being called Billie. She was in her early twenties, divorced, and sharp as a matzo, as they say. Jerry got her name, telephone number, and a brief bio in the first ten minutes of their conversation.

Billie had a roommate, a sort of plain-faced, plumpish, nineteen- or twenty-year-old cheerleader type who came from Kansas City and whose name was Dorcas Palmer. As we were introduced, she said to me, "I'll give you a dime if you know where my name comes from."

I pounced on the challenge and dared her. "Make it a quarter . . . and Dorcas is mentioned in the New Testament. She was a seamstress who sewed garments for the poor in Jaffa Palestine."

Dorcas said "Wow" and reached into her purse for a quarter. I waived the two bits and the four of us ordered a Heineken. After that, we were a steady quartet until the battalion was put on "alert," which came a week later.

My goodbye to Dorcas was uncomplicated. I promised to write and I did. Jerry's farewell to Billie could have come from *Madame Butterfly*. Somewhere in their dating history, he may have made a reference to "after the war," which Jerry insisted never happened. I sent Dorcas a friendship letter from Tunis. To my knowledge, Jerry never wrote.

Returning to Fort Dix after a three-year absence had an "Auld Lang Syne" spin to it. We had been here before as soldiers on the way to war. This time we were old and largely spent GIs on the way home. There was a sameness to the base. The barracks, the dining halls, the ball fields, the parade grounds, even the soldiers looked the same. The permanent personnel had that same tired look.

By an odd coincidence I discovered that Billie Syms, Jerry's onetime girlfriend, was still on the base. The Syms part was new. In our prior firmament, she was named Johnstone and was a manager of sorts who supervised the women barracks clerks. It was Billie who recognized me in the officers' club that Jerry and I had always avoided. She wore her hair somewhat longer. It was blondish and curly and went very well with her clear blue eyes. She was a gorgeous spectacle.

She came over to the bar where I was enjoying a beer. "Still drinking Heineken," she said and kissed me on the cheek. She was drinking wine that came from France, she said.

"You know your friend Dorcas is married to a creepy guy from Minneapolis. A 4-F. She has a little girl she calls Magdelene."

"Still faithful to the Bible," I said with a smile.

"Looks like it," she answered. She took a healthy drag on her wine. I thought she was about to bring up the subject that was on both our minds, and I was not mistaken.

She asked, "Is Jerry here? Did he come in on your ship? Is he on the base?"

"I don't think so, Billie," I replied. "We split up three months ago. I was transferred to USTAF headquarters in Paris. He stayed with the battalion. He made captain, you know."

"What's USTAF?" she asked.

"It's the highest Air Force headquarters in Europe," I answered.

"So he made captain?"

"Yes, he did."

"I wish I knew that. I would have sent flowers."

"He would have liked that," I said softly.

"He never wrote, you know."

"I didn't know that, honey."

She was crying. Her eyes reddened as the tears leached out. "Do you think I'll ever see him again, Bill?" she inquired softly.

"Oh, sure. You got the luck of the Irish."

"But I'm not Irish," she said with a smile.

"Well, maybe Jerry is."

"Not very likely," she said, almost like a whisper.

I changed the subject. "What's with the Syms moniker? What happened to Johnstone?"

"I don't talk about that, Bill."

She finished her wine, took my left hand, kissed it, and walked off. I never saw her again.

That exodus conversation took place on the Friday after Thanksgiving. The next morning I was mustered out. It felt strange being in uniform and not belonging anywhere. No orders to obey. No routines to follow. I supposed I would get used to it.

A couple of guys I didn't know were negotiating with a cabdriver to take them to New York City. I asked if they could use another passenger and they said sure. We ended up paying the cabbie five bucks apiece, which I thought was excessive, but they were happy with it. I was the first drop-off at a hotel on Twenty-third Street. The name escapes me but it had a history of housing literary figures like F. Scott Fitzgerald, Ernest Hemingway, and Henry James.

I doubt that Henry James ever set foot in this hotel. It was not a dump but it was not the Waldorf-Astoria either, and Henry James, the writer, had lots of money. Barrels of it, they say.

I had decided to spend the night in New York City because it was Saturday, the Sabbath. I knew my father and his brothers, my uncles Yankel, Benchik, and Mottel, were Sabbath observers and would undoubtedly show up at the Lackawanna railroad station to greet me. This would have violated their Sabbath observance, which I did not want to happen.

I phoned my sister Dorothy and told her I would be arriving next morning around noon at the Lackawanna depot. She was virtually speechless, which was not usual for Dorothy. She was sobbing like a schoolgirl.

I had a meal at Sardi's, which was a disappointment except for the ice cream. At a nearby table sat the first lady of the theater, Ethel Barrymore, who was working on a huge lobster that appeared to be chewy. She caught sight of me, smiled, and bowed her head in my direction. After dinner I dropped into a USD center and was given two tickets for *Porgy and Bess,* which I thought was a masterpiece. I never used that second ticket.

I didn't sleep very much that night. It was the anticipation of going home, I think, plus a very noisy party that seemed to go on and on at the end of the corridor. It was mostly attended by women who laughed or sang away the night like they owned it. The lyrics sounded interesting but they were definitely not Oscar Hammerstein who would never use that kind of language.

Next morning I took a cab to the Barclay Street Ferry going to Hoboken where the Lackawanna railroad started off. By the time we reached Montclair, I was deep asleep and had to be awakened by the ticket collector who told me we were just ten minutes outside of my destination. He helped me with my barracks bag and knapsack, and I slipped him a fiver that he pushed back into my hand. I protested but his grip was stronger than mine.

As I expected, my father and his three brothers were at the depot. My father embraced me first and after I was awash with his tears, I was passed on to my Uncle Mottel and then Benchik and finally to the youngest of my uncles, my father's youngest brother Yankel who was a veteran of the first world war. He kissed me twice and cried shamelessly. My father told me that my mother and aunts and my two sisters were preparing a Thanksgiving meal that would feed thirty. I don't know why I was not surprised. Nor was I astonished that Thanksgiving was being celebrated three days late. And that the turkey turned out to be a twenty-six pound goose, which is a story that has almost spiritual connections.

Years ago when we were kids, my parents celebrated Thanksgiving with a goose, a small goose to be sure, but a verifiable goose and not a duckling which has a shorter neck and legs. My father and my mother too knew that the turkey was a kosher fowl. My father, who owned a grocery store, sold turkey to his Christian customers "finished." That is, the bird was killed, plucked, and cleaned up ready to be put into the oven.

His Jewish customers, if they wanted turkey for Thanksgiving, had to buy it alive and take it to the *shoichet* to be slaughtered ritually and then defeathered and cleaned for its entry into the oven. In addition, there was the psychological factor. A turkey for Thanksgiving was a tradition that grew out of a Christian religious celebration, which created some sort of guilt among Jewish people. Thus a lot of them used chicken or goose in the place of the big bird. It wasn't until my bar mitzvah, which took place three weeks before Thanksgiving, that my mother roasted her first turkey. My sister Dorothy and I were not too enthusiastic.

The first order of business when I crossed the threshold of our house was a religious ritual that I think my father invented. He gave me a skull cap to replace my Army headgear. He went over to the large breakfront in the dining room and opened the drawer where he kept his gold watch and chain. He removed a manila envelope and gave it to me to open, which I did rather uneasily.

Inside were three sizable pieces of matzo, which were remnants of the *afikoman,* which is the Greek word for dessert. It is the last food eaten at the Passover Seder and has a special attraction for children.

When I finished eating that chunk, my father gave me two others. These were for the three seders I missed when I was overseas.

When my brothers came home, they went through the same ritual. My youngest brother came back to the States in June. He had been in Japan. When he was offered the *afikoman,* he asked my father if he could have his with jelly and my father gave him a fast no.

The night of my return, I phoned a friend in New York City who offered me a job in public relations at a hundred dollars a week. I took it sight unseen and stayed with it until May 1948 when Israel was born. But that's another story.

My Father's Grocery Store

Actually my father owned half of the store. The other half belonged to his partner who was his best friend—most of the time. On the negative days, he was his worst enemy. They were partners for more than fifty years and, as I said, they got along very well, considering. His partner's given name was Milton, a name he gave himself when he was drafted into the Army during the first world war. I think his Jewish name was Menachem, but I won't swear to it.

Pop's name was Dave. My mother called him Doovid and his *landsmen* (kinsmen) and close friends in the shul called him Doovidel. Doovidel is an affectionate term for Dave or David, and most of those who called him Doovidel loved him as did most of his customers. The customers, however, called him Mister because in addition to having great affection for my father, they respected him. Especially the black people. They regarded Pop as a friend rather than a storekeeper.

They knew that when they were short of money, which was most of the time, my father extended them credit and never once asked them to pony up with the money. They paid and always with a smile.

"Your father, he's gentle folk. We don't like that other fella," they would tell me when I delivered their orders in my Red Rover delivery wagon. More often than not, they gave me a penny or two for my "trouble," as they put it.

"That other fella," Milton, my father's partner, was an honorable man, but he rarely smiled and was often taken for a snob and a bigot—which he definitely was not. His best friend in the Army, he said, was a black man named Fred who was with him at the Army's cooks and bakery school. My father's partner became a baker and Fred a cook and was the best in the school, according to Milton.

Some years after the war, Fred came to our city to visit Milton who got him a job in Hotel Casey, which was the finest hotel in northeastern Pennsylvania. In a short time, Fred became the head cook and then the chef and became famed for his chowders and oysters Rockefeller. Pop's partner would get invited from time to time to dine with his wife Bertha as a guest of Fred's, and, according to my father, he would come back to the store the next morning redolent with the aroma of some fancy fish soup that lasted all day. My father was invited by Fred, too, but he would never eat anything that was not kosher.

Each partner excelled at his own area of expertise. Pop was the fruit and produce "maven," who learned all about God's green thumb from his many years as a horse-and-wagon huckster. Milton was the butcher, who learned his trade from his father who had a butcher shop in some shtetl in eastern Poland. While he knew all there was to know about beef, lamb, and poultry, his father had never dealt in pork. It was Fred who took Milton into the world of swine, and in no time at all the store became known for its pork chops and hams.

My father, who could also cut meat, was never comfortable with pork products. Too fat, he said, and avoided contact with a side of pork or a ham butt. Milton had no such inhibitions.

The store was open seven days a week from 6:30 in the morning to 11:30 at night. Each partner worked late every other night six days out of seven. Pop's day off was on Saturday, which allowed him to attend synagogue services at the Penn Avenue shul. Milton was off on Sunday.

It was an arrangement made in heaven. My father had his weekly tête-à-tête with God, after which there was a splendid Sabbath meal followed by the luxury of a two-hour nap. My father and mother were nap people. Every day Pop, after a hasty lunch, would lie down on the parlor couch with his Yiddish newspaper, and before you could say "Gesundheit" was off in some distant planet of slumber. My mother would follow my father into the parlor, lie down on the floor, cover herself with the Yiddish paper, and take off like Charles Lindbergh.

Milton, who considered himself more Americanized than my father, could picnic on a Sunday with his brothers and their families or go to a baseball game (which he never understood) or just sit around and loaf. Years later, Milton also took Saturdays off and in time became president of his synagogue.

When he became a Sabbath observer like my father, my sister Dorothy who was the oldest and bossiest of us kids took over the supervision of the store like she was a graduate of the Harvard Business School. I was the delivery boy and she barked orders at me as if she was General John J. Pershing. But I didn't mind too much. I was never that good behind the counter. I dropped things, broke things (especially eggs), couldn't find things like butter—which once made one of our customers (a Mrs. Hortense Moloney who ran a rooming house with suspicious renters) kick me in the shins. As I remember, I kicked her back and she slapped my face.

In the late twenties, which was the onset of the Great Depression, business took a bad turn. Especially for the store. An A&P, the archenemy of independent grocers, opened only a block away. We could not compete successfully with an A&P whose prices (and quality, my sister said) were below ours. We ran a cash-only store, and my father had to extend credit to many of his customers. Our cash flow bubbled slowly like a trickling brook, and my father and Milton did what many grocers had to do—find a new source of business.

There was only one way to go. This was the era of the Volstead Act—Prohibition. The sale of whiskey was verboten in all forty-eight states. Though the availability of liquor was largely diminished, America's thirst was not.

My father and Milton became minor league bootleggers, like so many of their fellow independent grocers. They had access to alcohol, which made them immediate players. I think it was my father who initiated the business. Milton was reluctant at first. "Did I fight a war to break the law?" he complained. My father reminded him that the war he fought was in the kitchen baking bread.

Pop plunged into the whiskey trough like he was in that trade all his life. The booze, of course, was manufactured in our bathtub. He gave it color with a couple of quarts of Sweetouchnee tea and then poured the mix into an old wooden wine barrel, which, according to my father, gave the liquor body and aroma. We used empty milk bottles that my mother scrubbed till they sparkled. "Always fill the bottle to the top," Pop instructed her. "Give good measure. They like that and will come back for more." And they did.

Business was brisk. Every night my father would prepare the next day's inventory. He made it a rule not to keep the stock in the store. When a *fleshel* (bottle) was needed, either he or Milton phoned my mother to send over a bottle of "juice." I was the delivery service and relished the role.

First, there was the intrigue factor. I was, I fancied, in enemy territory, which spelled danger and daring. Second, these deliveries were profitable. If the customer was in the store, he gave me a dime tip. (I think my father made that a precondition to the sale.) Frequently it was more than a dime, depending, I suppose, on how thirsty the customer was.

There were some deliveries that didn't go that well. One time, I believe it was in July, my mother got the call to ship a *fleshel* and "the customer is waiting." In a flash I was on my way. I hadn't gone more than fifty feet when out of nowhere a huge policeman with three stripes on his sleeve (I learned later he was a sergeant) grabbed my shoulder and said, "What you got there, sonny?"

I blanched, I trembled, I felt faint. I barely squeaked out an answer. "My father's lunch," I said.

He put out his ham of a hand and reached for the package I was carrying.

"Do you mind if I take a look see?" he said with a smile. "I don't think you got the right," I answered.

He grabbed the package out of my hand, unwrapped it slowly, and held up the *fleshel.*

"So this is your old man's lunch," he said with a grin.

"Gee, I must have taken the wrong package," I said.

"Well, sonny, I'm afraid I'll have to confiscate this bottle. It looks like it might be"—he hesitated momentarily—"a bottle of tea. Tell that to your old man. Tell him I'm a tea lover. He'll understand."

"Yes sirree, officer," I said.

"You will remember to tell him what I said, won't you?" he said with a wink.

"Yes, sir, officer. Have a good day."

"Oh, I will, sonny. I will that," he said and left.

From that time, my father and Milton had themselves a new partner. To even things out, they raised the price of a *fleshel* by 50 cents, which to most of their parched clientele didn't make any difference. To the others, they rescinded the raise. This probably made them the only compassionate bootleggers in the world.

Another time, maybe six months later, mom packed a *fleshel* in a Yiddish newspaper and sent me on my way. It was wintry and cold and there were ice spots on the street. I ran in the dark, and no more than fifty yards from the store I slipped on the ice and the *fleshel* flew out of my hand and onto the pavement. The bottle smashed like it was a grenade. I picked up the sodden newspaper and its contents and brought it to the store and told my father what had happened. There was fire in his eyes and he exploded in Yiddish.

"This was for Caferty, the janitor. He's running a crap game in the high school basement and needs schnapps. Go back to Mama and bring me two *fleshels*. And don't fall." Cafferty was a three-dollar customer. He paid a dollar more per *fleshel* than the average buyer. When I returned to the store, he gave me a buck, which ain't hay, as they say.

The Volstead Act was the law of the land until Franklin Delano Roosevelt was elected president in 1932. One of his first priorities was the repeal of the Prohibition amendment, which occurred during the early part of his first term. Repeal brought on a beer thirst to the country and somewhat diminished the demand for whiskey. The store was licensed to sell beer. I don't know whether it was the law or a stricture imposed by Milton, who would not allow the home delivery of beer and virtually put me out of business. But there I was, a relic of the old regime, a victim of Repeal.

Oddly enough, the illicit sale of homemade liquor continued for a while in the store. Orders came in but less frequently of course. It was either the bargain price of our stuff or the inconvenience of traveling to a liquor store to stock up.

Or maybe it was the Sweetouchnee tea.

Glossary

aliyah: a call to the Torah
arbis: chickpeas
avoyde: duties, tasks
azoy groys vie a genetz: as large as a yawn (or a sigh)
ba'al tefillah: cantor who chants the prayer service
ba'alei teshuvah: Jews who have returned to Jewish observance
benching: blessing after meals
brocheh: a blessing
Bruriah: wife of Rabbi Meir, a great Talmudic scholar
bubbeh: grandmother
Chabad: Lubavitch movement or practitioner
challah: Sabbath bread
chazzerai: junk
cheder: Hebrew school
cholent: Sabbath stew
chuppah: bridal canopy
claff: parchment in a mezuzah
davened: prayed
Doovedel: Dave
dreck: feces
emes gezukt: the truth of the matter
Far View: mental institution
fleshel: bottle, flask
gabboyim: synagogue officers
gonif: a thief
gribenes: cracklings of chicken skin
haray aht: wedding vow made by the bridegroom
Hashem: God

Kabbalah: Jewish mysticism
kadishel: a young boy who recites the Kaddish prayer
kapote: long, black coat
kashrut: Jewish dietary laws
kiddush: blessing over wine
kohane: priest
kopecks: minor coins, pennies
kuchen: onion roll
kugel: pudding
landsfrau: kinswoman
leffel: spoon
Litvak: Lithuanian
Lubavitcher: member of Lubavitch movement
luftmensch: intellectual
maven: an expert
mazel: luck
Meah She'arim: ultra-Orthodox part of Jerusalem
meichel: something delicious
melamed: a teacher of young boys
meshuggener: lunatic
mezuzah: small case containing prayers affixed to the doorpost
mikvah: ritual bath
milah: also *bris milah;* circumcision
mitzvah: a good deed
mohel: one who performs circumcisions
momzer: bastard
motzi: blessing for bread
naches: joy
niggun: melody
Petach Tikvah: city in Israel
pisher: one who urinates
poretz: a nobleman
prust: vulgar
Rabbenu Tam: commentator on the Talmud
Rashi: Biblical and Talmudic commentator
rosh chodesh: new month
schicker: a drunkard

schmaltz: chicken fat
Shabbos: sabbath
shalom aleichem: a greeting
shiduch: marital match
shmatte: rag
shmegegge: a jerk
shmendrik: a fool
shmuck: a jerk
shmutz: dirt
shoichet: ritual slaughterer
shtetl: village
shtreimel: fur hat worn by Chasidic Jews
shul: synagogue
simcha: celebration
talmid chochem: scholar
Tanach: Bible
tefillin: phylacteries worn during prayer
tichel: kerchief
Torah: Bible, scriptures
tsunami: seismic sea wave
tzimmes: a sweet side dish; a big deal
tzuris: troubles
vildah chayeh: wild animal
yasher koach: congratulations
yerid: market, fair
Yizkor: memorial prayers
zayde: grandfather